# TIED DOWN

## TROPHY DOMS NEW YORK #2

### KATE HAWTHORNE

# TIED DOWN

### KATE HAWTHORNE

Tied Down
Trophy Doms New York #2
by Kate Hawthorne

Copyright © 2024
Kate Hawthorne

Edited by | Jordan Buchanan

Cover Design | Amai Designs

# DEDICATION

*For those who are ready to let go.*

## CHAPTER 1
# BOSTON

THERE WERE WORSE THINGS IN LIFE THAN WORKING FOR MY BROTHER, living in New York being one of them, but there was no convincing him of that so I'd stopped trying. There was a time, back when we were both teenagers, when I'd seen the appeal of the city. Back then, anything was better than central California farmland and two parents who were content to let the goats do the babysitting. Kale and I had good parents, if not a little too agriculturally focused for most people's tastes, and much like living in New York...there were also worse things than being babysat by goats.

I'd always appreciated that my mom came from money and had been given the choice to stay or go, so when Kale and I got old enough to choose, we were given the same opportunity.

As a teenager, there weren't many things that sounded more appealing than getting the fuck off the farm and into the city with our grandparents. They had money and an endless supply of hot water in the showers, and there were boarding schools and fancy restaurants and buildings that were taller than the clouds. It was a relief, at first, to get the dirt out from under my fingernails and the hay out of my hair, but I was pushing thirty now and I'd replaced dirt with papercuts and hay with smog and pomade.

Truly, I'd started to wonder if my life was going to be a series of *the grass is greener over there* scenarios, over and over and over again until I died. I'd been debating moving back to California long before Kale met his boyfriend, Christian, and their ridiculously saccharine love story only accelerated that train of thought. Kale was my brother, my twin, my very best friend, but even with the bond we shared, none of that could be a forever thing. We were pushing middle age and Kale had always been luckier in love than me.

The dating scene was another horrible thing about the city. Most of the women I'd dated were after the money they thought they could get out of me and not anything fundamental that I had to offer. They recognized the last name, the address, the designer labels, without caring about the personality of the person. It felt hypocritical for me to call it out because it was exactly those things that had called me and Kale to the city in the first place, but now...

I was exhausted of the whole thing.

My last relationship had made it eight months before things went south. There hadn't been anything inherently wrong with Colette, beyond the fact we just didn't *click*. She was pretty and she was smart, and she had her own money, which was a refreshing change of pace from the other women I'd dated in the past. Fresh out of a shower, she smelled like sugar and lemons, and she was absolutely everything I should have wanted.

My relationship with Colette had been *nice*, it had been

*fine*, but I wanted more than that. I knew there had to be a woman out there who would kick up some inextinguishable spark in the middle of my chest that would burn us both to the ground one day. I wanted that incendiary kind of attraction, an obsessive kind of love. I wanted someone to dedicate my time and my heart and my life to, the same way Kale had done to the city. The same way he'd done to Christian.

And I knew that wanting those things while also craving a quiet life on the farm made my dreams unattainable, but I'd settle for bits and pieces of the whole if that was all I'd be allowed. Because the farm brought authenticity, and authenticity bred connection. At the end of the day, *that* was what I wanted more than anything else. That was what had been missing from my relationship with Colette. I didn't expect Kale to understand, especially not after he met Christian, and when he'd told me to take an extended trip home, I honestly worried if I went for a visit, I would never come back. And for as disillusioned as I was by the life I knew I'd never have, I wasn't ready to say goodbye to my brother yet.

With that thought in mind, I snapped the lid on my laptop shut and leaned back, closing my eyes and taking a deep breath. Kale had gone home an hour ago, excited to take Christian out to the ballet after dinner, so I'd taken my time tying up some loose ends from the meetings he'd had earlier in the day. I knew Kale had only offered me the job as his assistant to keep me in the city longer, but we both *knew* my departure was inevitable. The only thing up for discussion was the when of it all.

I rolled the chair backward, the wheels crashing into the overstuffed box of squash and potatoes our parents had sent over. It was the most recent delivery in the CSA box that we'd never asked for, and if I were being honest, the food from home was one of the things that made it hardest to be away. Without opening my eyes, I swiveled the chair around and picked up one of the zucchini, taking the time to appreciate the rough grit of the dirt and the vegetable skin beneath my fingers.

"Did you want some privacy?"

The question startled me, and I threw the squash in the air, flailing around trying to catch it before it landed on the floor, or worse...my lap. The zucchini from the farm had always been monstrosities and the weight of one landing right on my junk would have been an absolute disaster, ending with me at home on the couch and a bag of frozen peas between my legs.

When all was said and done, I caught the vegetable by the curly vine left around the stem, the thick base landing against the floor with a thud. Defeated, I tossed it over my shoulder and back into the box, angling my face toward the visitor who'd almost startled me into a child-free life.

"Ford." I spun the chair around toward the front of my desk. "Kale's gone home for the day."

My brother's best friend glanced past my shoulder at the dark windows of Kale's office, then looked at me with a sly smile. Ford was, as my brother often said, a nightmare, but I think there was as much love between them as between Kale and me. Ford was just taller and bolder, with a mouth that hadn't known a filter a day in its life. The man said what he wanted, what he thought, what he needed, with little or no thought to anyone else in the room. Sometimes it was annoying, the way he dominated conversations, sucking the air out of every room he walked into, and sometimes it was admirable, stirring some kind of feeling in my stomach that four years of college had never given me a word for.

Ford also, apparently, had a penchant for sleeping with Kale's assistants. The last one, Stefan, hadn't made it long at all before Ford had gotten his hooks into him, and Kale refused to employ people who fraternized with his friends. I was an exception in that his friends were all almost my friends anyway, and since I was straight, there wasn't any worry about me falling into bed with his charismatic problem of a friend.

"Not you, though? I hope he's not working you too hard."

The inflection on the last word didn't go unnoticed, but I shrugged him off. Whether I was interested or not—which I wasn't—Ford never bothered to dial down the flirting. It felt harmless to me, just some well-intended lines meant to send my brother into an early grave, so I didn't ever bother telling Ford to stop.

"He's working me fine," I assured.

"Did you *need* to get worked harder, Boston?" That smile of Ford's grew into something that barely reached his eyes, the mischief sparkling in his irises with the ask.

"That's what the zucchini was for." I stood up from my chair and turned around to get the box of vegetables in question. Ford groaned when I bent over, and my cheeks burned with the embarrassment of being watched that way. The flirting was one thing, but sometimes I wondered if there was truth behind the things Ford playfully propositioned me with.

"He's got jokes." Ford laughed, coming around my desk and taking the box out of my hand. He smelled like sandalwood. "You're funnier than your brother."

"I got the humor. He got the attraction to men."

"Well," Ford mused, eyes narrowed, "with both, you'd clearly be too powerful to contain. Taking the entire city onto their knees and then their backs."

I wondered what it would be like, sometimes, to be a man like Ford Carlisle. So unashamed of whom he was and what he wanted, saying the first thought that came to mind regardless of the audience or the impact.

"Seriously, though, Ford. What brings you by?"

I grabbed my pea coat off the hook on the wall and shrugged it up my shoulders while Ford followed me around with the dirty cardboard box of root vegetables in hand.

"I was looking for your brother," he said. "He's not answering his texts."

"He's at the ballet with Christian."

Ford scrunched his nose and huffed an annoyed breath out loud and hard enough to dislodge a chunk of dust and dirt from the box in his arms.

"I forgot about Christian," he said.

"That feels impossible." I checked my pockets for my things then reached for the box, but Ford took a step back.

"I've got it."

"You'll get your suit dirty."

Ford looked down like he'd forgotten he was even dressed, let alone in a suit that had most likely cost thousands of dollars.

"It'll clean or it'll get donated. What are you doing with these? Taking them home for some quiet one-on-one time?"

"I'm not quiet at all, Ford." I wrestled the box out of his arms. "Will you get the door?"

"You can't say things like that to a man, Boston." He

pulled open the door and then closed it behind us. "You'll give me a heart attack."

I ignored the insinuation, heading toward the elevator with Ford hot on my heels. Pressing the down button with my elbow, I waited for him to say something else. When he didn't, I asked, "Is all the wishful thinking finally taking its toll?"

"I have more stamina than you give me credit for," he said softly, standing much closer to me than I'd realized.

Suddenly, his breath was hot against my neck, barely above the collar of my coat, and it was impossible to breathe with the smell of him in my nose. Whatever expensive, spicy cologne he wore wrapped around the both of us, and when the elevator doors slid open, I practically ran into the small space to escape him.

The box of vegetables bumped into the far wall of the elevator and I spun quickly, just as the doors were sliding closed. Ford was still in the elevator alcove, a smear of dirt across the otherwise stark black wool of his suit coat. He caught my stare, a curious look in his eye that was gone as fast as I'd noticed it.

"Are you coming?" I asked.

The corner of his mouth quirked up and he shook his head. "I'll see you on Monday, Boston."

The doors slid closed, and I realized I'd been holding my breath. Sucking in a desperately needed lungful of air, I dropped my head against the mirrored back wall of the elevator, trying to get myself together.

What the *fuck* was that?

What just happened?

The elevator landed in the lobby, the doors whooshing open

so fast I lost my breath again. I shifted the box under one arm and pinched my nose with my free hand like I could somehow squeeze the scent of Ford's cologne out of my nose, but the insistent pressure of my fingers only served to drive the smell of him deeper. Behind me, another elevator arrived in the lobby, doors sliding open. Expensive-sounding footsteps came up behind me and stopped, and I shifted the box back into both of my hands.

"Do you need help with that, Boston?" Ford asked quietly.

"No, thank you." My voice cracked on the last word, and I cleared my throat, shuffling away from him and toward the wide open lobby space.

"Okay," he said, walking behind me. "Let me know if you change your mind."

With that, he brushed past me, entering the revolving door without even looking back at me. He was on the sidewalk without so much as a backward glance. I came to a stop to watch him go, waiting until he was far out of sight before heading out into the blustery fall night on my own.

## CHAPTER 2
# FORD

Sitting in an overstuffed leather chair on the main floor of The Black Door, the exclusive kink club my friends and I were all members of, I picked mindlessly at a hangnail on my thumb. I wasn't paying attention to the annoying scrap of skin, my attention was instead focused on a man across the room who, if I closed my eyes or had enough to drink, could have looked enough like Boston to get me hard. Not that Boston was the only person who gave me an erection. In fact, far from it. But I'd developed a bit of an unhealthy fascination with my best friend's twin brother from the moment Kale told me not to.

He should have known better, obviously, because telling me not to do something not only inspired me to do it, but to do it faster and better than everyone else. Kale's barely younger twin brother should have been off-limits because there had to be an age-old rule somewhere about not sleeping with people who shared DNA with your friends, but I was an only child and also not a fan of the word no.

"You're going to rip your skin off." Another one of my best

friends, Brooks, sank down in the empty chair to my right, passing me a tumbler of golden-colored whiskey.

I glanced at him, took the whiskey, then looked at my thumb, which I'd apparently done quite a number on. Lifting the wounded digit to my mouth, I sucked at the pearls of blood that had beaded around the edge of my fingernail, then chased the copper taste down with a swallow of liquor.

"Thanks for the drink and the warning," I said, smacking my lips after I swallowed.

"I didn't know you were coming out tonight."

I didn't know I was coming out tonight either. It was a Friday night and Kale was apparently off with Christian at the goddamn ballet, our fourth friend, Alex, was off still nursing some unspoken wounds that were going to come to light eventually, and I honestly hadn't even thought to see what Brooks was up to. I'd walked to The Black Door on autopilot after parting ways with Boston at the office.

Earlier at work, I hadn't gone downstairs to look for him, and I definitely hadn't meant to spend the whole time flirting with and flustering him, but sometimes the world worked in my favor. I'd sincerely been searching for Kale, who'd been extremely hard to pin down since he shacked up with his new boyfriend, Prince Christian of whatever little island Kale had found him on.

"I didn't mean to," I admitted, trying to shake Boston and his B-rate doppelganger out of my mind. "Kale is off with his Prince and I was bored."

Brooks gestured toward the swollen corner of my thumb. "I think there's better ways to entertain yourself than ripping your fingernails out."

"I had a hangnail," I said.

"Then go get a manicure."

I snorted, rolling my eyes and taking another sip of my drink. "It's too late for that."

"I can't believe you don't have a manicurist on speed dial," he countered.

"Do I strike you as the type?"

"You're wearing thousand dollar shoes and drinking two hundred dollar whiskey," Brooks said, eyes dancing with amusement. "You very much strike me as the type."

"Do *you* have a private manicurist?"

"Of course." He stretched his arm toward me, giving his fingers a bit of a shake before letting his wrist fall limply over the edge of the chair. "Hands are my favorite part of a man."

"Your favorite part of yourself?"

"No. That's clearly my cock."

I chuckled, choking on my own spit in a notably unattractive way. I chased the stray saliva with another swallow of whiskey, groaning as the liquid burned its way down my throat. I'd been drinking whiskey for years, but I'd admittedly never developed a taste for it. I liked to enjoy my drinks, my meals, my men, and whiskey had always been too sharp on the front end for my liking. I found it near impossible to go all in on something that made me feel like it wanted to burn my throat out of my body, though there was one particular brand I'd started to develop a taste for. Maybe that was part of the only child syndrome, but I liked things to be handed to me, and I liked them to be easy.

Boston, though.

Boston was far from easy.

My flirting with him had started harmlessly enough. I'd taken Kale's warnings to heart, believing that his straight younger brother was well and truly out of reach for me, but something had changed tonight. I'd been with enough men to recognize arousal when I saw it, when I smelled it, and Boston...

He'd been well on his way.

I would have been perfectly happy to do nothing besides tease him and torment Kale into an early grave, but Boston's body had responded to mine earlier. Whether his mind had caught up with his hormones or not, there was something there when he thought about me, and what kind of man, what kind of *friend* would I have been if I didn't guide him toward those urges and give him a safe place to explore them? Because, honestly, if Boston wasn't as straight as he and his brother imagined him to be, there wasn't a more qualified person to show him the ropes than me.

I knew Kale thought I was scared of relationships, but that wasn't the case. I was bored of relationships. I'd dated plenty in college and in my twenties, and that had been fine and good, but it wasn't exciting. It was always predictable and boring. The truth of the matter was while everyone had pinned me as a fuck boy, I was a romantic at heart. Not like I would ever let any of my friends know, lest they hold it against me, but that was the real reason I fucked instead of dated.

I'd spent enough time in therapy to know it was a result of being an only child with too much money and too much unsupervised time, but I didn't do things in half measures. When I was six, my parents decided I needed to learn how to play the piano, so I'd been enrolled in private lessons that took up every second of time I wasn't in school. I had mastered Haydn's piano sonata in B minor before my seventh birthday.

When I was fourteen and had wanted to learn how to paint, I found myself enrolled in a six-month intensive with teachers flown in from Italy to critique my technique. When I was much older and wanted to learn how to fuck, well...I had to resort to some more creative educational measures, but the end result was the same.

I'd thrown the same level of intensity into my relationships until I realized the reward was not worth the work. My first serious relationship after college was a perfectly tolerable man named Matthew, and while I enjoyed making him come his brains out, I didn't enjoy much else with him. He found my attention to be overbearing and controlling, and it was words like those that had led me straight to The Black Door. Harnessing the natural dominance in my personality to be better at something I already excelled at was one of the most enjoyable learning experiences of my life.

But none of those interests, those skills, those talents... none of it fixed the problem of not finding a man who could match my energy for the long term. It was always fun at first and then it was too much. *I* was too much, but one thing I would never do was apologize for that. I found it easier for everyone—mostly for myself—if I kept my extracurricular escapades to the physical side of things.

Flirt.

Fuck.

And, in the end, flee.

It had been so long since I'd been with someone seriously that I occasionally wondered if I'd forgotten how, and I'd found myself at The Black Door picking at an annoying hangnail wondering what that would be like with Boston Sheffield. A truly horrible daydream for multiple reasons, first of which being I didn't want to have a relationship and last of which being he was my closest friend's *straight* twin brother.

"That man over there is watching you," Brooks said, pointing his chin toward the far corner of the room and the man I'd been squinting at before his arrival.

"I was watching him."

Clearing my throat, I finished off the drink he'd gotten for me, hoping the burn of the whiskey would be enough to get me out of my head and back into my body for a while.

"Finish your drink," I said, clinking my empty glass against his. "I'll get you a new one."

Brooks tipped the rest of the drink down his throat, and I took both of our glasses to the bar to get another round.

"More of the same?" the bartender asked.

"One for him," I said, glancing up at the bottles on the wall behind him. "I'll have a vodka tonic with lime."

While I waited for our drinks, Boston 2.0 sidled up beside me at the bar, being far too forward and bold for my taste.

"I saw you looking at me earlier," he said.

He had a nice enough voice, and the way he enunciated his syllables confirmed he had a decent upbringing.

"I've been looking at lots of people," I said, tapping my fingertips against the bar.

"Not as hard."

I chuckled, angling my body toward him so I could get a proper look at him. Up close, he didn't look anything like Boston. He was too slim, too short, his hair was too pale and his mouth too thin. He wouldn't do at all.

"I thought you looked like someone I knew." I turned back toward the bar as the bartender slid both drinks toward me.

"Do you want it on your account?"

I gestured over my shoulder toward where I'd left Brooks. "Put it on his."

Picking up the drinks, I turned away from the man who couldn't be Boston even if he spent an entire life practicing and pretending. I made it two steps away before his fingers curled around my bicep, dragging me to a stop.

"Where are you going?" he asked.

"Get your hand off me," I warned, not turning back toward him.

The longer I talked to him, the more ways he proved how wrong he was for me. And while I didn't mind a challenge or a game sometimes, I couldn't stand people who didn't understand the fundamental rules of engagement at a place like this.

His fingers fell away from my arm.

"You're a good-looking man," I said, hoping it landed as a consolation, "but you're not my type."

"I could be."

"You definitely could *not* be." I frowned, shaking my head. "My type would never say something as humiliating as that."

"Asshole," he muttered.

"Like I said. Now." Raising one of the glasses in a mock toast, I shifted my grip so I could give him the finger. "Have a good rest of your night."

When I returned to my seat, Brooks was watching me with a curious look on his face. I passed him his whiskey and sat down, flipping the twist of lime off the edge of my glass and onto the ice.

"What?" I asked.

"What did he want?"

"He wanted to fuck." I watched as the man wandered over toward the corner of the room where I'd found him.

"He seemed like your type," Brooks said.

"And what's my type?"

"Breathing."

That earned an honest laugh, starting as a low rumble in my chest. Leaning back into the soft leather chair, I stretched my arm toward Brooks and clinked our glasses together. "I have standards," I assured him.

"Breathing *and* willing?" he teased.

"Exactly."

I was content to let my friends believe that about me because it was easier than sharing the truths of my dreams. The fantasies and the wants that kept me up at night, that almost always involved a comfortable home to share with a man who was a willing hole, but also so much more. Because that was another thing I'd learned as an only child—no matter how much you want it, you can't *always* have it all.

## CHAPTER 3

# BOSTON

I woke up the next morning with dirt on my pillow. Kale's zucchini had really done a number on me, but whereas I knew my brother would have been horrified at the prospect of getting his sheets dirty, it only made me miss the farm more. I made a mental note to call my parents at some point in the day, but since it was barely seven for me in New York, it wouldn't have even been four for them in California. While they were, of course, early risers, there were chores to be done first thing and I counted through that list—which I'd never forgotten—and settled on calling them sometime after lunch.

I flung my legs out of bed and grabbed my glasses off the nightstand, sliding them onto my face so I could blink my room into focus. My grandparents had bought an apartment for me after college, and I'd been living here ever since. It was nowhere near as large as the brownstone Kale had bought, but it was more than enough room for me.

A one-bedroom in a doorman building, just under twelve-hundred square feet, was plenty of space. The living room had an old fireplace and a bay window that overlooked the street below and the city beyond. It was lots of wood and white with exposed brick walls and dark brown leather. My apartment was as cozy as it could be, with blankets that my mom had woven from homespun yarn thrown over the back of the couch and half-drunk mugs of coffee on the low wood table in the middle of the small room. I had plants and a record player and a bookshelf of stories I'd fallen in love with in college and never been able to part with. My apartment was as much *me* as a place like New York City would allow, but Kale had been right. Walking away from the high-stress job I'd been in since college and stepping into a role as his assistant had done wonders for my outlook and my mental health.

Grabbing my phone off the charger on the bedside table, I scrolled through the alerts that had come through overnight while I padded barefoot into the cramped kitchen. Even a million dollars couldn't get me anything more than a short galley kitchen on the Upper East Side, but I didn't cook a lot, so the complaint didn't count for much. I normally got food at work or on the way home, or I went out with friends or my brother. My fridge didn't have much in it beyond a dozen eggs, courtesy of my parents, a gallon of milk, and a bag of mandarin oranges. The coffee was on the counter, next to the Keurig, and I brewed myself a strong mug of coffee.

I had a text from my brother about the zucchini, which I answered, assuring him the vegetables had been appropriately dispatched. I'd kept one for myself and dropped the others at the food pantry where my friend Shawn worked. It was between the office and my apartment, and Shawn was more than happy to take the farm-grown produce off my hands to help out. I had no idea what I was going to make with the giant squash I'd kept, but getting rid of the entire bounty seemed wrong. Even though we'd both begged our parents to stop sending so much, they'd never been good at taking no for an answer. I imagined that was how they found themselves on a farm in California in the first place, miles away from the parquet wood floors and massive oil paintings that decorated my grandparents' house.

I owed them a visit as well, I realized, but like the call to my parents, it could wait. My grandparents were great at some things, like showing love with money, but not others... like showing love with words. They wouldn't be sad that I hadn't come around in months, and even less sad if I delayed longer.

My coffee finished brewing and I carried the mug into the living room, taking a careful seat on the couch as to not spill on my lap. The sounds of horns and squealing brakes had already started to filter up from the street, and I sipped at my coffee, trying to pick the noises apart and identify them one by one. There were at least three yapping dogs, one angry cabbie, and two loud-talking pedestrians. I set my coffee on the table, next to the half-finished mug from yesterday morning, then went to the window to peer down onto the street and check my work.

There were four dogs, one cab, and a group of people talking so loudly over themselves it would have been impossible to separate the voices. Dressed in nearly matching suits, I wondered what the five men had to talk about so loudly considering the extremely early hour, but it was just another piece of the hustle and bustle in the city that had never appealed to me.

The men made me think of my brother and his friends...

made me think of Ford and the afterhours encounter we'd shared the night before, the way his breath had burned against the back of my neck while we waited for the elevator. The memory caused heat to stir low in my belly, and I jumped back from the window like the recollection of the event had burned me the same way.

Ford Carlisle was an enigma of a man.

I sometimes imagined that my brother idolized him, though not in a way that he'd ever confess to. But Kale and I were twins, and I knew him as well as he knew himself. So I knew without a shadow of a doubt that he admired Ford more than he'd ever admit. My brother hadn't always been so bold and brash, but Ford...Ford had come out of the womb like that. From the first time Kale introduced me to his friends, I'd reckoned Ford to be the ringleader, the troublemaker, and also the problem solver. He was also the playboy, and it was because of him I'd been able to convince Kale to give me a job.

Whereas Kale's favorite hobby was reading the newspaper and mine was people watching from the window, Ford's was sleeping with strangers. Sleeping with anybody, if I wanted to be honest. He favored men, which put me right in his crosshairs, but I was straight, so...

I was *straight*.

I'd never been with a man before, never even thought about it. But for a straight man, I'd spent a lot of time overnight thinking about how good Ford smelled and how his breath felt against my skin. Swallowing thickly, I stood up from the couch, not looking down so I wouldn't have to acknowledge the half hard cock tenting at the fly of my navy blue pajama pants.

It was fine.

It didn't mean I was into men.

Even though I hadn't been with a woman in years, I was still attracted to them. It wasn't like I had faked things with Colette when it came to the bedroom. I wasn't attracted to men, but I'd also never looked at a man long enough to see if I *could* be.

Ford wanted me to look at him.

Even if I did find myself suddenly attracted to more than one gender, which I found to be an unbelievable prospect, Ford would not be where I wanted to start. In the years that Kale and I had been in the city, I'd never seen Ford with the same person more than twice, and on top of that, he was my brother's best friend. One of them, at least. If I wanted to see if my attraction to men was a real thing, there were better places to test it than in Ford Carlisle's bed.

Unfortunately, thinking about Ford's bed took my semi right into full-on erection territory, the head of my cock poking through the loose button on the front of my pajamas.

"You've got to be kidding me," I complained to no one besides myself, shoving my pants down to my ankles and kicking them off. Ignoring my dick, I went into the bathroom and turned the water as hot as I could stand, and then stepped into the small shower. With the bathroom door closed, the small space was quick to transform into my own personal sauna, but even the heat and the humidity weren't enough to do away with the ache between my legs.

*Be rational,* I thought, pressing my back against the wall of the shower with a sigh. I closed my eyes and tried to think about other men who might be marginally attractive, but those thoughts only made me frustrated, my erection waning. I was mad because my subconscious didn't want to think about other men. It wanted to think about Ford.

That was fine.

It was normal.

Just because there was some weird hormonal thing going on where my body was responding to Ford in new and frankly terrifying ways didn't mean I had to sleep with him. Ford had always made his little flirting jokes at me, but that didn't mean I had to act on any of them. It didn't mean *anything*, because Ford acted that way with *everyone*. My dick hadn't gotten that memo, obviously, feeling more than special with the increase in attention. I washed my hair, washed my body, washed my face, but my cock refused to settle down.

"Think about Charlize Theron," I told myself, making a fist around my shaft and squeezing a little harder than entirely necessary. My brain was in an uproar, scrambled by the fresh memories of Ford's breath and his scent as soon as I forced the visual of a woman into my mind.

I didn't want to think about Charlize. Didn't want to think about Colette. As soon as I gave my mind permission to wander to Ford and his mouth, I was coming. I barely had time to recall the heat of his breath against that sensitive spot on my neck, just behind my ear, the way he smelled like expensive things and expensive sex. How I couldn't even breathe properly around him when he flirted at me like he had the night before. Didn't even have a chance to wonder what he would look like naked or how he would take my clothes off given the chance.

It was over.

The orgasm ripped through me with so much force it left me gasping for air, fingers scrabbling madly against the tile while my other hand raced up and down the length of my cock. With one hand against the wall, slipping and sweaty, cum shot out of my dick and painted the grout and the dark green tile in front of me. My toes curled, heat rising from the base of my spine and radiating out in shockwaves that didn't feel like they were ever going to die down in their intensity. I couldn't see, couldn't think, and again couldn't breathe.

Throwing my head back, I let out a noise I'd never heard myself make before. It was something feral, like a man possessed and pleasured, and then my knees gave out and I slid down to the floor. Cum still leaked from the slit of my dick, and I watched in awe as my balls found more and more to empty onto my trembling hand and my shaft. I'd never even had time to pretend it was Ford's fingers wrapped around my cock. It was still just me. My hand. My fingers. My fantasies.

"What the fuck? What the *fuck*?" I muttered the question to myself over and over again, cock still throbbing hot and hard in my hand as cum spilled over my knuckles. Water from the shower beat down against the top of my head, raining into my eyes and making it hard to see, but I didn't miss the wet swirl as my cum circled the drain before disappearing.

I'd gotten off thinking about a man.

With a shaking hand, I reached up above my head and tried to swipe the cum off the wall and let it chase the rest down the drain, but I'd shot so hard and so far, I couldn't reach it all. I was going to have to stand up and actually clean it off...face what I'd done.

I wasn't gay.

*Kale* was gay.

But none of that answered why I'd just come thinking about a man's mouth and hands on me. None of that mattered when my cock was still hard and my mind was still on the one man I knew I should never want. None of it mattered at all, but at the same time...everything had just changed.

MONDAYS WERE ALWAYS TEDIOUS. THIS MONDAY, MORE SO, BECAUSE I was making a concerted mental effort to not go downstairs and harass Boston Sheffield at his desk. My flirting with him had always come from a good-natured place, but I'd be lying if I said I was impartial about the outcome of things when it came to Boston. Flirting with him had at first started as a challenge, a way to piss Kale off more than normal, but something had changed on Friday in the way Boston reacted to my otherwise playful jabs.

As lunchtime neared, I gave up and rode the elevator down to Kale's floor with the intent to take him out to lunch —and also as an excuse to see his brother. It felt a little needy, especially by *my* standards, but desperate times and all of that. Or whatever. By the time the elevator reached Kale's floor, my palms were a little sweaty, which was a shocking new development. There was a nagging voice in the back of my head that wanted me to sit awhile and think about why I was so obsessed with Boston, but the elevator doors opened and I was on their floor, and there wasn't any time left for that. I wasn't a man who got sweaty hands over anyone, least of all a straight man who didn't know which way was up.

"Good morning, Kelsey," I greeted Kale's receptionist with a grin and mock salute. "Is Mr. Sheffield in?"

Her cheeks flushed. "Both of them."

"Perfect."

"I'll let them know you're coming." She reached for the phone and I gave her a pretend frown.

"No need."

I made my way around the desk and through the maze of cubicles and glass-walled conference rooms. Kale's office was in the back corner, split into two to accommodate him and still provide a private office for his assistant of the hour. Though privacy was debatable, considering most of the walls on his floor were made of glass.

I found the main door open, and I could hear Boston on the phone with someone before I even rounded the corner.

"Kale said I should come home for a visit, but I don't know when I'll have time," he said to someone, most likely his parents.

I'd spent many years teasing Kale about not just growing up on a farm, but also being named after the least enjoyable kind of lettuce in the world.

"Maybe in the spring...I can plan for it better...I know, I miss you both too."

I tapped my fingers on the doorframe, and Boston's head shot up looking like he'd just been caught in the act. His glasses slipped down the bridge of his nose and he used his knuckle to nudge them back into place, giving me a nervous smile before focusing down at his desk and pushing some pens around.

"I gotta go, Mom. Love you." He was quick to hang up the phone, only to turn his attention to a stack of papers he'd messed up in his rush and then made neat again.

"You good, Boston?" I asked, leaning against the door-frame, perfectly happy to watch him get more flustered with each passing second. If anything, his lack of composure made me feel better about how the weekend had gone for me.

On Friday, after an uneventful night at The Black Door, I went home alone and wanked over the fantasy of shooting my load all over Boston's thick, black-framed glasses. I woke up Saturday morning, still alone, and had a wank over the fantasy of coming in his mouth. For good measure, after lunch, I had another wank while thinking about what sounds he would make if he came in *my* mouth.

"Fine." He nervously scratched at the bottom of his chin.

"Is your brother here?"

Boston looked over his shoulder as if to check. "He went to the bathroom."

I looked over my shoulder then, but Kale was nowhere to be found. With a resigned sigh, I stepped into the office and closed the door behind me. Boston glanced at the door, then back to me as I settled into one of the visitors' chairs across from his desk.

"How was your weekend, Boston?" I asked.

He clenched his jaw, one of his cheeks going hollow as he bit it. "Why do you do that?"

"Do what?"

"Use my name."

I huffed a laugh out of my nose, unbuttoning my suit coat and getting more comfortable in the chair opposite him. "Do you dislike your name?" I asked.

"No." He shook his head, just barely. "It's just most people don't use names anymore when they talk to other people."

"I can give you a nickname if you want." I leaned forward, and Boston's body swayed back and forth. "I could call you sweetheart if you like that better."

At the endearment, his nostrils flared and his jaw went slack.

It was a bad word choice, because calling Boston something as delicate and intimate as *sweetheart* had my cock jerking back to attention in my pants as if I hadn't already beaten it to within an inch of its life over the weekend.

"Leave my brother alone," Kale boomed from behind me.

I should have been startled. Boston sure was. But I was so singularly focused on the man in front of me, I could not have cared less about Kale's arrival. I straightened up slowly, standing and redoing the button on my coat. I knew my cock was not flaccid, and Boston's stare flickered toward my fly since it was practically eye-level. He snapped his jaw closed and swiveled his entire chair away from me and toward his computer.

"You're just jealous that your brother was named after a place and you were named after the shittiest kind of lettuce."

"Boston's named after lettuce too," Kale said, brushing past me and into the depths of his sprawling corner office. "Don't you have the fucking internet?"

I headed around Boston's desk to follow after Kale, stopping with my fingers beside his keyboard.

"Are you really?" I asked him softly.

"Mom's favorite and Dad's favorite."

"Which one are you?"

He licked his lips, glasses slipping once again down his nose.

"Don't tell me," I said, reaching out and pushing his glasses back up for him. "You're a mama's boy, aren't you?"

"What do you want, Ford?" Kale hollered from his desk.

I chuckled, taking my hand back and walking away from Boston. I closed the door behind me, taking a seat in front of Kale's desk and stretching my legs out before me. His office was nicer than mine, which was fair because he worked a lot harder than I did. I didn't know how he got any work done, because if I had a view like him, I'd do nothing besides stare out the damn window and daydream about putting my cock into Boston's mouth.

"I wanted to see if you were interested in getting lunch."

"I would if I could, but I made plans with Christian," he said, hardly apologetic.

"Don't you see him every day and also every night?"

"I do more than just see him." Kale gave me a devilish grin.

"Aren't you bored of fucking the same man every night yet?" I asked, wondering briefly how long it would take me to get bored of fucking his brother.

"Fortunately not," he said.

"Well, that's positively droll."

Kale busied himself shutting down his computer and grabbing his things from his top desk drawer.

"Do you want to get together this weekend?" he asked. "Christian wouldn't mind going back to The Black Door, and I wouldn't mind seeing everyone."

"Wouldn't mind." I scoffed. "You know you can do both, right? Have a boyfriend and friends."

Kale dragged his tongue across the front of his teeth,

narrowing his eyes and glaring up at me. "I do both. You're here, aren't you?"

I gestured to all of the things he'd just shoved into his pockets. "And you're leaving."

"Friday night," he proposed, kicking my shoe as he walked past me toward the door between his and Boston's office. I stood up and headed after him, closing the door since it was clear he wasn't going to be gone for lunch, but gone for the day.

"Friday night," I agreed. "I'll tell Brooks and Alex."

"Alright." He looked at his brother. "You good the rest of the day?"

"I'll stay busy," Boston said.

"Or you can take a half day. That was the point of coming to work for me, wasn't it? Something less stressful?"

Boston looked up at his brother and let out a long and slow sigh. "I'll be good, Kale. You can go."

Kale pointed at me, brows knit together. "Leave my brother alone."

"I don't fuck straight men, Kale. Your brother's honor is safe in my hands."

Boston would sure be *something* if I ever got my hands on him, but I wasn't going to say that to Kale's face. The answer I gave must have satisfied him, though, because he said goodbye to us both and left without so much as a single look back. I debated sitting back down in front of Boston's desk, but ultimately decided against it, leaning against the edge instead.

"Anyway." I smiled down at him. "Where were we, sweetheart?"

Boston exhaled, looking past me. I watched him watch his

brother go, then with a resigned breath, he settled his stare on me. Cocking my head to the side, I studied him in a way I never had bothered to before. Sure, I'd of course known he was attractive, but I'd never really taken the time to appreciate his features. He was similar to Kale, with the color of their eyes and the color of their hair, but Boston had a little more meat on him. His cheeks were rounder, softer, his eyebrows a little bushier, his mouth a whole lot fuller.

"My weekend was fine," Boston said, and I was about to ask him what he was talking about when I remembered he'd never answered my question.

"What did you do?"

I decided I wanted to stay awhile, so I sat down after all.

"A lot of thinking." He took his glasses off and tossed them haphazardly onto his desk, then reached up and rubbed the bridge of his nose. I clenched my jaw, swallowing back a wave of unbidden fantasies that went far beyond all the ways I wanted to cover Boston in my cum.

"You look distressed, Boston."

He inhaled sharply, leaning back and giving a sideways shake of his head. Pressing his fingertips against his eyelids, he groaned and then dropped his hands into his lap and blinked his eyes open. That was the first time I noticed the soft purple discoloration under his eyes, the bags that I was all too familiar with. A byproduct of sleepless nights, too much liquor, and an overloud brain.

"Why does..." he trailed off.

"Why does what?"

"Can you just..."

"Can I just what?"

"Fuck." Boston flexed his hands into fists and then spread

his fingers wide, pressing his palms flat against his desk like he was about to lever himself over the top of it, but I couldn't tell if he wanted to kiss me or punch me. Maybe it was a little bit of both.

I'd have taken either.

"Do you ever just fucking stop?" he finally asked, blinking up at me with tired eyes. "Do you ever take a break?"

I swallowed and told him the truth. "No."

It wasn't in my nature to make anything easy for anyone. Not because I had malicious intent. In fact, it was quite the opposite. I'd worked hard my entire life for all the things I had, and I knew how sweet success tasted after the work was finished. I approached all parts of my life with the same philosophy, including flirting, including friendships, including sex.

There were men like Alex and Brooks, the kind who really got off on inflicting pain. And there were men like Kale, who got off on the authority and power of the whole thing. There were even men like Beamer, who preferred the other side of the coin entirely, and then there were men like me...the kind of man who was going to wring every ounce of pleasure out of your body over the course of the night and leave you begging for more.

Being with me wasn't easy, but it was always worth it.

In the end, at least.

"I can't think around you," he muttered.

"If things were different between us, you wouldn't have to," I said.

"What does that even mean?"

I sighed, leaning forward and picking Boston's glasses up from the desk. I wiped the damp sweat off the piece that sat on the bridge of his nose, then came around to the back side of the desk and dropped down so we were eye level. He inhaled a sharp breath, chin quivering as I inched closer and closer, and closer still. I could smell the coffee on his breath and the wintergreen mint he'd sucked on at some point in the morning. Closer still and I could smell his shampoo, his cologne. Carefully, I slid his glasses back onto his face, tucking his hair back behind his ears as I settled the frames.

His head lolled forward, pressing against my hand, which for some reason...I hadn't yet moved. His hair was unbearably soft between my fingers, and I allowed myself to lean closer and bury my nose in the silken, brown strands. I breathed in the scent of him, cock leaking against my thigh. This was more than I should have taken and definitely more than should have been allowed, but...

I wanted him.

"It doesn't mean anything at all, sweetheart. At least not for you."

Standing up had the unfortunate effect of bringing my half hard cock right to Boston's eye level again, and with his glasses back on his face, I knew he didn't miss the obvious bulge that had apparently taken up permanent residence between my legs. I wanted Boston Sheffield in a near animalistic way, and up until that moment, if there was something in life I wanted, I took it, but I couldn't take him. Kale had been right all along that fucking his straight brother was off the table. Any delusions I had otherwise were just that...

I took a step back, ready to make peace with mentally walking away from the person I wanted the most, but Boston reached out, curling his fingers around my thigh and stopping me in my tracks. We both gasped, both shocked at the touch. I slowly looked down at the way his palm covered the front of my leg, the way his fingers wrapped around the outside of my thigh.

"Boston," I said carefully, swallowing slowly so I didn't do or say the wrong thing. I was on the edge and I'd talked myself into going one way, but his fingers were desperately trying to shove me in the other direction. "What are you doing?"

"Why doesn't it mean anything for me?" he asked.

"Because you're straight, for one." I plucked at one of the fingers currently curled around my leg, ready to continue the list and remove his hand from me entirely. Before I could move on to the second reason—which damned if I could remember—Boston dug his fingers harder into my leg and looked up at me, brows knit together in confusion, asking the absolute last question I ever expected to come from his mouth.

"But what if I'm not straight after all?"

IT WAS LIKE THE AIR HAD BEEN SUCKED OUT OF THE ROOM WITH THE question. The only thing I could see was the small gap between Ford's lips as his chin fell and the only thing I felt was the searing heat of his thigh through the expensive wool of his slacks.

"Say that again, sweetheart," he rasped. His finger was still wrapped around mine, but both now pressed against his leg.

"What if I'm not straight?" I repeated.

My cheeks flamed and I wanted to cover them, to hide my embarrassment from his penetrating stare, but I worried if I let go of his leg, it would be the last time I was able to touch him and I didn't know if I could survive that. To me, the question of my sexuality had already gone out the window, and the quickly hardening cock between my legs was proof of that. Ford sported an erection too, hanging thick and swollen, inches in front of my face.

"Why would you think that?" he asked, his body unmoving.

My heart slammed against my rib cage and I slid my hand against his leg, curling my fingers around the back of his thigh. He felt stronger that way, sturdier, and I found myself wanting to lean in close and rest my cheek against the front of his leg while I held him. His muscle flexed beneath my palm, and I stretched my fingers around toward the inside of his thigh, trying to touch as much of him as I could without raising alarms for either of us.

"Do you want the honest answer?"

"Always."

"I jerked off thinking about you," I admitted, glancing up at him. It was hard to see his face with his dick so close to my eyes, radiating heat and want the way it was. I licked my lips, breath catching as I tried to stop myself from blacking out. My heart beat so fast, I couldn't even make out the separate pumps. Instead I heard one long and frantic thump echoing in my ears.

"Did you want to tell me more about that?" he asked softly.

His hand landed in my hair, and I could have cried with relief. His touch was tentative, like he was consoling a stranger at first, but then he tangled his fingers into the strands and I all but purred, pressing the top of my head up into his hand.

"I didn't mean to," I said. "But I couldn't stop thinking about how you smelled and—"

He cut me off. "How do I smell, Boston?"

"Expensive," I blurted, huffing out a nervous breath.

"How else?"

"Competent."

"How does a man smell competent?" he asked.

"Men who don't know what they're doing don't stand as close to other men as you do." I closed my eyes, thinking back to the last time I saw him in the office with an armful of vegetables and his breath burning the back of my neck.

"I want to tell you that you're wrong," he said softly. "That there's plenty of men who don't know what they're doing that pretend they do, but the fact of the matter is your assumptions about me are *not* wrong in the slightest."

I swayed forward, heart firmly lodged somewhere in the back of my throat. There was something I needed to say, but nothing came out when I opened my mouth. Ford's fingers were still working their way through my hair and my fingers had made it around to his inseam from the back. I tried to urge him closer, but he held his ground, a frustrated sound leaving his throat, and then he stepped back so fast he stumbled. The move caught me off-guard and I fell backward in my chair, the wheels gliding half a foot across the floor. With Ford farther away from me, I could breathe, even if it hurt, and I watched him scrub a hand down his face and look almost frantically around the room.

"Whatever you think you want, Boston, you can't want it with me." He took another step back, palming the erection that had tented his pants and tucking it back into place as best he could.

I didn't bother trying to hide mine. If anything, I wanted to look down at it longer and marvel at it. This physical reaction was proof of the one thing I'd most recently started to suspect about myself. Whether I would get hard for other men was yet to be seen, but I was achingly hard for Ford.

"I can," I rasped, swallowing my heart back into my chest, "and I do."

"I don't do things in half measures," he said, like that mattered.

"You do everyone in half measures," I countered. "Your reputation precedes you, Ford Carlisle."

"You're wrong in the assumption that I don't put everything I have into those moments and those people," he said, moving to take a step forward before dropping his foot back to the floor in place. There was a war waging behind his eyes, clear as day for anyone to see. "Just because I don't want to date them doesn't mean I do *anything* by half."

"I'm not asking you to date me," I said.

"You haven't asked me for anything." Ford worked his jaw side to side and gave me a jerky shake of his head. "And you can't."

"Why not?"

"Because you're straight." He held up a finger, ready to resume his list. "Because you're my best friend's little brother—"

"We're twins," I corrected, standing up and taking a step toward him. "Four minutes hardly counts for anything."

"Not the point."

I reached down and held the base of my cock between my finger and my thumb as best I could through my pants. I wanted him to see how hard I was, how much I hurt for him.

"And I don't think this happens to straight men," I said.

"I have it on the record that straight men do in fact get erections, Boston." Ford's mouth quirked into a wry smile, his stare flickering between my legs before darting back up to my face.

"You know what I'm trying to say," I protested.

"And you know what *I'm* trying to say."

"I just want to know for sure."

Ford rolled his eyes, looking once again at my cock. "I think you know."

"I want to *try*," I said instead.

He pursed his lips, shaking his head more urgently than before.

"No." Ford pressed his hands together in front of his chest like a prayer, fingertips pointed at me, then at the half-glass wall that separated my office from the rest of the floor. "No. And no."

I hadn't even thought about the fact we were basically standing in an observation room, given the ridiculous open floor plan of the space and the excessive use of glass. Thankfully, it was lunchtime and most of the people who worked on this floor had stepped away, but the realization that someone could have seen us was like a bucket of cold water dumped over my head. I stumbled backward, falling into my seat and covering my face with my hands. My erection was quick to soften, and I spun my chair so Ford could only see my back.

What the fuck had I done?

"Shit, Ford. I'm sorry."

I didn't need to see him to feel him close the space between us. He put one hand on the back of my chair and twirled me around to face him fully, dropping down so we were closer to eye level than if he stayed standing. I couldn't see his crotch like that, and I had no idea if he was still hard or if he'd also gone soft like me.

"You don't have to apologize." He reached forward like he wanted to touch my face, but then pulled back at the last minute, slapping his hand down onto the top of his thigh. "It's natural, Boston. Whatever you think you're feeling, whatever you want to explore. None of it's bad."

"Just bad with you."

He bobbled his head in reply, squinting at me like he wanted it to be the obvious answer even though neither of us truly believed it.

"For so many reasons, sweetheart."

"Please stop calling me that," I pleaded, squeezing my eyes closed. "This is so embarrassing."

"Boston." He set his hand on my thigh, giving it a reassuring pat, but the only thing I felt was the spread of his fingers and the warmth of his skin. It wasn't reassuring in the slightest. It was apologetic. It wanted more. It wanted the same things that I wanted.

"Please don't try to console me like I'm a child." I pressed the tip of my finger against the top of his fingernail until he took his hand away. I immediately mourned the loss of his touch. I was getting this all wrong. "I should have just downloaded that One Night Stand app like everyone else."

"You absolutely should not have downloaded One Night Stand," he said, tone stern and face stoic.

"Why not?"

"The men on that app are just there for sex."

"That's all *you're* there for," I said. I hadn't forgotten our earlier conversation or any of the things I knew to be true about Ford Carlisle. The man was a player in every sense of the word. There wasn't anything wrong with that. My brother had been much of the same until he met Christian and fell in love.

"A man on there would see a pretty boy like you and he'd take advantage, Boston."

"What if I want to be taken advantage of?

Ford practically growled at that, standing up and turning away from me with his hands tugging at the roots of his hair. "You don't," he bit out.

"How do you know?"

"You want someone to be your first, Boston. Is that what you're after? Those men would want to claim your virginity without taking care of it. I don't expect you to understand the difference."

"I'm not a virgin," I reminded him, standing up and meeting his gaze.

Ford was tall, but so was I, and something about squaring off with him toe to toe seemed to level the playing field a little more. I hadn't hated sitting when he'd stood, though. The thoughts of pressing against him hadn't gone away, but the feelings and the dynamic of being at the same level as him were different.

"Have you ever fucked a man?" he asked.

I shook my head.

"Had a cock in your mouth?"

I shook my head again.

"Your cock in a man's mouth? A man's ass?"

"You know I haven't, Ford."

"Then for all intents and purposes, you're a virgin."

"I've thought about it," I whispered.

Ford's face went pale, and he swallowed, Adam's apple visibly bouncing as he forced spit back down his throat.

"I thought about *you* that way," I said.

"Boston, please don't do this."

"I just want to understand what all of this means," I pleaded. He was right in front of me and I grabbed him by the lapels of his coat, giving him a shake. Ford's hands flew up, gripping my wrists and holding me still. Urgency and fear and arousal all mixed together in my stomach, bubbling up into the back of my throat. "I don't know what any of these feelings mean, Ford. It's terrifying."

"Sssh." He shook his head, pulling our bodies together and wrapping his arms around me. He stroked his fingers through my hair and down the back of my neck, down my spine, whispering comforting words to me the entire time. "Hush now, sweetheart. It's okay. It's okay."

"I've never..."

"I know," he interrupted, holding our bodies pressed together, his cock long and hard against the front of my hip. He was still erect, and my dick had already started to thicken again from nothing more than his proximity alone. I trembled, eyes filling with confused tears that I struggled to blink away before they fell.

"This was stupid of me." I tried to pull out of his arms, but he locked them down around me like a vise. "Ford, I'm sorry. Please just forget I said any of this."

"Boston."

My name came out of his mouth like a prayer, hot and dangerous against the shell of my ear.

"I couldn't forget any of this if I tried."

I NEEDED TO GO.

I needed to go like fucking yesterday, but Boston's dick was pressed right against me and had anyone ever felt as good and warm and perfect as he did? I rested my cheek against his ear, breathing in the fresh scent of his shampoo. He smelled like rosemary and mint and skin that I was desperate to taste.

"Promise me you won't download that app," I whispered, knowing it made me an asshole to ask that of him.

"What am I supposed to do then, Ford?"

The question was barely louder than a whimper, and he rubbed his forehead back and forth against the front of my shoulder. I tightened my arms around him.

There was no winning here.

If I told Boston no, he would go find someone else, a stranger most likely. He would find a man who didn't know him, didn't care about him, didn't want him the way *I* wanted him, and he'd get taken advantage of. He could get hurt, and not just physically. How could I live with myself if something happened to him? How could I look Kale in the face, knowing that I could have stopped something horrible from befalling his brother?

But if I told him yes, I'd be damning us both because, for as uninterested as I was in relationships with most people, there was no way I would share Boston with anyone else. There was no way that one time with him would be enough, and if I had to lie my way back into his bed to have him a second time or a third, I would do it. And then, in the end, I'd be the one hurting him instead of a stranger.

That, at least, would be expected.

Unfortunately for me, Boston wouldn't be the only one getting hurt when all was said and done. The fierce need to own and protect him already threatened to overwhelm me, and I had to fight every instinct in my body to not act like an unhinged caveman toward him. There were demands and promises on the tip of my tongue that I had no right even thinking about, let alone asking.

*Don't be with anyone else.*

*Only be with me.*

*Only* think *of me.*

*Let me show you what it's like to be with a real man, sweetheart.*

Beyond making him ask the actual question he'd been dancing around since I showed up at the office, I didn't want him to have another say in the matter. I wanted him to say yes and then trust me to make the rest of the decisions. When it came to Boston, it was as if I were two different men. The man I knew myself to be, and the man he made me *want* to be. They were a contrast to each other, fighting for supremacy while I swallowed dangerous words back down into the pit of my stomach.

"What am I supposed to do, Ford?" he asked again, and damn if the way he said my name didn't make me hard. He was begging for an answer, and it was right there... "Can't you just...can't we..."

Finally, a version of myself won out.

"Say it, Boston. Tell me what you want and I'll make it yours."

"I want you to show me what it's like to be with a man."

Before I could muster a response to that, Boston spoke again. "But I don't want you to be my boyfriend, Ford. Nothing like that. I don't...just...I just want the physical part of it. Okay?"

Something tight and hot twisted in the middle of my chest at his preemptive rejection, but this was fine. It was better. I wanted him in indescribable ways, ways that terrified *me*, and I couldn't imagine how Boston would feel if I were ever honest with him about the depths of my interest, and my obsession.

"Of course not," I agreed, even though it killed me.

There was no reason for Boston to look at me and expect any different. He knew what kind of man I was and that was all he wanted me for. I couldn't blame him for seeking me out to fuck when I'd spent years demonstrating to everyone around me that fucking was the only thing I cared about. Never mind the fact that fucking Boston had never been on the table before, because if it had, maybe I would have lived differently.

But no...

That felt disingenuous to even think about, because Boston had been here as long as Kale and it hadn't changed a thing before. I was the one who'd started to look at him differently, and then he started to look at me differently, and now we stood together in the middle of his brother's office, on the precipice of ruining both our lives and most likely...my heart.

The last bit was a secret I planned to take to the grave.

"I don't know what happens next."

I would have sworn Boston wiped his eyes across the front of my suit coat, but I didn't say anything, only protesting when he disentangled himself from my arms and put some much needed—but regrettable—space between us.

"Nothing happens here," I said, buttoning up my suit and making a weak attempt at smoothing my hair back into place. "And we can't tell your brother."

"I've never lied to him," Boston said.

"You lie to him about wanting to live in the city," I countered. It was a guess, something I'd picked up from observation, but also from eavesdropping. My suspicions were proved correct when Boston turned his attention toward his feet, fidgeting with the arm of his glasses.

"That's different."

"A lie is a lie, Boston."

"Well, I don't want to lie to him any more than I have to," he said.

"You have to."

He sighed, scrubbing a hand over his mouth and making his lips pop against each other. "I know."

"This isn't anything, so it's not that bad. Just sex, right? Like you said." I swallowed back bile. "Just like an instruction manual."

Boston gave me a weak grin. He looked like he wanted to be sick, and I imagined I looked much the same.

"Right."

It was impossible to ignore the way the mood of the room

had changed. Before, the air had been charged with arousal and electricity, making it thick and hard to move away from each other. When Boston's hands were on me, everything made sense, and now with the space and the nervousness...it gave me time to second-guess what I already knew to be subpar decision making.

"Boston." I cleared my throat. "Let's take a step back."

"Are you changing your mind?"

"I'm a man of my word," I assured him. "I just want you to be sure this is what you want."

He opened his mouth to answer and I raised a hand to silence him. The way he snapped his jaws back together, teeth clacking from how quickly he'd acted, made my cock twitch against my leg. My poor balls were experiencing whiplash, not sure if they were going to get to empty or not, and my head was starting to ache from all the directional changes my blood had been making.

"You know where I live," I said, walking around to the other side of his desk and scribbling my address on a post-it note. "There's the address if not. Come over tonight at eight if you're still interested."

He checked his watch. "That's hours away."

"It's enough time for you to catch your breath and make sure this is what you want."

I was being selfish, because I knew I'd backed Boston into a corner. He'd offered to go elsewhere and I'd taken that option off the table. All he had left to choose from now was me or lying to me, and I figured he had too much integrity for the latter. He didn't even want to lie to his brother, knowing what would befall me if and when Kale found out I'd taken him to bed.

He looked down at the post-it.

"Eight o'clock," he said.

"If you change your mind, we can pretend this never happened." I smoothed a hand down the front of my shirt and over the button on my coat. "No harm, no foul."

"I'm not going to change my mind." Boston looked at me head on, pushing his glasses up the bridge of his nose with a never before seen level of determination.

"I'll see you at eight then."

I didn't have it in me to tell him goodbye as I was barely holding on by a thread. I didn't know what I was going to do if Boston didn't show up at my house, because even though I'd said we could pretend it never happened, that was a lie. I was going to spend the rest of my life jerking off to the way his fingers had felt as they crept toward the inside of my thigh from behind, the way my balls had lifted in anticipation of what came next after someone touched me there, the way he'd held on to me, gasping and so needy for me to take control of the situation.

I didn't bother going back up to my office; my concentration was shot. Instead, I emailed my receptionist and let her know I would be out for the rest of the day, then rode the elevator down to the ground floor and practically ran out onto the sidewalk. Even with the fresh air—though calling it fresh was up for debate—in my nostrils, I couldn't shake the smell of Boston's shampoo out of my mind.

I walked to the drugstore to get condoms and lube. Even though I had some at home, you could never have too much. Then I went to a dingy no-name sex shop to kill some time. That ended up being a horrible idea because Boston was too fresh on my mind. Every toy I looked at, I imagined putting inside of him. From nipple clamps to blindfolds to the thickest butt plug I'd ever seen. I wanted hours, days, weeks with him so I could draw it out and show him just how good being with a man could be.

How good being with *me* could be.

But the longer I kept Boston in my bed, the more I would want him outside of it. I already wanted him outside of it, and that wasn't what he'd asked for. It wasn't who I was. I needed to find a way to give Boston what he'd asked for without drowning myself in the process.

I left the store empty-handed, not for lack of wanting, but because I already had most of the toys in a closet at home anyway. One thing I'd learned over the years was pleasure manifested differently for everybody, and what brought one person over the edge might not bring the next person anywhere close. I'd been with people who got off from spanking, from humiliation and degradation, and I'd been with people who got off on their back with their tongue in my mouth. I didn't judge and I was happy to please all of them in whatever way felt right.

I would do the same for Boston, but unfortunately for me, he had no idea what felt right. Walking home, I knew I should have been thankful that he was a blank slate. It basically meant I could have my way with him, but a blank check was a dangerous thing to give a partner, especially one like me.

If nothing else, I knew that even though I'd bought condoms like an overeager teenager, actual penetrative sex was definitely not going to be on the agenda tonight, so I detoured into Central Park on my way home to pick up a gyro from my favorite vendor near Columbus Circle. After paying, I found an unoccupied bench and sat down with a defeated flop.

Getting Boston naked was the only thing I'd been able to think about for the past week, so why wasn't I happier about the recent turn of events? If he'd been anyone other than himself, I would have already had him bent over with a cock inside of him, either mine or a plastic one. Maybe both. But I knew with Boston it was too much. Everything about him was amplified and exaggerated, including my interest.

This wasn't going to end well for anyone, but there was no going back now.

I stayed at work until five, if for no other reason than I didn't know what to do if I left early. There were still three hours before I was supposed to show up at Ford's house, which was plenty of time for me to question every life choice I'd ever made while I sat in Central Park and ate a gyro. But even as I beat myself up over the second-guessing and the doubt, I couldn't shake the thin strand of arousal that had curled around my spine at the same time I'd curled my hand around Ford's thigh.

He was so tall, so muscular, so sure of himself. Being attracted to Ford shouldn't have made sense, but there was no way to explain it. I didn't think I *needed* to explain it, though. It wasn't the 1950s anymore. While it was still problematic in some parts of the country to be in a same sex relationship, New York wasn't one of them. And I wasn't even going to be in a same sex *relationship*. I asked Ford to show me how the body parts worked, nothing more. Being intimate with a man was one thing, dating a man was something else entirely and I didn't know if I was ready to wrap my head around that piece of the puzzle.

By the time I worked through all of those mental conversations, it was barely seven. With a frustrated sigh, I decided to go home and change clothes. Maybe I'd feel more comfortable if I wasn't in my suit, if I washed the feel of Ford's hands out of my hair with a quick shower even though the whole point was to go to his house in an hour so I could have them there all over again.

I washed up and while I was getting dressed to go, my phone buzzed with an incoming text message. Immediately, my heart sank, thinking it was going to be Ford calling the whole thing off, but the truth of the sender was much worse.

It was my brother.

**Kale**: Do you want to grab a drink?
**Me**: Already in for the night, sorry.
**Kale**: Maybe Friday?
**Me**: Didn't you make plans with Ford on Friday?
**Kale**: Let me ask my assistant.
**Kale**: Did I make plans with Ford on Friday?
**Me**: Yes, and the rest of your friends.
**Kale**: Did you want to come?
**Kale**: Actually, scratch that. Tomorrow night for us?

I exhaled, trying not to read into why he didn't want me to come out with his friends on Friday night. I'd known all of them almost as long as he had. It wasn't like we were strangers. It was just Kale trying to make decisions for me based off what he thought was best. It was exactly what he'd done by giving me my job. He didn't think I should leave, so he made sure I would stay.

**Me**: Sure.

I put it on his calendar so he didn't forget, then sat on the edge of my bed to lace up my sneakers. I'd settled on something casual, just jeans and an old college t-shirt. I really didn't know what the dress code was for when you convinced your brother's best friend to teach you how to fuck a man, but I doubted Ford knew either. I didn't expect to be in clothes long anyway, so...

This was a ridiculous plan.

But my body wanted it and my feet carried me out of the house and down to the curb where I flagged a taxi. I climbed into the back seat on autopilot, and then I was in front of Ford's gorgeous brownstone, once again wondering if this was a mistake. I had money. My brother had money. My grandparents had money, but Ford...Ford had *money*. I knew how much buildings in this part of town went for, and Ford's was far from the smallest. I was in over my head with him in every way possible, it seemed.

When I knocked on his front door, it was eight o'clock on the nose.

He opened the door before I could knock a second time, once again stealing the breath from my lungs at the sight of him. Ford made my casual look overdressed as he stood before me in low-slung gray sweatpants and a crisp white undershirt. He was tall, and the smallest sliver of skin was exposed between the bottom of his shirt and the waistband of his pants and, further down, his feet were bare. Long and slender toes tapping against what looked to be real oak floors.

"Hey, Boston." He said my name like it was an endearment by itself. "Did you want to come in?"

I swallowed, clearing my throat and bringing my stare back up toward his face. "Yes, please."

He took a step back and I followed him inside. He was careful to move around me to close the door, the smell of him already fresh and sharp in my nose.

"Shoes off?" I asked.

"If you don't mind."

I toed off my sneakers and kicked them under the small side table just inside the door. Ford's wallet and keys sat in a wooden bowl beside some crumpled receipts, spare change, and a hot pink fuzzy mouse.

"I hope you're not allergic to cats," he said, tilting his head toward the hallway.

I followed after him, my socks slipping over the highly polished floor. Ford's house was narrow and deep, like most of the renovated units in the Upper East Side. He had at least three stories of room, though, and detailed black finishings throughout.

"What is your cat's name?" I asked.

"Milo. He's a beast of a Calico, but he mostly keeps to himself."

Ford made a left turn through a doorway which led into a decent-sized living room space that overlooked the back garden made mostly of gnarled vines and mismatched cobblestones.

"Sit down," he said. "Let's talk. Did you want a drink?"

"I probably shouldn't." I tucked myself into the corner of

his black leather loveseat. It faced a brick fireplace and a massive TV which hung on the wall above the mantel.

"You probably shouldn't be here either," he reminded me.

"I'll have a drink."

"Get comfortable. I'll be right back."

It was impossible to not get comfortable on Ford's couch. The whole room smelled like him, and it was the first opportunity I had to get a look at the man behind the playboy exterior. I would have never guessed he had a cat, but the proof was scattered all around the room in the shape of more fuzzy mice and a cardboard scratching post near the window. Ford returned quickly, two glasses of wine in hand. He passed one to me and then sat down next to me so close the outside of our thighs brushed. I tightened my fingers around the stem of the wine glass and took a quick swallow.

"So, you've thought about it," he said. "You're sure this is what you want."

"I told you it's what I want. You're the one that didn't believe me."

"You're right." Ford took a big drink of his wine, then stood up, a near mirror from the position that had gotten us both into this mess in the first place. "If you want to learn my way, you have to play by my rules, though."

"What are the rules?" I asked, taking another drink of wine. My hand was trembling and the rim of the glass clashed against my teeth when I brought it to my mouth.

"The rules are that I'm in charge, Boston. I decide what we do and when we do it. If you don't like something, you can ask me to stop."

"Isn't that normal?"

"The last part." His mouth quirked up at the corner. "Not the first part."

"I don't mind you taking the lead," I said softly, turning my attention toward my lap. Why was that such a vulnerable thing to admit out loud? We'd already established the fact I didn't know anything about anything when it came to being with a man. It made perfect sense that Ford would be the one to make the decisions and show me the ropes.

"I would like for you to get tested," he said, reaching onto the mantle and picking up a sheet of paper that was folded in fours. He handed it to me expectantly. "I already have."

I balanced the glass on the arm of the couch and unfolded the sheet of paper, revealing the letterhead of Ford's physician and his most recent STI panel from the week before.

"How often do you get tested?" I asked, folding it back up and returning it to him.

"Monthly."

"Do you use condoms?"

"All the time," he said. "And so will you, as long as we're doing whatever the hell this is."

I picked up my wine and took another careful sip, not wanting to shatter the glass against my teeth. "Are you going to sleep with other people while we're doing *whatever the hell this is?*"

"Are you?" he countered.

The idea felt absurd, and I couldn't help but laugh at him before I answered, "I'm not."

"Not even women?"

"No one," I said, shaking my head.

"Then neither will I."

The air in the room settled, and Ford took the wine glass

out of my hand. He set both of our drinks on the fireplace mantel, then extended a free hand to me.

This was it.

I slid my hand into his and let him pull me to my feet, bringing us once again face to face. He still smelled like sandalwood, but the wine on his breath was rich, and I had to make a concerted effort to root my toes into the floor so I didn't fall right into him.

"Lesson one," he whispered, plucking my glasses off of my face and setting them on top of his test results, "kissing."

My teeth chattered, only quieting down when Ford slowly cradled my face in his hands. He stroked his thumbs across my cheekbones, and I finally allowed myself to sway toward him. Ford's dark and appraising eyes traced over my whole face, and I was thankful my glasses were only for distance, because there was no way I wanted to miss out on seeing even one second of this.

The power vibrated out of his hands, barely restrained as he angled my face toward him, bringing his face closer to mine at the same time. The tips of our noses pressed together, and my cock jerked against my leg, constricted and held down by the tight elastic of my underwear. I shuffled closer, bringing our bodies flush, Ford's erection brushing over mine. I gasped, surprised by the heat of it, the thickness of it, and then Ford closed the rest of the space between us and ever so carefully slanted his mouth over mine.

I gasped again, swallowing his breath, the taste of him, right into my mouth, and he tightened his hold on my face, keeping me still. He hadn't yet put his tongue into my mouth. Instead, it was just our lips parted and touching, my heart slamming against my ribs like it needed out of my chest entirely. My lashes fluttered, eyes closing, and then Ford pulled away.

A whimper tore out of my throat and he was back, lips against mine once again, this time more urgent and eager to explore. He licked across the seam of my mouth with his tongue before sliding it inside and tangling with mine. I had never kissed a man, but I knew how to kiss, and I threaded my fingers into Ford's hair to keep him right where I wanted him.

Kissing him was electric, unlike any kiss I'd ever had before. I pulled his hair, pushing back against him, not trying to take control of the kiss, only trying to not be overtaken by it entirely. Ford groaned, hands sliding away from my face and down to my neck. He turned us both halfway around and then my back was against the fireplace and one of his thighs was firmly nudged between my legs. The position put the perfect amount of pressure on my cock, and I whined into his mouth, grinding against his leg.

"Kissing," he murmured, pulling back enough that I couldn't reach his thigh with my cock anymore.

"I know how to kiss," I said, desperate to lean back into him and taste his mouth again.

Ford kissed with the same authority he exuded in everyday life, with his curious tongue, firm lips, and strong hands. He used his entire body to kiss, which was not the only thing new for me, but I knew I could never go back to middle school make-out sessions after this. I was hungry for more of this, more of him. I still wasn't sure if the need would translate through to other men, but I was happy for the desire to revolve around Ford, at least for now.

"You don't know how to kiss *me*, Boston," he warned, nipping my lower lip between his teeth before sliding his tongue over the tooth marks he left behind. "And I don't know how to kiss you either."

"I bet you say lines like that to all the boys," I tried to tease, hoping the humor would ease the throbbing ache that felt like it had taken up permanent residence between my legs. I needed more friction from him. I needed more than just a kiss.

He didn't say anything back to my comment, making some indiscernible noise in the back of his throat instead. He pulled me off the wall and guided me back to the couch, sitting beside me and resting one hand on the center of my chest and the other lightly curled around my waist.

"Tonight we're just kissing, sweetheart," he whispered, pecking his way from my ear down to the corner of my mouth. "No humping, no hand jobs, just kissing."

Then he leaned in, slanted our mouths back together, and did exactly that.

I didn't want to open my eyes.

Like a fool, I'd sent Boston home after kissing him senseless for well over an hour on my couch. When was the last time I'd ever done that? Made out like it was the end goal of the evening? Probably not since some time in high school, but with my lips still swollen from the insistent way Boston had explored my mouth, I didn't want to wait twenty years to do it again. Sending a man away at the end of the night with an erection was rarely my style, but I told him it was kissing and I wanted to stick with the plan. The longer I drew out his education, I wagered, the more chances I'd have to be with him.

The way he'd looked at me as we said our goodbyes, standing there in the entryway, his lips slick with our mixed spit and puffy from how I'd sucked on them...his eyes glassy and dilated behind the clear frames of his glasses... it had been unmatched. Boston's hair was mussed from where I'd tangled my hands into it and tugged on the ends, his t-shirt rumpled from how I'd wanted to ruck it up and get my hands on his skin. I'd kept my fingers above his clothes as much as I could manage, only grazing a pinky over his hip one time when I tried to push him into a better angle so I could get my tongue deeper into his mouth.

I'd never shown that kind of restraint.

And I'd never wanted anything more.

"What's the next lesson?" he'd asked, feet firmly on the porch, the evening air dancing through his hair as it whipped across the front walk.

"Kissing without clothes," I murmured, reaching up and tugging his bottom lip with my thumb.

He let me.

I imagined he'd let me do anything to him, all in the name of learning, of course, and that was a terrifyingly powerful aphrodisiac. I was a dominant man in all things, but Boston made it even harder than normal to play by the rules.

"When?" he asked. "Tomorrow?"

"What an eager boy." I let his lip go and shoved my hands into the pockets of my sweats. My cock had been hard since before he'd even arrived, and there was now more than one wet stain on the front from where I'd leaked the proof of my arousal across the gray fabric. "Friday night, after I'm done with your brother, or Saturday night. It's up to you."

"That's forever." Boston rocked forward on his toes, body bowing as he pumped his hips at me. He was hard too, and I tried not to salivate at how massive the bulge between his legs looked. I knew he was hung. He'd been rubbing his erection on me all night, and it had taken a lot of willpower to not put my hands on it like some man off the internet would have.

No, I wanted Boston to have time to really appreciate the physicality of being with a man so he could be sure if it was what he wanted. I was not going to rush through things just to get him into bed for the grand finale, so to speak. I would go slow, so he could make an informed decision. At least, that was what I told myself as we agreed on Friday night after I was done with the boys.

By the time I made it back to the couch, I already had a text message from him. The sight of his name on my home screen made me laugh. He hadn't even been gone for a full minute, but the message he'd sent sucked all the air right out of my lungs.

**Boston**: Am I allowed to jerk off when I get home?

Even though, on a surface level, I understood what he was asking, I'd come up with stupid rules and a stupid plan, and he wanted to abide by all of them to get the full experience, the question still stirred something heavy and deep in the pit of my stomach. Boston had no idea just what the question did to me.

There was no way.

Palming my phone, I went into the kitchen to get the bottle of wine I'd opened on his arrival. Milo was sitting in front of his water bowl, clearly annoyed that I'd ignored his dinner time instead of my own. He gave me a loud meow, and I kicked his food bowl with my toe. He had plenty of kibble, but the bottom of the bowl was visible which was so far beyond the pale for his tastes. Once the stainless steel was covered, he let out another meow, swished me with his tail, and set to eating.

**Me**: What do you think?

**Boston**: I don't know. That's why I asked.
**Me**: You and I don't have *those* kinds of rules.

My phone stayed silent for so long, the screen went black. I exhaled, almost feeling relief, then I turned on the TV and took a drink of wine. The pinot noir blend would forever remind me of him now because I could taste the grapes on his tongue the first time I kissed him. I was going to order a case or ten of the particular vintage as soon as I was at my desk the next morning. That was a perfectly reasonable and sane thing for a man who was coaching his best friend's brother through the ropes of his potential bisexuality to do, right?

My phone flashed Boston's name across my screen, and I swiped the message open, choking on the next swallow.

**Boston**: Why not?

I set the wine and my phone down, then got up and walked out of the living room.

This was too much. This was...not sustainable, not even for a man like me. I could handle pretty much anything life threw at me, but I didn't see how I was going to survive Boston Sheffield. My own dick had finally gotten the better of me. I should have let him fuck a rando off a hookup app and washed my hands of the whole thing. But no. I'd been prideful and boastful, and a thousand different kinds of arrogant, and the only man I wanted was the one who didn't even understand the cost of what I'd agreed to give him.

**Me**: Call me when you get home.

I drank half the glass of wine, tried to watch whatever channel I'd turned on, but my brain was not having it at all. Thankfully, my phone rang less than twenty minutes later, Boston sounding a little breathless on the other end of the line after I answered.

"So, why don't we have those rules?" he asked after I said hello.

I bit the inside of my cheek. "Because you're in Sex 101 and that's more like Sex 208."

"That can't be more than three classes ahead, and I'm a pretty quick study," he said.

"It's a different *subject* entirely," I assured him, silently praying he would understand that while I couldn't tell him no, I simply could not play those kinds of games with him.

"It doesn't feel like it to me."

"Boston." I scrubbed a hand down my face, pinching my lips closed and squeezing my eyes shut.

"Ford."

"Are you home?" I asked.

"You told me to get home before I called you," he said.

"And you listened." I cursed under my breath.

"Of course I did."

I dropped my head against the back of the couch and stared up at the coffered ceiling, counting each square while I tried to steady my breath and slow my heartbeat.

I was already damned.

If Kale caught on to what Boston and I were up to, shit was going to hit the fan. As it stood, the reward outweighed the risk, but if I was already in over my head, I might as well commit to drowning myself entirely.

"Those rules would mean you do what you're told, Boston."

"I already am," he said. "You said only kissing, and we only kissed. You told me to go, and I went. You told me to call—"

"And you did," I finished for him.

"I know I told you I wanted to know what it was like to be with a man, Ford, but honestly...I think I just really want to know what it's like to be with you."

It was like all the air had evaporated. This wasn't what we'd talked about and it was nowhere near what we'd negotiated.

"This is just sex," I reminded him. "We agreed."

"I know," he said quietly, clearing his throat and sounding a lot like a wounded deer. "I know we did. I'm sorry..."

"Don't be sorry, sweetheart. You win." I shoved the waistband of my sweats down past my balls and fisted my cock. I put my cell phone on speaker and sat it on the arm of the couch. "If I go too far, just tell me to stop."

The spark of excitement was nearly palpable through the phone as Boston said eagerly, "You won't."

I barely heard him speak, all the blood rushing to the incessant erection between my legs. I gave a rough stroke up my length, groaning when precum leaked out of my slit and smeared across my fingers. It was the first time all night I'd well and truly touched myself, and I didn't think I had a lot of stamina in me.

"Get comfortable and get your dick out," I told him.

"Oh, fuck," he whispered, breath huffing loudly through the speaker and filling my living room. I turned the volume up as loud as it could go so I didn't miss a thing.

"Put your hand on your cock," I instructed him next,

forcing my own fingers to relax so I didn't strangle myself. "Tell me how you like to touch yourself."

"I've never thought much about it." Boston whimpered. "I just squeeze it and jerk off."

"But what types of things make you feel good?" I pressed my thumb against the flared tip of my cock, applying just enough pressure for it to hurt.

"Any touch on it makes me feel good, Ford. I'm easy."

I chuckled, even though I'd known off the bat nothing with him was going to be easy. My heart beat loud in my ears, and the warm leather of my couch creaked as I shifted my weight to stretch out my legs. I was dangerously close to coming, after having kept myself on edge all night to make sure Boston completed his lesson on kissing.

"Well, until you can figure out how to explain it to me, you'll only touch yourself the way I tell you to. Do you understand me?"

Boston sucked in a short breath. "Yes, Sir," he whispered.

I clenched my jaw so hard, I worried about shattering my molars. Hearing the honorific come from his mouth in that nervous baritone rumble was almost enough to undo me. Gooseflesh raced up the back of my neck, and I tightened my fist around my cock so I didn't come on the spot from words alone.

"You don't need to call me Sir," I told him, even though I liked it. I actually really more than liked it.

"It just felt right. I'm sorry."

"You can if you want to, sweetheart." I was quick to offer him the option because I was a selfish man and wanted him to say it again. "Whatever feels right is fine."

"I like when you call me sweetheart," he said quietly.

I wanted to dig a hole in the ground and bury myself before I said another word to him, before I gave another instruction or listened to another whimper tumble out of his mouth. Boston was fucking perfect for me in a hundred different ways and he truly had no idea how special that was. He didn't know how hard it was going to be to let him go when all was said and done.

"I'll keep that in mind. Are you ready now?"

"Yes," he rasped.

"I want you to lie down on your stomach, put a pillow beneath your hips and make a loose fist around your shaft." I closed my eyes, imagining Boston arranging himself on his bed, pillow propped beneath him, pushing his ass up into the air.

"Okay. I'm there," he said.

"Hold your arm still," I said. "Use your hips to fuck your cock into your fist."

Boston groaned, and a shiver wracked its way through my body.

"I'm already so close," he croaked.

"Then fuck yourself faster," I told him.

I spread my legs, bringing my hand to my mouth and licking my palm before reaching down and taking hold of my cock. I was probably as close as Boston was, if not closer. The sounds that filled my living room were some of the dirtiest I'd ever heard, and I knew that kissing Boston with no clothes on was not going to end with only our mouths joined.

"I'm close," I warned him, eyes rolling back as I stroked myself faster. "I want you to come first, Boston. Come for me, sweetheart. Let me hear it."

"Oh, fuck. Fuck." Boston cried out, cursing and moaning

as he reached his end. I imagined his asshole quivering as he got off, clenching and searching for something to fill it as he shot his load into a pillow.

"Just like that," I whispered, letting out a low grunt. "Fuck, you're such a good boy, aren't you? Such a good listener."

"Oh, God. Ford." He whispered my name and that was the end of me.

Cum shot out of my cock like a geyser, painting stripes up the front of my undershirt, all the way to my chin. I curled my toes into the floor, lifting off the couch to chase after the end of my orgasm. On the other end of the phone, Boston had quieted down and was making soft mewling noises that sounded almost like a purr. The unbridled sensuality of the sound was enough to milk the rest of the cum from my balls, and when it hurt to touch myself, I let my hand fall on top of my thigh.

"Boston."

"I'm here." His voice sounded muffled, and I pictured him with his face buried in the pillow, ass still up in the air.

"*Use* your hand this time," I said, pinching the bridge of my nose with my dry hand.

"This time?"

"You're not done yet, sweetheart. I want you to come again. This time, roll onto your back and stroke yourself."

He groaned. "It hurts."

"It's going to hurt until it doesn't," I assured him. "You can stop if you want to, but I'd like for you to try again."

"Do you think I can handle it?" he asked softly.

Fuck, I wanted him back in my house. On my couch, in my bed, anywhere. I wanted to brush his hair out of his face and whisper words of praise and promise in his ear while he hurt himself with the pleasure of it all.

"I know you can."

Boston gasped softly, and I listened to his moans and sighs, appreciating the way they crescendoed into a beautiful and desperate cry as he came a second time. My own cock was still hard, but I let it be, perfectly happy to listen to him get himself off at my command.

"How did that feel?" I asked, minutes after his breathing had settled down to normal.

He huffed into the phone like a bull. "It was a lot."

"That's not an answer."

"It felt really good," he said, breathless. "Thank you."

I finally swiped the drying cum off my chin with my thumb, then sucked it into my mouth, biting the pad after I'd gotten it clean.

"You don't have to thank me, Boston." I stared down at the wet cum splatters on my shirt, keeping the last part of the thought to myself.

*And I really wish you wouldn't.*

Instead, I told him what I knew he wanted to hear, what he needed to hear. And it wasn't a lie. It was very much the truth, just one I had no place speaking.

"You are absolutely perfect, and it was entirely my pleasure."

## CHAPTER 9
# BOSTON

I DIDN'T SEE FORD FOR THE REST OF THE WEEK, WHICH I IMAGINED was by design. After our phone call jerk-off session, we'd stayed in touch over text, but nothing as intense as those conversations had been. I'd gotten off plenty of times since our phone call without asking, and I wondered if that was allowed, but I couldn't bring myself to ask about it on the off chance my brain was trying to take things too far. There was no way Ford cared about what I did with my body when he wasn't around or on the phone. That was just some unanticipated kind of wishful thinking on my part.

I'd spent a lot of time during the week trying to unpack why I'd even thought about texting him to get the okay in the first place. Sure, it made sense when we were in the heat of the moment, but asking for his approval for a shower jerk-off Wednesday morning felt a little over the top, even for me. The feelings around the way Ford wanted to control my body were only half the battle I'd been fighting, though. The giant elephant in the room was that he was, of course, a man.

I'd kissed a man.

I'd kissed him for hours and we both had erections, and I'd really wanted to do more than just kiss him. When he talked me through how to get myself off later that night, I'd pictured him beneath me, pretended my fist was his body. Just thinking about it was enough to make my cock thicken in my pants...less than opportune considering I was walking down the street in the middle of after-work rush hour on a Thursday.

I didn't have a destination in mind, but I found myself in front of the food bank with a bag of gyros in hand just the same. Since my parents had started sending Kale and me produce in more volume than we'd ever be able to work through, I'd ended up on a first-name basis with one of the administrators—Shawn. He was my age, born and raised in Brooklyn, and fully dedicated to serving those who struggled to serve themselves. Shawn was also funny and kind, and he reminded me of all the things I missed the most about home. Thinking about home reminded me that I did want to plan a visit back, no matter what Kale had to say about it. I could deal with that next week. There was enough on my plate already.

I was halfway up the steps when the massive front door swung open, the comforting smells of vegetable soup and fresh bread rolling down the stairs in waves.

"Is that you, Boston?" Shawn asked with a laugh. "I hardly recognize you if you're not carrying your weight in home-grown produce."

I chuckled, finishing my ascent of the steps. "I have dinner."

Shawn was at the top with a small family, a mother and two children who each clutched fresh and clean stuffed animals in their arms. He spoke softly to the mother, a reassuring hand on her shoulder, before stooping down to say something to each of the children. The three of them left, passing me with nervous smiles as they went.

"No vegetables today," I told him. "Just two wraps that need eating, and I was in the neighborhood."

Shawn checked his watch and inclined his head toward the inside of the building.

"They were the last to go and I'm just finishing up a batch of soup to freeze. Did you want to come in?" he asked.

I nodded my agreement and followed him inside. He latched the door locks behind me, and we both headed into the kitchen. There was an enormous pot on the stove, boiling and bubbling away. Shawn flipped the burner off and slid the pot onto the counter with an exhausted sigh.

"Just have to let it cool first," he said, jumping up onto the edge of a counter. I leaned against the fridge, unwinding the loose knot of my scarf. I reached into the bag and handed him one of the foil-wrapped treats.

"One for you," I said, reaching next for mine. I crumpled the bag and tossed it in the industrial gray trash can at the end of the counter.

"Thank you for this," he said, unwrapping his sandwich. His stomach growled so loud it echoed off the stainless steel appliances in the kitchen. "I didn't realize how hungry I was."

"You never do."

Shawn was far too busy putting everyone else ahead of himself. It was an admirable trait, if demonstrated with moderation, which Shawn rarely had. The food bank had been both a blessing and a curse for him. With surprisingly uninvolved owners, the entire operation fell on the shoulders of him and the other administrator, both of them grossly underpaid.

I'd offered on more than once to make donations, but Shawn had voiced concerns to me months before that the community donations weren't making it back to the kitchen itself. Instead, they were lining the pockets of the owners, but there wasn't much that Shawn could do. If he left, it was the community that would be punished, and he was too good of a person to let that happen.

"It's been a long couple of weeks," he said after inhaling half the gyro. "But the zucchini you brought by has been great. Made some soup with it, and some pasta sauce."

"And you still had a ton left over," I added with a grin.

"Not wrong." He pointed at the fridge I was currently resting against. "But we'll get it used before it goes bad. There's always people looking for fresh produce."

"You should partner with a local farm," I suggested.

"Local?" He scoffed. "Have you looked around lately, Boston?"

"Well, not *local* local, obviously." I finished off the last bite of my gyro and pitched the wrapper into the trash can. "But upstate somewhere or something."

"That's a lot of work, and Lisa and I don't have a lot of time."

"I wish I could do more to help."

"You bring us food," he said with a smile, ever the optimist. "Which is more than most. And you come help serve, which is also more than most."

I sighed, appreciating the sentiment of his messaging, but feeling helpless just the same.

"Unless you have plans to move upstate and open your

own farm, Boston, you already do plenty, so don't worry about it." Shawn finished his gyro and dropped the wrapper into the trash next to mine. "That was so delicious. Thank you for bringing it by."

"Honestly, anytime." I thumped my head against the cool stainless steel behind me. "I did come with an ulterior motive, though. Not sure if that cancels out the good deed or not."

"Everyone has ulterior motives." He turned away from me and plunged a thermometer into the soup. "And we have plenty of time, so what's up?"

I'd debated if I wanted to talk to Shawn about Ford. Shawn and I were new friends, barely friends, and he didn't know much about my family history or current situation. He didn't know me as the straight twin, didn't know me as anything besides the man I really was. I worried if I confessed to someone who knew me more or knew me for longer, that the reception to my confession would be less than well received. If I sat with that, though, I knew it wasn't true. No one cared that Kale was gay and no one would care that I was probably bisexual or demisexual.

The problems were all in my head.

"I don't even know how to say this," I muttered, taking my glasses off and pinching the bridge of my nose.

"Generally putting words together to form a sentence is a good start." Shawn slid off the counter and shoved me out of the way so he could get into the fridge. He pulled out two cans of soda and handed me one before returning to his perch.

"I've kind of been...I don't know." I exhaled and popped the top on the can, taking a big swallow to buy myself time. "Talking with someone lately."

"Talking like dating?"

"Talking like talking," I corrected. "Not dating."

"Talking like we're talking?" he asked, a brow arched toward his hairline, "because you're not that great at it."

I laughed, shoulders sagging under the weight of my secret, the weight of my needs.

"Talking with intent," I clarified.

"A hook-up then?" he asked.

I nodded.

"That feels like a very normal thing, Boston." Shawn sipped his drink. "Is that not normal for you?"

"Not really."

"I don't mean to be forward, but what part of it?" He cocked his head to the side and scrunched his nose. "I don't want to pry, but I assume this is the conversation you wanted to have with me."

"It is," I said. "The prying helps."

Shawn laughed again. "I can ask leading questions, if that helps."

"It might."

"What's his name?"

I'd just raised my soda and taken a drink, but when the pronoun came out of Shawn's mouth so easily, I choked and sputtered, spitting soda out onto the floor. Shawn's eyes went wide and he jumped off the counter again, coming over and patting my back until my breathing went back to normal.

"Shit," I mumbled, setting my soda on the counter and reaching for a rag to clean up my mess.

Shawn went to the ground beside me, covering my hand with his and bringing my frantic swiping to a stop.

"Boston," he said my name gently, the way I'd heard him

talk to scared parents and anxious children before. "What about what I just said caused that reaction?"

"How...how did you know he was a he?"

Shawn pried the rag out of my hand and sat on the floor. I slid down onto my ass next to him, stretching my legs out and mentally comparing my pressed wool slacks to his well-worn jeans.

"I just assumed." He let out a high-pitched squeak of a laugh. "Was I wrong?"

"A week ago you would have been."

"Oh." A smile formed on his face, and I dropped my head against the fridge and stared up at the glaringly fluorescent lights in the ceiling above us.

"What makes this one special?" he asked, bumping me with his shoulder until I scooted over so we could both lean against the fridge.

There were undoubtedly a thousand things that made Ford special, but considering the rules of our relationship—or lack thereof—I didn't want to spend too much time thinking about any of them. I was already far more invested in the man than I should be, considering we'd agreed there was no future in it for us.

"He's not special," I lied. "He's just my first."

My face burned, and I angled my head to the left, hoping Shawn wouldn't be able to see the color blooming on my cheeks.

"Do you want confirmation that this is totally normal? Even if you're a bit of a late bloomer?" he asked, patting my thigh.

"I don't know," I admitted. "I just haven't talked to anyone about it and I think I'm losing my mind."

"Because you're attracted to a man?"

"Because I haven't told anyone," I said.

"What about your brother?" Shawn asked. "From what you've told me, the two of you are close and he's gay, right?"

"Yes to both, but the man in question is a friend of his."

Shawn laughed, kicking the dirty edge of his sneaker against my shoe. "I think they write books about this kind of thing."

"How do they end?"

"Happily," he assured me, using my leg to leverage himself back up to his feet. He checked the temperature on the soup and made a pleased sound. "Come help me batch this out and we can get out of here."

I knew where the storage containers were, so I pulled four of them out and lined them up on the counter while Shawn busied himself with the ladling and the pouring. He checked the temperature again before putting on the lids, then we put the containers into the fridge. Shawn didn't ask me any other questions while we worked to clean up the kitchen and turn off the lights, and I didn't offer him anything to go on until we were out and standing back on the steps.

"There's nothing wrong with being attracted the same gender, Boston," he said, giving me a soft rub across the top of my shoulder blades. "It's not the 1980s anymore."

"I know." I ground my molars together, giving him as complacent of a smile as I could manage. "I know."

"Did you want to get a drink?" he asked, an unexplained flicker of *something* in his eyes.

"I appreciate the offer, Shawn, but I think I'm good for now."

The look in his eyes vanished as fast as it appeared, and he gave me a small and apologetic-looking nod.

"If you change your mind, you know where to find me," he said, reaching out and giving my shoulder a squeeze.

"Thank you for that," I said, "and thank you for listening."

"That's what friends are for, right?" Shawn cleared his throat and headed down the steps, leaving me at the top to watch him go.

The conversation replayed over in my head, his words echoing more truth than lie the longer I thought about them. There wasn't any reason for me to be ashamed of being most likely interested in men now. What I didn't know, though, was why Ford was the only man who stirred up that attraction. Why he was the only one who made me want more than I ever had before?

When Shawn touched me, he might as well have been my brother. And I knew I hadn't spent a very long time thinking hard about what kind of men I found attractive or whether my blood burned when they touched me or not, but I worried even I had...

It would never compare to how I felt when I was with Ford.

**CHAPTER 10**
# FORD

THE BLACK DOOR HAD ALWAYS BEEN MY FAVORITE PLACE. IT HAD A good atmosphere, strong drinks, and generally great company. Even if my friends found little toys to entertain themselves with and wandered off, I'd always been content to admire the sights...and more often than not, the sounds. I also couldn't think of a single night I'd left the club without a companion, and I wasn't sure how I was going to get out now without arousing suspicion.

"Are you ill?" Brooks asked, collapsing into a chair beside me.

We'd been out for a couple of hours already. After drinks and some mindless chatter, Kale had taken Christian off somewhere, Alex had disappeared to sulk, and Brooks had found a brawny-looking little thing who wanted a spanking. My dear friend had been more than willing to oblige, but now found himself unentertained and plenty sober.

"Do I *look* ill?" I asked, raising a brow at him from behind the brim of my whiskey.

"You look alone," he said.

"I look like the whole pretense of this little outing was a waste of time," I countered, rolling my head from side to side to crack my neck. "Kale is too far up his little prince's asshole to notice, though."

"Don't act like you'd be any different if you met someone new."

I thought about Boston and checked my watch. It was almost eight, which meant I had another half hour to endure their escapades before I could try to make an escape.

"Just like Beamer did with that West Coast husband of his?" I asked. "I suppose it could be worse. Kale could have absconded to a Mediterranean island to rule alongside Christian."

"Christian is too far back in the line of succession to ever take the throne," Brooks said.

"You've done research?"

"I told him," Kale said, coming to sit on the small loveseat opposite the matching chairs Brooks and I occupied.

"Where's your boyfriend?" I asked.

"Taking a piss." Kale gestured toward the bathroom. "Which he is allowed to do without my attention."

"Sounds like you're missing out on a real opportunity," Brooks teased.

"I see his cock plenty," Kale said. "I don't need to hold it for him while he takes a leak."

"Wouldn't it be the other way around anyway?" I tilted my head to the side, nose scrunched in thought.

"Cock holding is entirely unnecessary," Kale grumbled, "much like this entire conversation."

"Don't blame us. We were left to our own devices," Brooks said.

"I was just commenting that you're the one who invited us out, but you haven't even been bothered to spend any time with us," I said, finishing off the amber liquor in my glass.

"You've always been fine on your own."

"That's not the point."

"What is the point?" he snapped.

"You're acting like Beamer, and we all remember how butt hurt you were over his behavior with Dalton Fox," I said.

"I didn't relocate."

"You didn't have to."

At that moment, Christian sauntered over to us, sliding down onto the couch and tucking himself against Kale's side. His eyes were barely more than hooded slits, his cheeks flushed and his lips swollen.

"You sure he was taking a piss?" I asked.

"I know what he was doing," Kale said, brushing Christian's hair back and kissing his forehead. "The question remains, though, what are *you* doing?"

"I just asked if he was ill," Brooks offered, entirely unhelpfully.

I'd not only had enough of the conversation, but also enough of the company. I would rather sit home alone and twiddle my erection while I waited for Boston to show up than endure another minute of this drivel.

"I am feeling a bit feverish." I set my drink down on the table between my chair and Brooks' and stood. My fingers were steady when I buttoned up my suit coat and smoothed my hand down my stomach. "I think I'll call it a night."

"Don't say I don't spend time with you," Kale said, almost teasing but not quite committed to the bit.

"We can get lunch next week."

I said goodbye to them both and made my way back to the street. It was getting too cold to walk, so I flagged down a cab and counted buildings as we headed uptown to my house. I got home at ten to eight, not surprised in the slightest to find Boston bundled up on my porch, a scarf wrapped around the bottom of his face and steam covering the lower half of his glasses with every breath. I tipped the cabbie and practically ran through the gate and up the steps to the door. Boston's hands were shoved into his pockets and the visible apples of his cheeks were pink from the cold. I fought every instinct in my body to yank the scarf down to expose his mouth so I could kiss him senseless on the spot. My hand was halfway raised when a shiver wracked through his entire body, making me aware of just how cold the evening air really was.

"How long were you waiting?" I asked instead, unlocking the door and giving him a shove inside.

"Not terribly long," he said.

"You should have texted me."

"Would you have gotten here any faster if I had?" Boston unwound the scarf from around his face, revealing flushed cheeks and a perfectly kissable mouth.

"I would have told you where the spare key was," I said, finishing the job of unraveling the scarf from around his neck. I hung it on the coat rack by my door, then carefully divested him of his coat and added it to the same hook. He was still dressed for work, with brown oxfords, navy slacks, and a white button-up rolled up to his elbows.

I shrugged out of my pea coat and hung it up, then stripped myself of my suit coat, which I dropped on the small cushioned chair beside my shoe rack.

"Did you want a drink?" I asked, rubbing my hands

together to get them warm—and to keep them from touching him too soon.

"I want to kiss naked." Boston shoved a folded up piece of paper at me. "I'm all clear, by the way."

It suddenly felt like the Sahara Desert had relocated to my throat. It was dry and vast and impossible to swallow when I opened up the paper and read through Boston's thorough STI panel. I refolded it and handed it back to him without a word. Not because I didn't have anything to say, but because it was impossible for me to speak.

I'd spent the whole week thinking what Boston and I had already done together was the point of no return, but somehow with him here in my home again, it felt forgivable… unavoidable. This next step, though? Getting him naked and onto my bed where I had free range to touch the parts of him that up to this point I'd only imagined? It was far more damning than anything before it had been.

"And I want more of the rest of it," he said, clearing his throat and turning his attention toward my stairs.

"What's the rest of it?"

"The parts where you tell me what to do," he whispered.

I closed my eyes, angling my head toward the ceiling and biting my lips together to act as one more failsafe designed to stop me from saying something I had no right to even think about, let alone give voice to.

"Please don't change your mind," he said softly, reaching out and tracing the tips of his fingers over the top of my hand. "I still want this."

"I know you do."

"Do you?" he asked.

"Very much, sweetheart."

How was Boston Sheffield so perfect for me? So willing and ready for everything? I'd been with eager men before, but it had always felt scripted, contrived. Like they were playing a part that they imagined I expected of them. There was none of that with Boston. He was honest and sincere, and he was just...horny. And curious, which was quickly proving to be a dangerous combination for me.

"Please."

"Right," I agreed, opening my eyes and letting myself look at him.

It was a mistake.

The fog had evaporated off his glasses, revealing dilated eyes that were dark with a want so tangible if I stared at him too long, I could imagine it wrapping around me and strangling us both. But he touched me again, a soft dance of his fingertips across my knuckles, up my hand, to the top of my wrist, and I was gone.

"Let's get you upstairs then," I said, words rough and unrecognizable to my own ears.

I turned my hand, threading our fingers together and leading him toward the stairs and up to my room. He held on to me tightly, all nervous energy and arousal...another risky pair. Not just for his feelings, but also the two of us. I did my best to ignore it, pulling him behind me into my room.

"I don't know what I expected, but it wasn't this," he said, breath hot against the back of my neck.

He was so close.

I tried to see my room from his eyes, wondering how the wide plank wood floors and the four poster bed against the exposed brick wall would read to someone who didn't know me well. My bedroom was sparse, but comfortable, with expensive white bedding on the king size mattress, and a matching bedroom set. I found my space entirely ordinary and predictable.

"Did you think I slept in a sex dungeon?" I asked, pulling him ahead of me and deeper into the room.

"I did imagine there to be more leather."

I chuckled, plucking open the buttons on my shirt until it was halfway undone. Boston had his back to me, still surveying the room, from the plants on my dresser to the art on my walls, and the cat bed beside the door to the en suite. Milo, of course, was nowhere to be found.

"Sorry to disappoint," I murmured.

Boston spun, startled like he'd almost forgotten I was there. His stare quickly traveled from my face to the exposed V of my chest.

He shook his head, letting out a nervous breath. "I'm not disappointed."

I scratched my collarbone, and Boston's eyes followed the path of my fingers. The man was primed and ready, a live wire about to explode. I wasn't too terribly far behind him, the anticipation of the week proving to be more of a drug than I'd expected. I should have had him take his own clothes off, but I didn't seem to be able to make good decisions when it involved him, so I beckoned him closer. With far less space between us, I had to bite the inside of my cheek to slow myself down, to remind myself that Boston was practically a virgin and sex was definitely not on the table for us tonight.

"Can I undress you?" I asked, gently pressing my finger against the top button of his white dress shirt.

"You don't have to ask."

"I'll always ask," I promised him, popping open the first button.

He sucked in a quiet breath, and I worked my way down until I reached his waistband. I went for him with both hands then, giving the tails of his shirt a tug until they came free of his pants. We worked together to get the rolled cuffs back down his forearms, and then his undershirt, and then I reached for his belt. I couldn't look at him long, because Boston was unequivocally gorgeous, with a farmer's body that he'd never quite outgrown. He was muscular and broad, far stronger than his brother—I knew that from sight alone.

"Pants next?" I asked.

"That's part of undressing," he murmured.

"You're so brave," I said, giving his belt a tug until the tine popped loose from the leather hole, then I pulled the belt off of him entirely. Dropping it on the floor with his shirt, I undid his fly and let his pants fall to his ankles.

"Not brave," he said, mouth flitting into half of a smile. "Just ready."

I'd have to be brave enough for the both of us then, because this was the most terrifying thing I'd ever done.

"You do the rest of it, Boston," I said, gesturing to his feet, "and then you can do me next."

GeTTING OUT OF MY SHOES, SOCKS, AND PANTS WAS LIKE RUNNING ON autopilot. I kept my underwear on because it felt weird for me to be naked and for Ford to be dressed, but when I reached for him, he grasped my wrist and stopped me dead in my tracks.

"I said the rest of it." His voice was rougher than usual, lower, more dangerous.

"Ford." My protest was weak, and I think we could both tell my heart wasn't really in it.

My heart was actually in my throat, threatening to choke me to death over the whole affair. I tried to swallow around it, and Ford guided my hand down to the waistband of my tight boxer briefs. I was already hard, had been for hours, and my cock pressed insistently at the stretchy cotton fabric that tried desperately to keep it at bay.

"I'm fairly certain you'll like it, sweetheart." He traced his finger along the inside of my wrist and then lightly across the point where my hip met the waistband of my underwear. Gooseflesh tore through me, and I swallowed my heart back into my chest.

"It's just a lot of being seen," I murmured, eyes rolling back at the tenderness of his fingers against my skin.

"Isn't that the point?" He took a step closer, trailing his hand up my ribs and over my chest until his fingers wrapped around the side of my neck. I leaned into his hold, happy for how grounding the closeness of him made me feel.

"I'm not sure of the point anymore," I admitted, but Ford cut off the sentiment by pressing his lips against mine.

The moan that left my mouth should have embarrassed me, but Ford must have liked it. He yanked me toward him, our chests crashing together, leaving me painfully aware of my nakedness against his clothing. Heat simmered in my stomach, annoyed that there were layers between us still when I'd been so looking forward to kissing him naked and being able to get my hands on him.

Ford nipped my lower lip, tilting my face toward the ceiling and kissing his way along the underside of my jaw. I realized he'd been right all along. I should have taken his clothes off like he'd asked and then we would have been one step closer to the thing I'd been daydreaming about all week. But, to be fair, more than once I'd let my mind wander to more than just kissing naked.

With a growl against the pulse point beneath my ear, Ford gave me a gentle shove back, effectively ending the kiss. I swayed on my feet, lips parted and still chasing after him for more.

"The rest of it," he repeated slowly, letting his hand slide down my chest. "And then, me."

I wasn't going to argue a second time with him. I shoved my underwear down so quickly that I stumbled, falling into his chest. Ford chuckled, wrapping his hands around my biceps to help me steady myself, but I was on him before he could move away. Tearing madly at the buttons of his shirt, the belt around his waist, I knew I should have taken it slower so I could catalogue and appreciate the maleness of him, but I was far too gone with arousal to care about any of that. Maybe when the newness of him had worn off…I'd make sure to remember it all before our time was through.

Beneath his tailored slacks, Ford wore a tight pair of black briefs with a geometric gold pattern around the waist. The fabric was soft and thick, but not anywhere near strong enough to contain the erection that had grown between his legs. He was big down there, probably bigger than me, but I wouldn't know for sure until I took his underwear off. They were the last scrap of material between us, and I glanced up, throat going dry at the hungry way Ford watched my fingers work across his skin.

"Slow. Down," he said quietly. "We have the rest of the night, Boston. I don't turn into sugar at midnight."

"I'm sorry, I just…"

"Kiss me," he said, and I did.

It was already easy to slant my head at the right angle so our mouths could cover as much real estate as possible, easy to part my lips and make way for his tongue to slide against mine to explore the backs of my teeth. He threaded his fingers through the hair at the base of my neck, steering my head to get his tongue even deeper into my mouth, and I finally found a hold of his waistband and shoved his underwear down to his thighs.

He shimmied his legs to get out of them entirely, then walked us backward to the bed, mouths still fused together. Fear curled around the base of my spine when the backs of my knees hit the bed, but Ford shifted so he landed on his back and I landed on top of him. This was a position I'd found myself in more than once, though generally with a smaller body beneath mine, and Ford had one throbbing addition that was very new to the experience.

His erection brushed against mine as I found a comfortable straddle over the top of him, and he groaned into my mouth so loudly that my bones rattled. This was really happening. I was kissing a man, I was naked with a man, and I was so fucking hard for this man I couldn't even think straight. I'd never done any of these things before, but my body screamed for *more*. My hips pumped, grinding down against Ford and chasing after friction to ease the ache in my cock. His hands came around my waist, curled tight into the dips of my hips.

"Kissing naked," he said against my mouth.

"We are."

"*Just* kissing naked," he said.

"I don't know if I can," I admitted, breaking away from the kiss and burying my face in the crook of his neck to catch my breath. It wasn't much better there. I'd only traded the lure of his mouth for the intoxicating scent of his skin, either of which was likely to be my end. But as I breathed against his neck, Ford relaxed his hold on my waist, petting his fingers up and down my sides, across my shoulders, down the swell of my back toward my ass and back up again.

"You have to, sweetheart," he whispered, kissing the side of my head where he could reach me.

Untangling myself from his arms, I flopped onto my back, tossing my glasses toward the nightstand with a sigh. I covered my face with both of my hands, but there was no escape. The smell of Ford was still in my nose, the heat of him burning hot against the outside of my arm. My cock twitched in the air, needy to get back to the warmth of Ford's thigh for some more friction. Ford rolled onto his side to face me, using the tip of his finger to draw swirls over my hip and the outside of my thigh. "You're gorgeous."

I closed my eyes and turned my head to the side. "So are you."

"No." He shook his head, a small smile dancing across his lips. "Truly, Boston. You're breathtaking and it's really fucking hard to take things slow with you."

"You don't have to go slow." The words were high-pitched, even to my own ears, and my cheeks burned with shame over my eagerness.

"Oh, sweetheart." Ford brought his hand to my face and dragged his finger across my cheekbone. "Not everything is for you."

He leaned back in again and kissed me. Softer that time, more cursory, like he'd never been inside of my mouth before. The kiss wasn't hurried, wasn't rushed, and I could have melted into the bed, melted into him, for how torturous it was. My body burned with a need that I'd never experienced before, synapses crossing and misfiring at every possible connection point.

My eyes fell closed and I pressed myself deeper into the kiss. Ford hooked his leg over my hip and pulled me against him, bringing back the smoldering heat of his cock against my thigh. I couldn't stop myself from pumping against his leg, which earned a smile and another soft kiss to the corner of my mouth.

"You can touch me, Boston," he rasped, and it wasn't until then that I realized I hadn't been.

With our mouths still slanted together, I gave myself leave to explore the hard angles of Ford's slender body. He was strong, the muscles pulled taut beneath his skin and quivering, like it took work for him to stay still beneath my touch. I propped myself up, changing the angle of the kiss so I could work my hands up his ribs and his stomach. Against the tips of my fingers, his nipple hardened, and the groan he loosed in response to my touch was low enough to vibrate my bones.

It was the sexiest thing I'd ever heard in my life.

I levered myself back on top of him, feeling far bolder and less afraid than before. I turned my attention to the swell of his biceps, dragging his arms up over his head so I could reach every exposed inch of muscle and skin on him. When I reached his wrists, I gave an experimental press down into the sheets, and Ford growled, moving faster than I'd ever seen and flipping me onto my back.

"Don't get ahead of yourself, sweetheart," he chided, tearing his mouth away from mine and kissing my cheek, my chin, my jaw, down my throat and up my neck. My hips bucked off the bed, and I was helpless to control my own body. When Ford touched me, when he kissed me, licked me, my body responded like he was talking directly to my cells and my nerve endings. Every place he touched me sizzled, and I wanted more than anything for his fire to consume me entirely.

"I can't help it."

He licked a hot stripe from the dip of my throat to the underside of my chin.

"I need you to try harder," he whispered. "I'm not a good

man, Boston. Please don't give me the chance to prove that to you."

Ford kissed my lips, then dropped his forehead against mine, breathing heavy. I could feel every inhale. When his stomach expanded, his weight bore down on me and when he exhaled, I could breathe again. An embarrassing amount of precum had leaked out of my cock, smeared against my stomach and Ford's.

With surprisingly steady hands against his hips, I settled under his weight and closed my eyes. His cock jerked and twitched against me, every move drawing some new and guttural noise from the back of his throat. I could taste the tension with every breath against my cheek, and I slid my hands up his back, appreciating the planes of his shoulders and the muscles there.

"I'm trying," I promised.

Ford nodded, rolling his forehead across mine before pushing himself up so his hands were pressed flat against the bed on either side of my head. He stared down at me, the dark pools of his eyes nearly indecipherable. Maybe it was because I wasn't wearing my glasses, but I was certain there were answers there that I simply wasn't seeing.

"I know."

Ford kissed the tip of my nose and rolled onto his back. I looked down my chest, finding both of our cocks hard and long, pointing toward the ceiling. Ford's was longer than mine, but not as thick, with a bit of a curve near the base. I fisted the sheets to stop myself from reaching for it, the tug of the high thread count material not going unnoticed. Ford raised his ass, giving me more fabric to gather between my shaking fingers.

"What are your initial thoughts?" he asked, sounding like we were negotiating a business contract, not orgasms or my exploration of the male form.

I swallowed, blinking his ceiling into focus.

Even though my interest and fascination with men was new, I really hadn't thought too hard about the mechanics of being intimate with a man. I understood it would be different in some ways, similar in others. And when I'd propositioned Ford to let me learn on him, I hadn't been thinking toward what the last lesson would be. I knew there would be kissing and touching and, in the back of my head, I knew there would also be sex, but I hadn't put together just how badly I wanted that until I'd felt the heavy press of Ford's body against mine.

"I think I want to do a lot more than just kiss you naked," I admitted.

Ford huffed out a laugh that sounded like it died somewhere in the back of his throat. I exhaled until my lungs collapsed and rubbed the bridge of my nose.

"Yeah," he agreed. "I was afraid of that."

I KNEW THAT SPENDING THE NIGHT IN BED WITH A MAN WAS *NOT* THE next step after naked kissing, but there was no way I was going to let Boston leave unless he requested to go. I'd asked him to not give me the chance to prove to him how bad of a person I was, but every moan and sigh and buck of his hips drove me closer to the point of no return.

Hell, who was I kidding? I'd blown past it the first time he grabbed my leg in his brother's office.

"Ford." My name was a single syllable and it still cracked as he whispered it at me.

"What do you need, sweetheart?"

We'd been lying on our backs for what felt like hours to catch our breath, and at the sound of his voice, I rolled onto my side to watch him instead. He was gorgeous, chest still heaving with every inhale and his cock still jutting proudly out from the dark thatch of hair between his legs.

"Am I allowed to ask for things?" He angled his head toward the side to face me.

"That's how we got here, isn't it?"

Boston made a bemused noise. "I want to come," he whispered, licking his lips and looking back up at my ceiling.

I should have known it was coming. I *did* know it was coming, no pun intended. Kissing, kissing naked, the next step was going to involve either a hand or mouth around Boston's thick cock, and then...

I couldn't dare think that far ahead, lest I embarrass myself.

"Tonight was supposed to be kissing," I reminded him.

"We *have* kissed." Boston looped his thumb and finger around the base of his dick. "This is what kissing got me."

It was hard to understand why every step with Boston felt like one more pace toward damnation. Harder even still to understand why I was fighting against him—and myself—so vehemently. That hadn't ever been my style, and it shouldn't have been an exception with Boston. He should have been an absolute dream come true—a handsome man with no experience who only wanted me for my body and sometimes called me Sir? I couldn't have drawn up a more perfect textbook definition of my dream man, though I probably wouldn't have made him my best friend's brother.

"Don't move."

I flung my legs out of bed and walked from the room without looking back. I needed to breathe, I needed a drink, and I found myself in the kitchen, bent over my sink and my stare trained out the window toward my back yard. Even with space between us, my cock still ached for the man in my bed, the man in my heart...

Fumbling for the half-drank glass of wine I abandoned earlier in the night, I poured the room temperature red down my throat with one long swallow. The problem wasn't with

Boston. He was as perfect as he could be, as eager and willing as I'd want him to be. The issue sat solely with me and my borderline obsession with him. I could only focus my energy in one place, I realized. I could pretend it was okay for things to just be physical between us, or I could be good and go slow. For some reason, I found myself utterly incapable of managing both. Pacing from one end of my kitchen to the other, with the ever elusive Milo weaving his way between my ankles, I had to decide which was going to win out.

In the end, the decision was an easy one.

When I went back to the bedroom five minutes later, Boston hadn't moved an inch. He still loosely grasped his cock around the base and his eyes were still staring up at my ceiling. At my return, his eyes shifted toward me, but beyond that, the only movement was his chest on every long and drawn out breath.

"We need to talk." I sat down on the edge of the bed, reaching past him for a pillow, which I dropped on his lap.

Boston moved slowly to sit, trying to hold the pillow down over his legs and his cock. He moved into a cross-legged position, and I handed him his glasses from the nightstand next. Carefully, he slid them onto his face, the corner of his mouth flickering into an unsure smile before falling away.

"Did I do something wrong?" he asked softly, gazing down at his lap.

"I don't think you ever could." I covered his nervous hands with my own, lifting his toward my mouth and brushing a kiss over the tops of his knuckles before letting them fall back on top of the pillow.

"What, then?"

"I know you think of me as a tool," I started, scrunching

my nose at how unfair the description felt, even though I was at a loss for a better word. "A means to an end."

"Ford, no."

"That's what we agreed, Boston. It's fine. I mean, it's not fine…" I groaned, tilting my head to the side and scratching my temple. "I'm not as capable of fulfilling my half of this agreement as I thought I'd be."

The only sounds in the entire room were Boston's trembling exhale and the rapid heartbeat that echoed in my ears.

"It's so hard for me to control myself around you," I said.

"Then don't."

"You don't know what you're asking."

"I told you before, I'm not some blushing virgin, Ford."

I brushed the back of my knuckle across his cheek "You're blushing right now."

"I just want to fuck. We agreed, didn't we?" He rolled his eyes like he was disgusted with me. He looked so much like his brother, but also so different at the same time. Boston and Kale were clearly fraternal, but their mannerisms were so similar sometimes. "Your reputation has preceded you for years, so I don't understand why it's such a problem for you to fuck *me* when you don't have an issue fucking everyone else."

I knew what he was doing. He wouldn't have been the first to try and test me, to push my buttons to get their way. But Boston was coming at it from a place of rejection and not a place of restraint. He didn't understand the war in my head. He couldn't.

"That's not what I'm saying," I corrected.

He rolled his eyes, flinging the pillow to the side. He was still half--hard, even with the argument between us.

"This was a stupid idea," he muttered, shifting to get out

of bed, which was the absolute last thing I was going to allow him to do in that moment.

I moved without thinking, flinging one leg over his lap and grabbing his jaw with the other hand. His eyes went wide, and I forced him onto his back, pressing him down hard into the sheets with an extra jerk of my arm.

"You're not listening to me," I warned.

I had to let go of him, flexing my hand into a fist and letting it fall onto the bed beside his head. Dominance was like a second skin to me, something I could never truly separate myself from. Not that I wanted to. But there were circumstances and situations where I found it hard to control. Heat rolled up my spine at Boston's half-hearted protests, and I imagined a hundred different ways to disprove what he'd just accused me of. If he were anyone besides himself, his ass would have already been purple from the spanking.

"I don't want to *just* fuck you, Boston. I don't want to be a cock you use to learn about how to suck other cocks. Do you understand me?"

My arms trembled from holding me up alongside the weight of my confession. Beneath me, past the clear lenses of his glasses, Boston's pupils were dilated, eyes searching my face for any hint of lie or manipulation in my words.

"I bet this is how you treat everyone," he whispered, lashes fluttering as he gave his head a small shake. "You want everyone to feel special."

"You're wrong." I climbed off of him, getting off the bed to stop myself from using my hands to show him just how wrong he was.

"Ford." The sheets rustled behind me.

"In fact," I went on, turning on my heel to find him

kneeling up on the bed. "I'd much rather the men I'm with *don't* feel special. It makes things easier."

"Does it?"

My mouth was dry as cotton, and I licked my lips, wondering how this virgin of a man—who up until two weeks prior had thought himself straight—was able to unman me with such a natural grace and skill.

"I haven't been able to stop thinking about you," I said, rubbing my hand over my bare thigh, the spot he'd held me in Kale's office when we'd hatched this whole plan in the first place. His stare flickered to the contact point, then back up to my face. "But I can't *just* fuck you, Boston. It's...it's not possible."

Boston blinked slowly, worrying the corner of his mouth with the tip of his tongue. Neither of us spoke and the air grew thick with the truth of my confession. He breathed heavily, entire body moving with how much work it took to fill his lungs with air, and I fisted my hands together behind my back.

"What are you asking for then?" he asked softly.

Flashbacks of our conversation in Kale's office bounced around my mind, when I'd forced him to use his words to admit what he wanted from me. Look where that had gotten us. I wasn't delusional enough to think that me leveraging my own confession back at him would make much of a difference. We were already on a crash course for hell.

"I want to fuck you, sweetheart, more than anything, but I don't *just* want that."

"Are you saying you want to date me?"

When was the last time I'd dated anyone? I couldn't even

remember. I doubted my memory went back that far. But dating Boston raised a whole new set of problems, separate from the set that came from taking my best friend's brother to bed. I could hear the hesitation in his voice, though. See it in the way his back bowed and he moved away from me. I needed to do damage control or I was going to lose him entirely, and in all the scenarios of how things played out between us, that wasn't ever an option.

"You said you wanted to know what it was like to be with a man." I cleared my throat, rubbing my clavicle and giving him what I hoped read as a calm and collected smile. I didn't want him to know that inside I was panicking over him slipping through my fingers like sand. I'd done it again, gotten in over my head, and...

"I did," he said softly, interrupting my downward spiral.

"Fucking is only part of that." I wanted to drive the point home, make sure he understood what I was trying to sell him on. What it meant for us both.

"You're not wrong." His shoulders relaxed, and he sank down, dropping his ass onto his heels.

"And maybe I want to know what it's like too."

"What what's like?"

"Being with someone for more than sex,"

Boston inhaled sharply, lifting his glasses and rubbing the bridge of his nose. It had to be a nervous habit, a tired one. He shifted, landing on the bed and straightening his legs out in front of him with a sigh. He looked a little less likely to leave, and I dared a step closer.

"When was the last time you did that?" he asked.

"I can't remember."

"Why me?" Boston dropped his glasses back onto the

bridge of his nose. "How do I know you're being for real with me right now?"

"Believe me, sweetheart, it would be plenty easier for us both if I just took you to bed and washed my hands of the whole thing after."

He winced at the dismissive way I talked about our arrangement, and I closed more of the space between us, hating to see the look on his face but desperate for him to understand how what we'd agreed to before was different from what I was asking for now.

"But I'm not interested in that," I said. "In fact, the idea of you being intimate with another man makes my skin crawl."

He swallowed.

I sat down beside him on the bed, both of us still naked like our plan to only kiss on top of the sheets had ever been within the realm of possibility for a man like me. The outside of our thighs brushed together, and I relished how warm and soft his skin was against mine.

"And what about the idea of me dating another man?"

"Please don't ask me that," I whispered.

"Be honest with me."

"I don't think there's a man on this planet who's good enough for you, Boston, least of all me," I said.

Boston threaded our fingers together, looking down at the places his fingers settled between the swell of my knuckles. I turned our hands over, squeezing him tightly and appreciating the feel of his hand in mine. I couldn't remember the last time I'd dated anyone, let alone the last time I'd held someone's hand.

Fuck Boston Sheffield for bringing these feelings out in me. He was too good and too innocent to be with a man like me, but I was too horrible and selfish to let him walk away. I was no longer interested in admiring him from afar. I wanted to own him entirely, and when the time came for him to walk away from me, I wanted it to hurt. I promised myself in that moment that I would bear the brunt of any pain I brought him for the rest of my life. This was something a man like me shouldn't have wanted, but the idea of being intimate with Boston, of having a relationship with him, it sounded like a reprieve from the loneliness that had shaped my life up to that point...and the sorrow that would come after he left me.

"Okay." Boston had been quiet for so long, the gentle cadence of his voice startled me.

"Pardon?"

"I've never thought about being with a man before," he said. "Not physically and definitely not as a boyfriend or anything like that."

At his use of the word *boyfriend,* the skin on the back of my neck stood up, but I shook my head to clear it off. This was what I wanted. This was the best case scenario. This was what I'd come in here to ask him for, so why did it feel so wrong now that he was leaning toward agreement?

"But I've thought about both with you," he went on. "So, as long as you're willing, I'd like to try."

"I don't think I have a choice in the matter," I told him. "I don't know *why*, but I need to have this with you."

"Have you ever dated a man before, Ford?" He brought our hands—still joined—to his mouth and kissed them the way I had earlier.

"Not with the intent that I have for you." I licked my lips, entranced by the way his dusted across the tops of my knuckles.

"So, you're my first and I'm yours?" He lowered our hands to his lap, the hard, searing heat of his cock burning the top of my wrist.

God, he was perfect. So innocent and unsuspecting, but so capable of speaking up for the things he wanted and needed. At every turn, Boston surprised me, and this conversation wasn't proving to be an exception to that rule. He was going to be my undoing either way; there was no point in fighting my demise any longer.

"Yes," I rasped, untangling my hand from his and pushing him down onto his back. "I'll be your first, sweetheart."

"Will you be gentle?" He pulled his glasses off and tossed them back toward the nightstand, arching his neck to bring our mouths closer together.

"I'm not fucking you tonight, sweetheart."

"Of course not. Just naked kissing, right?" Boston lifted a brow and I leaned down, kissing the smug arrogance right off his face.

"Just naked kissing."

And dating.

And trusting.

And sharing.

And *owning*.

And also, probably...falling in love.

Except for a coffee date with Shawn on Sunday afternoon, I spent an embarrassing amount of my weekend in front of the full-length mirror in my closet, pinching, pulling, and tugging at my skin. I felt different inside, in ways I wasn't sure how to explain, and I was desperate to see if that had shown up outwardly at all.

Closing my eyes, I slumped back against the rack of hanging slacks, falling into them until my shoulders hit the wall with matching soft thumps. I stretched my legs out in front of me, batting the clothes out of the way so I could continue my pointless appraisal. There wasn't anything different about my body, save for the lightest pink rash on the underside of my jaw from where Ford had spent an inordinate amount of time rubbing his face against me on Saturday morning. If I touched the abraded skin and closed my eyes, I could smell him in my nose, feel the heat of his body pressing into my side, the hard swell of his cock against my hip. Just thinking about it was enough to make my own cock hard again, which wasn't shocking. I'd pretty much had a permanent erection since the first time he kissed me.

In the other room, my phone pinged an alarm at me, an annoying reminder that I had five minutes until I was supposed to leave for work. Begrudgingly, I rolled onto my hands and knees and then up to my feet. I didn't pay attention to the slacks I picked—they were blue—or the shirt—it was gray. I picked a pair of gray and pink polka-dotted socks, then shuffled into the bedroom to turn off my alarm.

I spent the walk to Kale's office mentally trying to convince myself it was time to accept the truth of the change that had happened to me. It was all internal, all tangled and messy in the center of my chest, and it was all made up of feelings I'd never had before. Even back when Colette and I were together, I'd never felt for her the things I felt for Ford. Colette was nice and she was pretty and she was fine, but with Ford, the need for him boiled in my marrow. Having him was a matter of life and death and that was frightening and exhilarating in equal measure.

At first, I was scared because he was a man, but I couldn't think of a better man to be my first. No matter what Ford said about himself, he had integrity and he was an honest man. He'd never lied to me about who he was or what he wanted, and even on Friday night...he'd been truthful. He wanted more from me, and I didn't think it was possible to tell him no. Not like I wanted to. I found myself starved for all of the things he talked about, the things he promised.

But more than anything else, parts from our first kiss kept coming back to me and burying themselves deep into my brain. When I called him Sir. When I liked it. He wanted to shield me from that life, but I had spent almost thirty years hiding from myself; I didn't have it in me to continue. I knew Ford was into kink, knew my brother was as well. It wasn't something I'd ever thought about for myself. I didn't jerk off thinking about being on my knees for someone, or at least I hadn't until recently. Everything in my life was changing, and I knew myself well enough to know how fast that could get out of control. I needed a way to ground myself, or I would get swept up in the feelings and the newness of the whole thing and who knew how that would end.

When I got to the office, everything was dark. Checking my watch, I confirmed Kale wasn't due for another hour at least. I got myself some coffee and settled in, checking his calendar for the day to make sure there wasn't anything pressing in the morning, and then I started my research. Googling kink and men and New York produced an overwhelming amount of results, most of which felt a lot like prostitution at best and grooming at worst. There were encyclopedia websites where I taught myself some more robust definitions of words I'd heard before, and then I found some videos...

I texted myself that link so I could come back to it when I wasn't at work.

I wasn't supposed to have erections at work.

Kale blew into the office later than expected, just before eleven, with a hickey on his neck so fresh I could still see Christian's spit shining against his skin.

"Did I miss anything?" he asked, tearing his scarf off and tossing it onto the coat rack behind the door.

"You don't have any meetings until one today," I said.

He hung his coat then turned toward me. I pressed my

fingers against my neck, raising an eyebrow. Kale cursed under his breath, slapping his hand over the fresh bruise.

"Your meeting can be moved to a call," I offered.

"Please and thank you."

Kale rubbed his neck like the hickey was a marker and he'd be able to get it off if he tried hard enough, and I imagined that was one of my brother's best qualities. He hated being told no, and he would rarely take it as a final answer. He'd practically stormed a castle to kidnap Christian, and there was something painfully romantic about that.

Ford didn't strike me as the romantic type.

"What's wrong?" Kale asked, narrowing his eyes at me.

"What do you mean?"

"Your entire mood just changed." He gestured vaguely at my face, and I adjusted my glasses.

"I just didn't have breakfast," I told him.

"Do you want to order us lunch from the cafe?" he asked. "I feel like it's been a while since we've hung out and I also feel like you're hiding something."

My pulse spiked and I prayed my face hadn't flushed. "I'm not hiding anything. I'll get sandwiches, though."

"I'll get settled in." That was as much of a goodbye as he was going to give in business mode, which was fine.

I hated the implication the changes I'd been struggling with over the weekend were somehow physical. Not that I was ashamed of it or the things Ford and I did, but I hadn't even thought about how to tell my brother about it, let alone strangers. Did I even have to come out? What was I coming out *as* in the first place? Thinking about it gave me a headache, and I tried to wash it down with a burning swallow of coffee.

I pulled up the website for the lobby cafe and ordered

sandwiches, chips, and drinks for me and Kale, interrupted by my cell phone flashing and vibrating along the desk with a call.

"Hey, Mom," I answered, sliding an earbud in and leaning back in my chair.

"You're up early, Boston," she said.

"It's almost lunch here. I've been up for hours."

"So have I." She chuckled. "How are things?"

"Fine." My back went straight, like someone had stabbed a sword down the center of it. "Why?"

"Just making conversation, dear. But, also, a mother knows."

"A mother knows what?" I asked.

"Mothers intuition, I don't know. You know how you and your brother have always known each other's secrets? It's kind of like that, but not as strong."

"Kale doesn't know my secrets," I protested, looking nervously over my shoulder at his closed office door. "I don't have secrets."

My mom answered that with silence.

I reached back to rub the bottom of my neck, and I imagined grabbing the sword handle and tearing it out so I could relax.

"Have you decided when you want to come for a stay?" she asked, masterfully changing the subject.

My shoulders relaxed and I tossed my glasses onto the desk.

"No, but soon," I said. "Maybe in a couple of weeks."

"That's very soon," she agreed. "Whatever you like, but that feels rushed."

I'd already pulled up the airline website on my computer.

"Rushed in what way? We've been talking about this for months."

"Is right now the best time to be away?" she asked.

I swallowed, hating the way she knew there was something going on, knowing there was some reason for me to not up and leave the state.

Behind me, Kale's door cracked open and he stuck his head out. I swiveled around to see what he wanted.

"Brooks is bringing up the sandwiches," he said.

"Mom, hold on," I said to her before answering my brother. "Is he joining us?"

Kale scrunched his nose. "Just you and me. He was just coming by to drop off a contract."

"Okay."

In my ear, my mom was talking again. "Was that your brother?"

"Yes, Mom."

"How is he?"

"Very involved with his boyfriend," I said. "We're having lunch shortly. It's been a while since we've seen each other."

"I thought you worked for him."

"Outside of work," I told her.

"So, a couple weeks?" she asked.

"For what?"

"For your visit."

My mom was absolutely giving me whiplash with this conversation, but I glanced up at the screen on my computer once more. The flights weren't that expensive, and while I wasn't necessarily keen to not have Ford within kissing distance, I also didn't think the space would be a bad thing. Maybe it would give me an opportunity to think through all of the changes and be sure I was making the right decision.

"Delivery." Brooks knocked on the metal door frame and gave the bag of sandwiches a little shake.

I smiled and waved at him, pointing at the earbud.

"Mom, I'll book something and let you know soon," I said.

"Hello, Mrs. Sheffield," Brooks called out, dropping the food onto my desk and leaning down to make sure his voice carried.

"Who's that there?" she asked with a laugh.

"It's Brooks."

"Ah." The pleasure in her voice was palpable. "Astor. How is he?"

"He's as fine as Kale is," I told her.

Brooks smiled, clearly impressed that my mom was asking after him. But that was her way. She was thoughtful and had a mind like a steel trap. She remembered all of my friends' names, all of Kale's friends' names, and I honestly believed she cared about the answers when she asked after them.

"I'm better than Kale," he said with a smug smile.

"I'll talk to you later, Mom. Love you."

"Love you, dear."

I disconnected the call and dropped my earbud onto the desk beside my glasses.

"What brings you up this way?" I asked Brooks.

"Had this contract for your brother." He waved a manila envelope and dropped it on top of the sandwiches.

"Did you want to give it to him? He's just..." I trailed off, gesturing over my shoulder toward his office with my thumb.

"Gotta run," he said, standing up and mimicking the gesture I'd made, but over his shoulder instead. And that was when I realized Ford was standing in the doorway, filling as much of the space as his slender and strong body allowed.

"Boston," he said slowly, stare transfixed on me and the corner of his mouth fighting a smile.

"Ford," I murmured, clearing my throat.

Behind me, Kale's office door opened, but Ford didn't look away from me. His stare danced across my face, dragging slowly up the curve of my jaw, and I wondered if he could still see the burn on my skin from his five o-clock shadow.

"I'm hungry," Kale said.

"So am I." Ford was still looking at me.

I exhaled a trembling breath, then blinked long and hard, hoping it would break the trance between us. I couldn't stand up and take the sandwiches into Kale's office with a half-plump cock hanging between my legs, and the longer Ford studied me, the harder it got.

"Thank you for bringing up the sandwiches," Kale told Brooks, clearly unaware of the sexual tension that existed between me and Ford. "Should we plan for The Black Door on Friday again?"

"That works for me." Brooks fidgeted with the button on his jacket.

"What about you, Ford?"

Ford licked the corner of his mouth and finally looked away, his stare flickering up toward my brother behind me. "Not sure yet," he said softly.

"What?" Brooks and Kale both asked in unison. "Since when are you not down for a night out?"

I rubbed my throat, letting my chin fall toward my chest. It was impossible to keep my head up, to look at him. This wasn't something we'd talked about Friday night when we'd decided *dating behind my brother's back* was a good idea. How were we going to hide it? How *long* were we going to hide it for? What was the ruse?

I flicked a look at him, the whole turn of the conversation working wonders at deflating my cock. Standing from my chair, I grabbed the folder from Brooks and the bag with our lunch in it.

"That's not what I said." Ford stood straighter, squaring his shoulders like he'd forgotten himself for a second, but quickly recovered. "It all depends on if Boston is coming or not."

He winked at me, and my heart hitched right up into the back of my throat.

"Stop trying to fuck my brother, asshole," Kale warned, but he rolled his eyes as he said it. He didn't think the threat was real. "He's straight and he's off-limits."

The quirk in Ford's mouth finally won out, his lip curling up into the slightest tease of a knowing smile. My cheeks burned.

"Of course he is." He dragged his tongue across the front of his teeth, then clapped Brooks on the back. "Are you ready to go?"

"Yeah. Yep." Brooks gave a general wave toward me and Kale. "Enjoy your lunch. Get that contract red-lined before the end of the day."

"See you later, Boston," Ford said, voice low like a promise.

I tried to play it off like I had before, but I wasn't as good of an actor as he was.

"Not if I can help it," Kale said, cutting off my chance to

find a reply anyway. "Come on, Boston. I'm starving. Let's eat and you can tell me why you're acting like you've been body-snatched."

"DOES KALE KNOW YOU'RE SLEEPING WITH HIS BROTHER?"

The elevator doors closed just as Brooks' voice tipped up into the end of his question. My back went rigid and I cleared my throat, looking at my reflection in the closed door of the elevator. Brooks studied me, and I blinked slowly, wondering what my tell had been.

"I'm not fucking Kale's brother," I said.

Boston and I had done plenty of kissing, but we'd not gotten anywhere near the main event.

"You're not *not* fucking him."

The elevator stopped two floors down and let on a woman who looked old enough to be my grandmother. She gave Brooks an appreciative onceover, which wasn't surprising. The entire group of us were rich, but Brooks looked like if you cut him, he'd bleed green dollar signs. It was a result of how he'd been raised and the life he'd been handed, paired with the work he'd done for himself. Philanthropy and domination had proved to be a formidable mix, and Brooks wore the results of it daily.

"Boston isn't gay," I said, choosing my words carefully.

In the reflection of the three of us in the door, the older woman's eyebrows sent up, but she didn't give any other sign that she'd been eavesdropping. Though, an elevator was far from the private kind of place I'd hoped to have this conversation. Not that I'd wanted to have it at all, but Brooks was persistent and he was just getting started with me.

He let me simmer in my answer until we reached the lobby. I followed the other passenger out to the sidewalk, and Brooks walked aimlessly beside me, hands shoved into the pockets of his slacks. I didn't say a word to him until we'd turned the corner and the office was a comfortable amount of space behind us.

"Neither am I," Brooks said thoughtfully. "That's never stopped me from putting my dick into another man."

"Nothing stops you from that," I teased.

He chuckled and slowed, pulling a hand from his pocket and grabbing my forearm. I came to a stop and we stepped toward the building, out of the flow of everyone else who was ready to go get lunch and not get the third degree about their bedroom habits from their best friend.

"Kale may have not noticed because he's too love-struck with his little prince, but I saw the way you smiled at him—"

I opened my mouth to argue, and he raised a hand to silence me, continuing, "And I saw the way he blushed when you did it."

"It's a crush, Brooks," I offered, wondering how much I had to give him before his curiosity was satisfied.

"In which direction?"

"Does it matter?" I asked.

"Alex had a crush on Beamer, and he's been sulking for months over that."

Brooks arched a brow, and I sighed. Alex and Beamer had just fallen into bed together before Beamer's long-forgotten husband came out of the woodwork and swept him off his feet. To say Alex had taken it hard was an understatement, and our other friend was still reeling from their brief time together—and also the ending of that time. He'd been much less present in our friend group than before, though he had started to show his face again, which was reassuring to the lot of us.

"They're different," I protested.

"Alex found something in Beamer that he hadn't had before," Brooks went on, unfazed. "I imagine a straight man falling into bed with someone like you feels much the same."

"Are you warning me to be careful with him?"

"So you *are* fucking him." Brooks crossed his arms over his chest, tipping his head back and narrowing his eyes at me. That short and smug, arrogant little asshole had talked me right into the confession he'd wanted from the start.

"We aren't sleeping together," I said.

He pursed his lips and blinked slowly at me. There was more and he knew it, but he was going to make me say it. What a cruel twist of fate to have Doms for friends who pulled the tricks out of your own arsenal and used them against you.

"Yet," I grumbled, shaking my arm out of his hold and starting off again down the street. We hadn't even talked about what we were going to get for lunch and I didn't even care anymore, as long as they had a drink menu.

"Kale is going to murder you," he said, jogging to catch up to me and then falling in step beside me.

"Kale is not going to find out."

"How long do you think that's going to work out for?"

"As long as I need it to," I snapped, stepping off the curb and into the crosswalk. The light was about to turn red, and I briefly wondered if I could lose Brooks in the traffic, but he was small and quick, catching up to me before I'd made it far at all. Two doors past the curb, he grabbed my arm and shoved me toward the open door of a restaurant neither of us had ever been to before.

"Two for lunch?" a chipper hostess asked as the sounds of the city died down behind us.

"Please and thank you." Brooks flashed her a devilish smile which left her blushing and muttering to herself as she walked us to a small bistro table in the corner of the restaurant.

It was unfair for all my friends to act like I was the playboy of the group, when Brooks was just as guilty of fucking his way through the eligible bachelors and bachelorettes of New York. Unlike me, he chose to dabble in giving back to others outside of the bedroom, and apparently that made me a fuck boy and him a saint.

Seated at the small table, I flicked at the silk flower arrangement in a small and dusty vase between us before pushing it toward the wall. It was impossible to get comfortable, given the size of the table and the penetrating weight of Brooks' stare, but I tried my best until he put me out of my misery by asking another question.

"What were you thinking, Ford?"

"I wasn't," I answered honestly. "But if it makes any difference at all, Boston propositioned me, not the other way around."

"Every time you open your mouth, it's a proposition."

"Not with him." I shook my head and frowned, remembering the years of flirting that I'd only recently ramped up. I'd started it to annoy Ford, but Boston was so damn pretty when he blushed, and...

Shit.

Brooks made a pleased noise in the back of his throat, and I touched the top of my thigh, able to vividly recall the pressure of Boston's fingers wrapped around me the day he asked me to teach him how to fuck men.

"That was just in fun." I arched a brow, prompting him to argue with me about the intent of my flirting.

"And now? Is it fun?"

"It's complicated, and I shouldn't even be having this conversation with you."

The hostess brought us waters and I drank half the glass in one go, even though the cold drink did nothing to ease the dry ache in my throat.

"He's straight," Brooks reminded me, as if I wasn't painfully aware of that little fact.

"That isn't a topic for us to discuss." I cocked my head to the side and set my glass back down on the table, finally reaching to undo the button on my suit coat. "If you want to talk to Boston about his sexuality, you're more than welcome."

"I want to talk to you about what you're doing with our best friend's younger brother."

"Younger by four minutes," I grumbled.

"You know how Kale is about him."

"He's an adult."

The line of questioning was quickly veering into sounding accusatory, and I wasn't interested in engaging Brooks at all if that was how he chose to speak to me. This wasn't high school, it wasn't even college. All of us were grown adults, well into our thirties, and capable of making educated decisions about who we took to bed. Just because I'd never been discerning in the past didn't mean I was a predator.

"You have to tell Kale," Brooks said.

"I don't have to tell Kale shit." I cleared my throat, realizing I'd accidentally raised my voice to levels not becoming the quaint little restaurant setting we'd found ourselves in. I lowered my voice, leaning closer. "I don't have to tell Kale shit. This doesn't involve him."

"I won't tell him, Ford, but he's going to find out."

While I wanted to appreciate Brooks' concern, I also wanted to throw him out a window. I loved all of my friends, I truly did, but the level of oversight was quickly becoming too much. I pushed myself against the back of the chair, eyeing Brooks warily while I mentally tried to jog through the past few years of our friendship, wondering if they'd always treated me this way...like I was a danger to others.

I knew I had a reputation.

I was glad for it because, if people knew what to expect with me, there was less chance for confusion and misunderstanding. Less opportunity for someone to fall in love when all I'd wanted to do was fall into bed. But that didn't mean I was a careless man. If anything, it spoke to the level of transparency and consent I chased after for my partners. If you knew what you were getting, there wasn't any room to be let down when you didn't get more. But then there was Boston, and how easily he was able to get everything he wanted out of me.

"I appreciate the concern, Brooks, truly I do, but everything is under control," I promised.

Everything was not under control, but not in the way he worried. Boston had one up on me, and he had since the very first time he touched me. The man played me like a fiddle and I practically begged him for more. I didn't have much help for the state of my emotions once we moved on from naked kissing and onto something like blow jobs, let alone sex. And to have stacked the emotional relationship piece on top of the physical?

"I don't think I believe you."

I gave him a fleeting and weak smile. "Brooks, if anyone is going to get hurt here, it's me, alright?"

The hostess—who was apparently also our waitress—came back to the table, which was the reprieve I needed from the intense scrutiny of Brooks' stare. I ordered a martini and a club sandwich, doing my best to avoid looking across the table at my friend until he'd ordered and we found ourselves alone again. I chewed my cheek until I tasted copper, and then glanced up at him with my chin tucked against my chest.

"You're telling the truth," he said slowly.

"You can rest easy at night knowing that Boston Sheffield has one up on me, okay?" I worried the hole I'd gnawed in my cheek, grateful when the hostess was quick to return with our drinks. The vodka absolutely burned the cut in my mouth, and I was thankful for the grounding pain of it. With a wince, I took a second swallow before returning my drink to the table.

"Do you...*like* him?"

It felt disingenuous to say I *liked* Boston. I was very nearly obsessed with him in an unhealthy way that was going to be the death of us both. At every turn, he proved to me that he was more than capable of handling whatever our relationship was in a reasonable way, and I was the one treading water and trying to pretend I wasn't gone for him and the way his stare went hazy after he took his glasses off. The way the softest smile took up residence on his face once he was able to bring my features back into focus. I rubbed at the center of my chest, like that would do anything to ease the ache that bloomed when I thought about Boston.

"I don't know," I answered.

I could have very well already been on the way to loving him, but that answer would have gone over about as well as a wet blanket.

"You're playing with fire, Ford," he warned, picking up his drink and swirling the ice around the glass before lifting it to his lips and taking a sip. He didn't take his eyes off me the whole time, and I was acutely aware of the judgement behind his stare.

"Yeah," I agreed, polishing off the rest of my martini. "I know."

KALE UNWRAPPED HIS SANDWICH AND SMOOTHED THE WHITE PAPER out like a plate in front of him. I was slower with mine, more careful, like if I pulled at the tape wrong it would set off an alarm that told my brother I was in some weird kind of pseudo-relationship with one of his best friends.

"Does Ford bother you?" he asked, opening up the bread and plucking off the pickles. He tossed them toward me without asking because, in addition to being the straight brother, I was also the pickle brother.

"In what way?" My voice cracked, but Kale didn't notice.

"Any way." He glanced up and smashed his sandwich back together, taking a bite a chewing before he finished his thought. "But I meant with the flirting and all of that. I've told him a thousand times you're not into men."

Something in the center of my chest constricted, twisting like a rag getting wrung out. I hated lying to my brother, but I wasn't a fool. I knew better than to tell him about Ford, and especially knew better than to tell him before Ford and I were on the same page *about* telling him. Whatever was happening between me and Ford was so new and fragile, something neither of us had expected and something Ford hadn't even wanted. Keeping it secret, just for the two of us, felt like the best way to make sure it was sustainable. There was definitely another secret, though. One that *was* my place to tell, and probably needed to come first anyway.

"I might not *not* be into men," I said, following the bombshell up by taking a huge bite of my sandwich that made it impossible for me to speak.

Kale's head snapped up, his jaw slack and eyes wide, then he narrowed his stare at me, one brow winged right up into his hairline. Chewing felt like I had resistance bands around my jaw, but I managed to get through the bite and get it swallowed.

"Explain," Kale said, once my mouth was clear.

"I've been wondering lately, and I just think that maybe it might not be fair to say so definitively that I'm not interested in men or people who aren't women."

"There's a lot of qualifiers in that sentence," he murmured, stare still fixed on me. "Have you met someone?"

Obviously, I'd known Kale my entire life. He knew me almost as well as I knew myself, sometimes better, and I knew what I could lie about and what I'd never be able to get away with. He was smart enough to know that my interest in men wouldn't have come out of nowhere, that it would have been triggered by one man in particular. I cursed myself for not having the foresight to know that about him, and I took another huge bite of my sandwich to buy myself some time.

"That's a yes," he said, taking a bite of his own sandwich while I worked on swallowing down mine.

"It's a yes," I confirmed.

Now Kale was chewing, and it seemed to me that was a perfectly acceptable way for us to battle through this conversation. The time to chew would hopefully stop either of us from saying something that we couldn't take back.

"Where did you meet him?" Kale asked.

I finished the bite I'd been working on and decided to stick as close to the truth as I could. "The office."

The corner of Kale's left eye twitched, and I fidgeted with my glasses, lifting and settling them back down in the same spot on the bridge of my nose.

"He works in the building?"

"Yes."

I managed another bite, dreading how the conversation was going to go after we were both out of food to act as a buffer. For good measure, I shoved one of Kale's pickles into my already full mouth.

"Who started it?" he asked.

I swallowed. "I did."

Kale sucked in a breath, clearly caught off-guard by the answer, but it was as much the truth as it was a lie. Ford had been flirting incessantly with me, but I was the one who'd touched him first, who'd propositioned him, who'd negotiated him into bed. He hadn't taken advantage of me in any way. If anything, I'd taken advantage of him, even if it hadn't been intentional.

Well, it had been intentional.

Deliberate.

But not malicious.

"What brought this about?" he asked, shoving another

bite of sandwich into his mouth before he'd even finished asking the question.

I didn't think there was an easy answer, even though the truth felt a little murky to me. Especially when Ford wasn't around. When I was with him, everything made sense in a way it never had before. I wished this was a conversation he and I could have shared before my brother started in on me about the whole thing. It was impossible to not hear the accusation in my brother's voice, even if he meant well. He'd always been protective in an unfair way, considering we shared the same birthday and the same opportunities.

"I thought he smelled nice," I admitted honestly, "and he made it hard to breathe."

"Did he smell like chloroform, Boston?"

I huffed a dry laugh, shaking my head and popping another pickle into my mouth.

"No, not like chloroform. But I mean...being near him took the air out of the room."

Kale dragged his tongue across the front of his teeth and I knew he couldn't argue about it because I was certain whatever he'd just gone through with Christian had to be comparable.

"And I assume it wasn't Chanel No. 5," he said.

I shook my head again and he let out a long and slow breath.

"If it's any consolation, I don't think I'm gay."

He rolled his eyes at me. "I don't care if you're gay. I just want you to be happy."

Little did he know, but sooner or later I was most likely going to be putting the validity of that statement to the test.

"It's too new to say one way or the other." I put the last bit of sandwich into my mouth, watching Kale carefully while I chewed. He didn't say anything, so after I swallowed, I told him, "But it's nice for now."

"Are you being safe?"

"Please don't do this." I shook my head, reaching up from underneath my glasses to rub my eyes.

"It's just... you know that when two boys love each other very much..." He stopped, unable to manage his laughter.

I balled up my sandwich wrapper and threw it at his face. It bounced off his cheekbone and landed on the floor near his feet. "I wasn't born yesterday."

Kale snatched my wrapper off the floor and tossed it into the trash can, then gathered up the scraps of his sandwich and added it to the pile.

"This is so exciting. Like losing our virginities all over again."

"Your virginity is so far gone it's not even an afterthought," I said.

"Not yours!"

I clasped my hands together in front of my face, the sides of my pointer fingers pressed against my lips and reaching toward my nose. "I'm begging you, Kale."

He must have seen the disgruntled brotherly love flash across my face because, for whatever reason, he relented. Leaning back in his chair with a laugh, he fondly rolled his eyes at me. "I'm here if you want to talk about it," he said.

"Thank you."

I stood up and gathered my things, ready to go jump out of a window instead of spend another half-hour with my brother. I wanted to talk to him about life and other things, but not under the weight of the confession I'd just lobbed into the space between us. There would be another day and another time.

"Unrelated to this revelation, I may need a few days off soon," I said.

He waggled his eyebrows at me. "Romantic vacation?"

"I owe Mom and Dad a visit."

At the mention of our parents, his expression sobered, and I gave him a small and sad smile in return. I knew my affinity for the farm had him nervous. There were lots of times that I'd stayed up late, imagining leaving the city and moving back to the farm for a while with our parents, but I wasn't sure if I was bold enough to actually go through with it. I'd recently started to wonder if it was farm life that appealed to me or the comfort of being taken care of, but it was too hard to think straight when Ford was in my orbit so I hadn't put too much thought into it.

"A visit?"

"I'm not going anywhere, Kale," I assured him.

He looked somewhat mollified, but not anywhere close to calm.

"Just let me know when," he muttered.

"Thank you." I pushed my chair in and went to the door, ready to get some fresh air when his voice behind me brought me to a quick halt.

"Boston."

I glanced over my shoulder at him.

"Don't let Ford know about this new development with your sexuality," he warned.

I pulled my bottom lip into my mouth, worrying it between my teeth while I debated the best thing to say.

"I'm not scared of him."

"He has a way of getting what he wants," Kale said.

Yeah, so did I apparently, but I wasn't going to lob that one back at him just yet.

"I'm not going to quit my job over your over-sexed best friend, Kale." It was an honest promise and as much of the truth as I could give him. "You don't have to worry about that."

I hadn't promised not to sleep with him, and Kale thankfully didn't catch on to the deliberate oversight.

"Let me know about your trip," he said. "And we'll get lunch again soon."

"Dinner," I offered, gesturing vaguely at the glass and stainless steel that made up most of his office. "Better ambiance."

"Fair enough." Kale's phone rang and he looked down at the caller ID with a smile. "Will you close the door on your way out?"

"Sure thing."

I latched the door behind me and walked as normally away as I could. The glass walls of the office would have given him a direct line of sight to my desperate escape if I'd broken into a run like I wanted to. I made it to the elevator before my composure started to crumble. I was in the lobby when my hands started to shake, and I had one leg still in the revolving door before my body gave out entirely.

I ran out the door and spun, bracing myself against the wall of the building, desperate to catch my breath. Thankfully, it was New York and nobody cared that I was on the verge of a panic attack in the middle of the day. Nobody except Kale's third best friend, Astor Brooks, who strode around the corner with a smile on his face and Ford right beside him.

When I saw them both, I turned away, threading my fingers into my hair and starting off toward the opposite end of the block.

"Boston," Ford shouted after me, the clack of his dress shoes against the concrete loud and insistent as he ran up behind me. He smoothed one hand against the small of my back and grabbed my wrists with his other, pulling my hands down and turning me toward him in one easy motion.

Immediately, my stare flew to Brooks, who watched us from the other side of the door with a tight and unreadable expression on his face.

"What are you doing?" I asked, trying to shake him off me.

"He knows," Ford said, fighting against my flailing arms. "He knows, Boston. Brooks knows."

"Why did you tell him?" I croaked. I could breathe, but I didn't know for how long. My heart was angry, slamming furiously against my ribs with every beat.

"He didn't," Brooks answered, coming to my other side and leaning against the wall to my right. He folded his arms in front of his chest and sighed so loudly, I heard him over the cabs honking in the street.

"How?" I rasped.

"Because I have eyes," Brooks said, "and I'm not head over balls for a prince the way your brother is or he would have noticed it too."

"I told Kale I'm attracted to men," I blurted, scrubbing my hands down my face and dislodging my glasses in the process.

Ford carefully unfolded them from both of my ears and cradled them in his hand.

"How did that go?"

"He was ready to give me the birds and bees talk again." I let out a nervous laugh. "Then he told me to make sure I never told you about it."

Brooks chuckled, and Ford glared at him.

"Kale isn't stupid," Brooks said. "The two of you are more obvious than you think, and if you want to keep this from him, you're going to have to do a lot better."

"I didn't even think..."

"Ford looks at you like he wants to eat you for dinner and you can't keep a blush off your cheeks to save your life," Brooks answered my unspoken question.

Ford exhaled softly and handed me back my glasses.

"I don't want to lie to him about this, so whatever is going on between the two of you, keep me out of it."

"With pleasure," Ford deadpanned.

Brooks shook his head, distaste clear as day across his face.

"I'm serious," he warned. "The two of you need a better plan and a book full of alibis if you want this to work."

With that, he leveled one last glaring look at Ford, a softer, more sympathetic glare toward me, and he disappeared past the revolving doors and into the building.

"So, I assume there's no point in asking how your lunch date went?" Ford asked, teasing me.

I slid my glasses back onto my face and blinked him back into crystal clear focus. The knot that had been wringing itself dry in my chest unwound completely at the sight of him, and for the first time in my life, I started to wonder if it was home I missed or just the feeling of home. And more than that, if the feeling of home could be a person.

"About as well as yours, I'd imagine," I muttered.

"Do you want to come over later? We can get dinner and talk about..." The corner of his mouth twitched and he gave me an apologetic shrug. "Talk about all of this, I guess."

"Yeah." I swallowed hard. "I think we should."

## CHAPTER 16

# FORD

SITTING ON MY COUCH, BOSTON LOOKED MORE NERVOUS THAN HE had when he asked me to teach him how to sleep with another man. I passed a tumbler of whiskey into his hand and sat down beside him, tucking one leg beneath me and angling my body toward his so my knee bumped the outside edge of his thigh.

"I figured we would have had a little more time to keep this between us," I said by way of apology.

He sighed and took a small sip of his drink. "I'm honestly surprised Kale wasn't the one who caught on first."

"Your brother is a meddler," I confirmed, flashing him a quick smile. "I am sorry, though. Brooks caught me off-guard and I try my best to tell the truth when people ask me questions."

"It's okay." He waved me off with a frown. "I just thought I would have had more time to process everything."

"You can have all the time you need."

"What are we doing, Ford?" Boston turned toward me, his knees bumping into mine. He fidgeted with his glasses, that nervous habit that was somehow so endearing at the same time, so I reached up and took them off. He could see enough without them and I needed him to sit with whatever feelings were making him so uncomfortable.

"I was under the impression you wanted to date me," I said.

He arched a brow. "And what do you want?"

Heat pooled low in my belly and I had to look away from him or else he'd see the truth in my eyes. I did want to date Boston. I wanted to fuck him and tie him up and make him cry and weep with pleasure, but I also wanted to find a way to embed myself in the swirling grooves of his fingerprints, the hollows of his bones, and the depths of his eyes. I wanted more than to just *date* him, but it was too soon for me to be that honest.

"You," I said simply. It was as much the truth as I could offer him. "What do you want?"

"A farm."

I couldn't stop the laugh from bubbling up from the back of my throat and spilling into the space between us. Hurt flashed across Boston's face, but he was quick to hide it, rolling his eyes at me instead and taking another swallow of his whiskey. He groaned—most likely from the warm taste of the liquor—and relaxed against the back of the couch, tumbler balanced on the top of his leg.

The answer shouldn't have been such a surprise. Some of the first things I'd noticed about Boston were the way he always smelled a little bit like the earth and how he wasn't scared of dirt on his clothes or beneath his fingernails. Not even a thousand dollar suit could hide the broad swell of his chest that was clearly made for hauling hay and bags of dirt or feed.

"Why a farm?" I asked.

"The farm is home." His brows knit together and he snapped his mouth closed like a fish on a line. He glanced up at me from beneath the dark fan of his eyelashes, looking like there was another answer on the tip of his tongue that he was fighting against letting out.

"Your parents' farm?"

"Maybe one of my own," he said. "I've just always...the farm used to feel like home."

I didn't ignore the past tense of his statement, but I didn't directly call it out either.

"Does New York not feel like home?"

"It's been home for almost as long as I can remember, but it's not the same."

"No," I agreed, "I imagine it's not."

"I'm going back for a visit soon," he said, raising his glass back to his mouth. Some of the amber liquid remained on his lower lip after he swallowed, and I leaned forward to taste it. Boston's eyes were quick to close and his chest moved toward mine like we were magnetized. I kissed him quick and soft, dragging my tongue across his lower lip with a pleased moan.

"Don't stop," he whimpered, chasing after me when I leaned away.

"Sweetheart, I'll go for so long you'll wish you never said that."

Heat bloomed on his cheeks and he blinked his eyes open, staring up at me with hearts in his eyes.

"But we have to talk first."

"Talk fast."

"I thought you wanted to do more than fuck." I swallowed, ignoring every cell in my body that wanted to throw him down on the couch and give him exactly what he was asking for.

"Why not both?"

I chuckled, turning and leaning against the mantle.

"The farm is home," I repeated his sentiment from earlier, and he tilted his head to the side like he wasn't so sure. "How long are you going for?"

"I haven't decided."

"Alright."

"Is that okay?" he asked.

"It's not up to me."

"Isn't it?"

He set his glass down on the side table and folded his hands together in his lap. Expectantly. The little minx was trying to coax me into sex, which was admirable and shocking all at the same time. Here I thought he was innocent and pure, but he'd surprised me at every turn with the bold way he asked for what he wanted and initiated what he needed. But sex and orgasms were one thing, walking the line of submission that we'd flirted with so far was another entirely.

"We can talk about that after we get your brother out of the way," I said.

His shoulders sagged. "Do you think Brooks will tell him?"

"No, but...if this lasts." Fuck, I wanted it to last. "He's going to find out. Whether we tell him on our own or he catches us. And it's important that we're on the same page about what we say."

"We say we're both consenting adults and who we fuck and who we date isn't up to him," Boston said.

"Alright."

"Is that settled?" he asked, swaying forward again.

The answer was there between us, but for some reason it didn't feel like enough. But maybe, in this moment, it was that simple. There would be fallout and arguments most likely, and lots of explaining, but that wasn't here and that wasn't now.

"Boston, I..."

I couldn't shake the unsettled way the whole situation had me feeling, but I was hard-pressed to admit the truth of my hesitance.

"Ford," he said my same softly, prompting.

I wondered briefly if Boston was a switch. If *I* was, because the way he could take me apart with the simplest of words was alarming.

"I want to make sure that you're really committed to this," I choked out. "To me."

"I've offered up my virginity, Ford. How much more committed can I be?"

"That was just sex," I reminded him.

"But it's not now." He stood up and took a step toward me. Always so fucking sure of himself. "And I'm still here."

"You know I don't date, Boston."

"But you said you'd date me."

I nodded, feeling like the room was spinning out of control around me. Where was my confidence, my competence? Why was Boston closing the space between us like he was the deci-sion-maker and I was the one who belonged on my knees. And that was it. Like a flash of recognition, I understood that Boston was offering me everything I'd been missing in every partner before him. I would have gotten on my knees for

Boston if it made him happy because all I wanted was for him to be happy. If it made him happy for me to lean into my dominance, I would give him that. If it made him happy to argue with me about paint swatches over cocktails, I'd let him.

"I *am* dating you," I corrected. "And I need you to understand how big that is for me because I don't..."

"Are you saying I'm special?"

He was right up on me, filling my space and breathing my air, and I would have given him all the breath in my lungs if he needed it.

"Very," I rasped.

Boston's mouth settled into the softest and happiest smile I'd ever seen. Reaching for him, I cradled his face in my hand and he leaned so gently into me I thought if I moved too fast, he would break. The shift was subtle and vulnerable, and a new, unspoken emotion swelled in the center of my chest. This was more than obsession, more than ownership. This was something else entirely.

"Can we go back to talking about you telling me what to do?" he asked, angling his mouth to the side and pressing a kiss against the edge of my palm.

"What about it?" I asked.

"Everything."

"Boston." I sighed, taking a step away from him and scrubbing a hand down my face. The connection from our touch was severed and I sucked in two desperate lungfuls of air.

"Am I too much?"

"Not in the slightest." I shouldn't have moved away from him, but he made it hard to think. He was so different from everyone I'd known before him and while the nuts and bolts of sex and domination were the same, the instructions were far more complicated than I was used to. "I don't want to go too far."

"I'll tell you to stop."

"I don't want to hurt you."

"I won't let you." He grabbed my hand and kissed the tips of my fingers, slowly lowering himself down to his knees. With my fingers still tangled with his, Boston stared up at me, all full of earnest honesty and curiosity, and beneath all of that, a dark and dangerous kind of arousal.

"I can tell you what to do in bed," I said, carefully studying the micro-expressions on Boston's face. "I can order dinner for you, pick your clothes...but I'll never tell you that you can't go home if that's what you really want to do."

Boston licked his lips, palms clammy against mine, but his grip sure and steady just the same.

"What else can you do?"

My tongue stuck to the roof of my mouth, but I forced myself to swallow.

"I can ruin you for any man who comes after me," I whispered.

It was the one promise I could make him and keep, but the unspoken addendum was that Boston was going to ruin me too.

"How would you do that?" he asked, bringing my fingers to his mouth. He traced his lower lip with the pads of my first two fingers, dragging them back and forth until I shook him off and pinched the hollows of his cheeks together.

His nostrils flared and his hips bucked. I didn't need to look between his legs to know that he was hard, to know that his cock was long and constricted in his pants and aching for friction.

"I can make you come better than them," I promised. "Longer, harder...more."

"I believe you." He managed to get the words out even with my fingers pinching his face. "I trust you."

The control I'd been hanging on to snapped, and I was done with patience, done with propriety, done with trying to do things right.

"Are you ready for your next lesson?" I asked.

"Yes, Sir."

There he was again with the honorific that he used, not because I told him to or demanded it of him, but because it felt natural for him. The way it rang to my ears had a decent amount of blood centering between my legs, and I made a show of palming my quickly growing erection over my pants.

We'd done enough talking for the night.

Boston was steadfast in his commitment to being in a relationship with me, and between the two of us, I was the only one scared of how his brother would react upon finding out the truth. There was no point in trying to get another answer or a longer explanation out of him. For Boston, it was simple, and I needed to take *that* lesson in stride. I envied him, I realized. He had a straightforward way of looking at the world that I'd long since lost. For Boston, it was black and white. There wasn't any gray, at least not when it came to who he was and what he wanted.

He'd come to me to teach him, but I was already learning from him.

"Open your mouth and stick out your tongue, sweetheart. Tonight you're going to learn how to suck cock."

IF HOME WAS A FEELING, LIKE I'D BEEN THINKING EARLIER, IT MIGHT as well have been on my knees at Ford's feet. In front of him, I found myself wrapped with the same feeling of security and comfort that I'd always related to the farm, but it was also laced with something so much *more*. Looking up at him, my chest swelled with happiness, with an absolute feeling of rightness that I didn't think New York was capable of producing for me. Maybe I'd just been looking in the wrong places—and the wrong people—the whole time.

It didn't matter that Ford was a man and it didn't matter that maybe it wasn't socially acceptable for me to kneel for him the way I was, but it was impossible to fight against the overwhelming sense of ease that washed over me when he let me call him Sir. I didn't know what it meant, didn't understand much of what we were doing, but when I opened my mouth for him, it was like early mornings on the porch back home, watching the navy blue sky turn the most perfect shade of pink when the sun finally crested the horizon. When he tugged at my bottom lip, pulling my mouth open wider, it was the same as sitting around the hand-carved wooden table in my parents' kitchen and enjoying a plate of fresh-cooked eggs.

It was easy.

It made sense.

"Stick out your tongue." Ford's voice was rough and scratchy, completely at odds with the cool and collected look he wore on his face.

I stuck out my tongue and tipped my head back. My eyes closed, and I exhaled through my mouth, an indescribable sensation of serenity flooding into me like the gentlest tide. Ford unzipped his pants, the rich musk of his sweat and soap rushing into my nostrils on my next inhale. I groaned. It was impossible to not. My body registered a visceral and primal reaction to the closeness of him and, without thinking, I reached up and—once again—gripped his thigh.

It was my fingers against his leg that had gotten us both here in the first place. The swell of his muscle was grounding, and I flexed each finger against him, one at a time, until I could imagine what the touch would feel like if we were skin against skin.

"If any of this is too much, just tell me to stop," he whispered.

I nodded, sticking my tongue our farther.

I was ready.

Beyond ready.

Ford gently set the head of his cock against the tip of my tongue, and I blinked my eyes open so I could watch. There was something utterly entrancing about staring down the length of my nose at the thickness of his cock and the way it protruded from his body before disappearing into mine. I wanted him to give me more, but he just tapped his crown against my tongue over and over and over until I had sweat beading at my temples and I was ready to go mad.

"Don't suck yet." Ford inched himself deeper into my mouth, pressing his shaft against my tongue as he slowly thrust toward the back of my throat. "Just get used to the feel of me. The taste of me."

Spit pooled in my mouth, trailing down my chin as he stretched my jaw with the thickest part of his cock. He couldn't have been more than halfway in when he spoke again. "Close your mouth around it, Boston."

He didn't have to tell me twice. I sealed my lips around his erection with a handful of inches still not inside, and immediately my own cock swelled in response. There was an ache in my jaw that I didn't hate and to say my mouth felt full was an understatement. It was all-consuming to have another man's cock in my mouth...to have Ford's cock in my mouth. I huffed a breath out through my nose, sounding more like an agitated bull than a man.

And I was agitated, because I wanted more than a taste. I wanted to take him so far into my mouth that I choked a little. I wanted tears to leak out of my eyes from the feel of having him inside of me. But more than that, I wanted...no, I *needed* to do what he told me to do. For as much as I wanted to taste him in the very back of my throat, what I needed was to follow his instructions.

Between my legs, my dick pressed insistently against my fly. I was so hard it hurt, half from the feel of him in my mouth and half from the hard press of the floor against my knees. I was only uncomfortable if I thought about it, so I wiped away the tension in my calves and focused instead on the burning piece of Ford that rested calmly against my tongue.

"Your mouth is so fucking hot," Ford rasped, stroking my hair away from my face before threading his fingers through it and tugging my head back an inch. I hollowed my cheeks and blinked up at him, giving him the first proper taste of suction. He shivered, lips twisting up into a barely restrained grimace when the flared crown of his cock smashed against the roof of my mouth. I still had my fingers wrapped around his thigh and his muscles trembled beneath my touch.

I whimpered around his cock and he licked his lips, looking up at the ceiling before focusing his attention back on my face.

"Suck it, sweetheart," he whispered.

I tested out the grip he had on my hair by pulling back until his flared tip was against the backs of my teeth. He didn't use the hand in my hair to control me, but it had me feeling steady just the same. I wrapped my other hand around the exposed inches of his shaft and slid my mouth back down until I reached my thumb and forefinger.

Ford cursed under his breath and precum leaked out of my own cock in embarrassing volumes. It didn't take long for me to find a pace that worked for us both, because while I'd never sucked a cock before, I'd had my own sucked plenty of times and I at least had some semblance of what would feel good. I sucked him sloppy, with spit dribbling out my mouth and between my fingers, and I sucked him loudly, not bothering to try and hide the moans that fell out of my mouth when the tip of his cock fucked toward the back of my throat.

I was dangerously close to my own orgasm when Ford tightened his grip on my hair and gave a rough tug, yanking my head back. He fisted his cock and jerked himself with short and angry thrusts, eyes narrowed on me the entire time.

"I want to come in your mouth," he grunted, and I stuck out my tongue, giving him a target.

His eyes rolled back into his head and his hips gave one last jerk forward. Ford's hand stilled and, for a brief moment, nothing happened. The only thing I could hear was my pulse hammering in my ear, and then a low rumble from Ford as cum shot out of his already soaking wet slit. The first spray of cum landed on my tongue, the second against the corner of my mouth, my cheek, the third against my chin. Ford put his cock back into my mouth and the rest of his seed landed against the back of my tongue, the roof of my mouth, the inside of my cheeks.

It wasn't the first time I'd tasted cum before. I'd tried mine on more than one occasion, but it wasn't anything like Ford. His orgasm was salty and hot, thick and...I sealed my lips around his cock, half over his white-knuckled grip, and I sucked him hard, doing my best to milk the rest of the cum out of him.

I understood the human body and knew well enough that I hadn't *made* the cum he'd shot into my mouth, but at the same time...my brain wasn't interested in those facts. I had made that cum; I'd gotten it out of him. It was as much mine as his, and I was focused on sucking out every drop. It wasn't until he gave a soft push against the top of my head and slid his cock out with a wince that I realized I might have been hurting him. I licked my lips, blinking up at him and waiting for whatever was going to come next.

"How was I?" I asked, voice cracking.

His lashes fluttered a little bit, and he traced his swollen and purple cockhead across both of my lips. I opened for him again and he slid back into my mouth, all the way to the back of my throat. He was hard, but not as thick after his orgasm and while it hurt to have the whole of him inside me that way, it was not a hardship to bear. That was where he wanted to be and that was where I would have him.

"You were treacherously perfect, sweetheart." He let go of his cock and cradled my face into both of his hands. His cock spasmed against the roof of my mouth and I sputtered around him, not trying to get away. Not that I could, anyway. The hold on my face wasn't just affectionate.

I took the praise for what it was, huffing out breath after breath from my nose. The well-trimmed thatch of hair around the base of his cock tickling my nostrils, and I slowed my breathing and closed my eyes. I didn't want him to pull away from me. I couldn't stand the idea of space between us. If being on my knees for him was like coffee on the porch, I had no idea what this was. It was better and more than anything I'd ever felt in my life.

A sense of pride and belonging bloomed inside of me, and I closed my eyes with a happy sigh. Ford's fingers stroked across my cheeks, even as his cock finally began to soften against my tongue. Neither of us moved, but I suckled at him more and more the softer he got, fighting against the inevitable slide and release from my mouth.

When his soft and sticky dick slipped free, both of us groaned, and I pressed my cheek against the rich wool of his slacks, wrapping my arms around his leg. He hadn't even taken his pants off for this. He'd only taken his cock out of his underwear before feeding it to me and there was something so unexplainably hot about what we'd just done...with our clothes still on. Down lower, my own dick throbbed in time with every frantic beat of my heart, the pain of not coming already morphed into something bigger than I could ever be.

"Boston."

Ford cleared his throat and gave a shake of his leg. I loosened my arms enough for him to slide down to the floor beside me. He didn't say another word as he hauled me into his lap and scooted us both back against the wall. Ford arranged me between his legs, his cock warm and soft against the small of my back, and then he busied himself with the fly of my slacks, shoving his hand behind the waistband of my underwear.

His touch was scalding hot against my inflamed erection and I cried out, bucking away from him. Ford tsked quietly in my ear, strapping his arm around my chest and pressing my back against him to restrict my movement.

"It's all right," he whispered, giving a tight, quick tug up my shaft.

"It hurts," I told him, dropping my head against his shoulder.

Ford kissed my temple, ignoring my pleas and stroking my cock with the tight and dry grip of his fist.

"It hurts," I said again.

He uncurled his fingers and raised his hand in front of my mouth. I knew what he wanted without being told. I licked his palm from the base of it to his fingers, and then he was back between my legs with his spit-slicked hold around my aching shaft.

"Do you want me to stop?" he asked, not relenting.

I shook my head and two strokes later my vision went white.

The force of my orgasm was terrifying, and I was only

aware of the tight hold of Ford's arm around the front of my chest, his hand around my cock, and the searing hot spurts of cum that geysered their way out of my shaft as he wrung an orgasm out of me.

Everything hurt and everything felt perfect, and as my faculties returned, I was aware of Ford helping me to my feet, walking me up the stairs and into his bedroom. He helped me with the buttons of my shirt, the laces on my shoes, and then my head hit the pillow with the softest thud imaginable. Ford was between my knees, head bowed down as he cleaned the cum off my cock with his tongue. He didn't suck me, and I was glad. I wanted to remember it if he did and I didn't think I'd remember much from this. The moments were flashes of awareness that I'd slowly piece back together in the morning, I figured. All I knew in that moment was I'd used my mouth to make another man come. I'd done it on my knees, and I'd never felt more powerful and *right* in my entire life.

THE HOUSE WAS QUIET, SAVE FOR THE V-8 VOLUME OF MILO'S purring in my ear. After Boston left, I threw myself down on the couch in a dramatic fit of pining, and Milo was quick to take advantage of the new place to lie, jumping on my chest and bumping his head into the bottom of my chin over and over until I patted the top of his head.

Boston had spent the night, half-naked in my arms, then he'd let me make him coffee before getting dressed in the same clothes he'd worn over the night before and giving me a blistering goodbye kiss. With my eyes closed, I traced my fingertips across my lower lip as Milo insistently shoved his head into my palm.

"What am I doing, Milo?" I asked.

My cat purred louder, curling up and swatting my chin with his tail before he coiled himself into a circle and laid down in the center of my chest.

Boston had me more tangled up than anyone ever had, and I wanted to hate him for it, even though I was much closer to another and just as powerful four-letter word. The mere idea of it was preposterous. I'd known Boston for years, but I didn't *know* him. My brain was running on endorphins around him...or something. But even as I tried to tell myself that, I couldn't understand where I'd gone so off-track.

Boston wasn't the first man I'd taken to bed that I found myself fond of, but my feelings for him were amplified as loud as Milo's never-ending purring. I could feel the hints of it in my bones, like it was a real and tangible thing beneath my fingers. That was the only reason I'd agreed to date him, which felt like not the best idea I'd ever had. New York was a big city, but it wasn't that big, and we both knew we were on borrowed time. He was content to play with fire, one way he was very much exactly like his brother.

In the pocket of my pajamas, my cell phone buzzed against my thigh and I fished it out, finding a handful of ignored text messages and one new one from Boston letting me know he'd made it home.

**Boston**: Taking a shower, then meeting a friend for lunch.
**Boston**: Can I jerk off in the shower?

My eyes rolled back a little, and I groaned, shoving Milo onto the floor so I could sit up. He landed with an undignified-sounding meow, then he sauntered out of the room in search of what I assumed to be less sentient places to sit. There was a box in my office that he favored and I hadn't had the heart to toss it out yet.

**Boston**: I don't know why but ever since you, I've been horny all the time.

I scrubbed a hand down my face, so far over my head I was drowning.

**Me**: It's like you're going through puberty again.
**Me**: You can jerk off but you can't come.
**Boston**: That's mean.
**Boston**: What's the point?
**Me**: There's plenty of points. One, because you asked and I gave you your answer. Two, because I'm a selfish man and I would rather lick your cum off your stomach than let it wash down the drain. Three, because if you get yourself close and don't finish, I imagine I'll see you sooner rather than later.
**Boston**: I could have stayed longer???

I swallowed, leaning forward and digging my elbows into the tops of my knees. I held my phone loosely in my hands, staring down at the unnecessary volume of question marks that followed his question. I would have let him stay forever.

**Me**: If I wanted you to go, I would have asked you to go.
**Boston**: I didn't want to overstay.

I didn't think he could.

**Boston**: Why didn't you tell me to stay?

That was a fair question, all things considered. Because I didn't want to look desperate and needy and it was one thing to control his orgasms, but another to monopolize his time. Before I could think myself into a deeper hole than I'd already dug, my phone rang.

"Boston," I greeted.

"Why didn't you tell me to stay?" he repeated the question from his text message like I would suddenly have an answer.

"I don't know," I admitted.

"I thought *this* was more than just sex."

"This is," I agreed.

"I didn't mean *us*," he said. "I meant the...controlling stuff."

"The dominance, Boston. You can say it."

"The dominance," he whispered.

I pictured him on his knees with my cock in his mouth, eyes open and pupils shot. I groaned to myself, cursing my own stupidity under my breath. There was no real explanation I could give that he would accept. I could say that I didn't want to scare him off, that I wanted to ease him into things, that I wanted him to only experience the best parts of me, but none of those were the whole truth. At the end of the day, the real reason was one I'd struggled with every time he pressed his mouth against mine. Boston kissed without a care in the world, like no harm could ever come. There was a courageous kind of innocence about him, and if I were being honest, I envied it. Because, at the end of the day, I was scared shitless.

Scared of the way being with me came so naturally to him.

Scared of the way I wanted him in my space...in my life.

Scared of the changes taking place inside of me every time I looked at him.

"It's been a while since I've played that way outside of sex," I told him.

"How long?"

I huffed out a breath that almost sounded like a laugh, had it not been laced with so much self-deprecation.

"College, probably," I said.

"Why?"

"It's a little early for the hard-hitting questions, sweetheart."

"I just want to know you," he explained, and it was impossible to not picture that same earnest and hopeful—and a little bit hungry—look he had on his face every time he looked at me these days.

"I'm not sure what to tell you," I said. "I don't think the man I am right now is the man I used to be."

"Who is the man you used to be?"

"I thought you were going to have a wank and a lunch date." I pushed up from my spot on the couch so I could go into the kitchen and refill my coffee. It was too early for this level of introspection, but apparently the bedroom wasn't the only place I couldn't tell Boston no.

"I will," he said, "eventually. Who is the man you used to be?"

"You know the kind of man I used to be." I filled my empty mug to the brim with a fresh round of hot coffee and turned to rest my ass against the counter while I waited for it to cool to a drinkable temperature. "The life of the party. Always down for a good time."

"But not a long time." Boston laughed at me.

"Not a long time," I agreed with a frown.

His laughter was quick to die down, and he cleared his throat. "But now?"

"Now, I don't know if a long time would be long enough," I told him honestly.

"Am I that good at sucking cock?"

I laughed, the boldness so out of character for the man I'd

thought I knew, but maybe I wasn't the only one being changed over the course of our relationship.

"My arrogance is rubbing off on you," I teased. "You've changed too."

"How?"

"You never would have said that to me two weeks ago."

"I didn't know I was attracted to you two weeks ago," he said.

"That's a lie and you know it, sweetheart." I raised my coffee and took a tentative sip. It burned my tongue, but nothing hot enough to scar. "If you think hard enough about it, you'll find out that I wasn't the first."

"You were, Ford."

I wanted to argue with him, but the insistence and surety in his voice stopped me in my tracks. I admired how certain he was about me, when every day with him had me feeling less sure of myself. At first, I'd been content to hide this little obsession of mine, but to have Boston know and for him to imply the feelings were mutual? For me to have met a person who wasn't scared off by my intensity, my needs?

I'd never imagined myself with a partner because the shoes were always too big to fill. I wanted too hard, too much, too fast. It was overwhelming and scary, not just for myself but for others, so I'd never given anything a chance to go that far. But it was impossible to pump the brakes with Boston.

"I can hear you thinking," he murmured.

"You're the pushiest submissive I've ever met."

"I don't think I *am* submissive," he said simply.

"You get hard when you call me Sir," I reminded him, getting hard thinking about *him* getting hard. Was the rest of my life really meant to be this vicious and never-ending cycle of arousal?

"I get hard other times too," he said.

I could tell there was more in that comment, but I hadn't had enough coffee to unpack it yet.

"And yet you still want me to assert my dominance in this relationship outside of the bedroom?" I pressed.

"Yes," he rasped. "I like it. It makes me feel…"

The silence stretched between us and when I was tired of waiting, I prompted him to finish the sentence.

"Makes you feel what?"

"Safe."

I screwed my eyes shut and scrunched my nose up in a painful grimace. The irony of Boston feeling safe with me while I was absolutely terrified when I was with him would forever remain one of nature's cruelest tricks.

"Are you there?" he asked.

"I'm here. Yes."

"Did I say something wrong?" There was that quiet and tentative man I'd always thought him to be.

"Not at all," I promised him. "This is new for both of us."

"Next time, tell me stay if you want me to."

"I will."

"When am I going to see you again?" he asked.

"When do you want to?"

He chuckled. "Depends on the next lesson."

Fuck.

How was he continually able to disarm me like that? I didn't know which way was up, but what was worse…I didn't care. I'd already resigned myself to letting Boston Sheffield tie me down and ruin my life, I might as well go big.

"I thought our next lesson could be a date," I said.

"I know how to date."

"That's not what I meant." I grabbed my mug and took a big swallow of my coffee. "I just meant I wasn't thinking about lessons, I was thinking I wanted to take you on a proper date. Since we're...since we're in..."

"A relationship," he helpfully supplied, voice barely louder than a whisper.

"If that's what you wanted."

"It's what we agreed."

"If it's what you wanted," I repeated, desperately searching out more than his consent, but also his interest.

"It is."

There was a small silence, and I found myself wishing we were having the conversation in person and not over the phone so I could see his face, so I could read his mannerisms, his tells. "A date would be good."

"Tonight?"

Boston hummed. "That works."

"I'll pick you up at seven?"

"That's perfect, Ford," he said softly. "This was a round-about way of me getting ready for that shower wank."

I couldn't help but laugh at that.

"No coming," I reminded him.

"No, Sir," he said. "No coming."

"I'll see you at seven."

I disconnected the call before he could say goodbye, before I could say something any more embarrassing than I already had. I was so out of my element with this man, but I couldn't go to any of my friends for advice. They wouldn't accept a nameless or faceless suitor if I brought it up, and there was no way I could let anyone besides Brooks know what was going on between me and Boston.

That only left one person.

It was early in California, but I was desperate.

I collected my phone and my coffee, then carried it all back to the couch where I collapsed against the cushions with a groan. The whole room still smelled like sex, smelled like Boston. Ignoring the way my cock threatened to tent the loose fabric of my pajamas at the memory, I scrolled through my contacts and called the one person who had kept a secret better than any of us ever could.

I called Beamer.

I HUNG UP WITH FORD AND GOT INTO THE SHOWER, MY MIND RACING a hundred miles a minute while I turned on the water and climbed under the hot spray. Curling my fist around my cock, I jerked myself once, twice, and then had to stop. The conversation was too fresh in my head for me to get another stroke in without being able to hold off the orgasm Ford told me I wasn't allowed to have.

The past week had been too much and not enough at the same time. What had started as an interest in seeing if my attraction to men was something worth looking into had turned into me in an actual relationship with one, and not just that, but a secret relationship. And not just *that*, but a kinky one too.

My brother didn't think I knew about those kinds of things, but we were the same age and even though we weren't identical, we were cut from the same cloth. Just because I hadn't done things in the past didn't mean I wasn't aware of them, didn't mean I hadn't spanked Colette for fun on our anniversary once or twice. The thing with Ford, though...it was drastically different. There was no arguing or trying to convince myself otherwise.

All the changes should have scared me, but every decision, every step, only convinced me I was going in the right direction. I believed Ford when he said it was all new for him too. He had his reputation, and I definitely had leaned into that when I asked him to teach me some things in the first place, but I could see it in the tense spread of his shoulders or the wrinkles around his eyes when he started to feel out of his element with me. It was his uncertainty that made it safe for me to feel my own, and I was grateful for it.

So, in the shower when I only got five more strokes before my balls shifted and raised between my legs, I slapped my hand against the tile and groaned over the misery of it all. I didn't need to touch myself to remember the heat of his dick in my mouth—or how hard having him there made me. Since our very first kiss, I'd been perpetually hard. It was difficult to concentrate on work, near impossible to look at my brother with a straight face, and I knew I needed to get my act together. I hoped lunch with Shawn would help calm my nerves a little, and the upcoming trip home would hopefully give some much needed room to breathe.

I made quick enough work of washing up, then grabbed a towel out of the warmer and padded barefoot into my bedroom. Standing in front of the closet, I texted Ford to let him know I remained full of cum, which earned me a devil emoji in reply, then I turned my attention to my closet. We were just going to grab sandwiches at a little coffee shop across the street from Shawn's apartment on my lunch break, but I needed to get to work first. The city was blustery and cold, so I opted for a pull over sweater and slacks, a scarf, and my black pea coat, hoping it would be enough to get me through the day.

The morning at work went by fast enough. Thankfully, Kale had started coming in later and later because he struggled to tear himself away from Christian in the morning. Honestly, I couldn't blame him. Leaving Ford's bed was torture, but we all had appearances to keep up. I slogged through work and told my brother I was going to take a long lunch since Shawn was off and home in Brooklyn.

It took me about an hour to get from the office across town to the coffee shop, and I met Shawn on the sidewalk out front. His coat wasn't as thick as mine, and he cupped his hands around his mouth to blow into them while he waited. When he saw me, his hands fell away and he smiled, opening up his arms for a hug once I got close enough. Shawn smelled like soup and industrial cleanser, and it was a familiar scent in its own way.

"How have you been?" he asked, holding the door to the cafe open.

We both stepped inside and I shook off the cold, unraveling the scarf from my neck before pulling it off the rest of the way.

"I've been good," I said. "Really good, actually."

"Your face looks like there's a story there," he said.

"Just that friend of my brother's." I stepped toward the menu. "Did you want to order? My treat."

"Well, if you're paying..." He waggled his eyebrows and shouldered me out of the way to get to the front counter.

We both ordered sandwiches and drinks, and Shawn carried our plastic table number to a spot in the corner by the front windows. I shrugged out of my coat and hung it on the back of my chair before I turned to him.

"Tell me about the friend," he said.

"I want to, but…" I didn't know how to bring up what I wanted to say first, but it didn't feel fair for me to have the conversation we were about to have without addressing what I felt to be the elephant in the room. "Can I ask you something first?"

"Always, Boston."

"When you asked me to get a drink with you when I saw you last…" I trailed off, watching a flush rise in Shawn's cheeks that gave me as much of an answer as I needed. "Did you mean you wanted to get drinks with me as more than friends?"

Shawn looked down, tapping his thumbs against the edge of the butcher block table before letting his hands fall onto his lap.

"It's against the rules to date benefactors of the kitchen," he muttered.

"I hardly believe my produce drops make me a benefactor."

"It's the whole fraternization thing," he said.

"We're fraternizing right now," I countered.

Shawn looked up, brows knit tight together and mouth twisted into a miserable-looking frown.

"I don't want to tell you anything that's going to hurt your feelings," I said.

"I hurt my own feelings, Boston." He gave me a tight smile and the girl who'd taken our orders came over with our sandwiches and drinks. She took the number and left us once again in the awkward and stilted quiet of our conversation.

"I didn't even realize I was attracted to men until Ford," I tried to explain.

"Being attracted to one man doesn't mean you have to be attracted to all men. You don't owe me an explanation or a reason for not being interested in me."

"But you had hoped?" I pulled one of the plastic-topped toothpicks out of the middle of my sandwich and tossed it onto the table.

"Every man in the city hopes, Boston. It's impossible to look at you and not hope." Shawn yanked his toothpick out much less gracefully, then shoved half his sandwich into his mouth. It reminded me of the awkward conversation I'd had with my brother at work, and I was dedicated to not having a do-over.

"I don't want to talk to you about Ford if it's going to make things weird," I said.

"You're not the first man who has said no to drinks and you won't be the last. I assure you I can survive this." He adjusted the bread on his sandwich and gave me a sincere smile. "I think you're a phenomenal guy, and if we're just friends, then we're just friends."

Shawn hadn't lied to be me before, so I didn't really have any option besides to take him at his word.

"Thank you," I said.

"Now tell me about Ford."

"He's unexpected," I said, setting down my sandwich and reaching for my peach tea. I took a long swallow through the straw while I tried to gather my thoughts. "But I like it, I think. The whole thing is unexpected."

"And he's your brother's friend?"

"Since college."

"Do you think your brother is going to be more upset that you're sleeping with his friend or that you're sleeping with a man?" Shawn asked.

"I told him I wasn't straight and he took it well. But he's not going to be pleased when he finds out what man I'm exploring all of that with."

"Why not?"

"Ford doesn't have the best reputation when it comes to relationships and I don't think Kale wants me to get taken advantage of."

"Is Ford taking advantage?"

I thought about how demanding I'd been through the whole course of things with Ford. It was laughable for anyone to even dare to imply that he'd taken advantage or manipulated me. For as dominant as he was, I'd been driving the getaway car from the start. Thankfully, he didn't seem to mind.

"Not at all."

"Then it doesn't sound like there's a problem," he said. "It sounds like you're trying to make a problem."

"I'm definitely not trying to do that. It's just uncharted territory for the both of us. We're going on our first date tonight. Do you have any tips?"

Shawn let out a low laugh and dropped the crust of his sandwich onto the tray. "Are you seriously asking me for dating advice?"

"I've only dated women!" I pushed my food away and used my fingertips to rub the bridge of my nose, pushing my glasses toward my forehead. "I don't know if it's different."

"I mean it's very different, but it's also not different at all. I think every relationship has its own dynamic and so what works for one won't work for another."

That was an absolute understatement.

With Ford, it was so fucking easy to go onto my knees for him, to call him Sir, to let him order me around the way that got us both hard. But it was equally simple for me to tease him and push back at him, to try and take control of the situation and order *him* around. They both felt like right choices, even if I leaned more one way than the other.

"Don't overthink it," Shawn said, and I rolled my eyes, bringing myself back to the present. "Where are you going on your date?"

"I don't know. Probably some place expensive. That's his MO."

Shawn scoffed. "And it's not yours?"

"Most of my money is my grandparents'," I said. "Ford's is his own."

I didn't mean to imply that I didn't work hard for what I had, but I'd definitely had a couple million helping hands along the way. I knew I had more than most and my friendship with Shawn reminded me of that, though he never tried to make me feel bad for how I lived.

"Fair enough." He picked at the last bits of his sandwich before leaning back in his chair. "Speaking of family, when can I expect our next vegetable delivery?"

I grinned, rubbing the back of my neck. "I'm actually going to be taking a trip to the farm in the next week or so. I'll see if Mom has anything good to send."

"I appreciate it, Boston. Everyone does."

"It's the least I can do," I said, and it was the absolute truth. "At least until I get that farm upstate, right?"

Shawn laughed and finished off the rest of his lemonade. "One day you'll come around to the idea," he said.

"Never say never."

I'd come around to the idea of being with a man, so I didn't really think anything was off the table for me at that point.

"Oh!" Shawn clapped his hands together, a mischievous smile flashing across his face. "I do have one piece of dating advice for you."

"I'm all ears."

"Bring him flowers."

I cocked my head to the side, not sure I'd heard him right. "What?"

"When was the last time someone bought you flowers?" he asked.

"I don't think anyone ever has."

"And I doubt anyone has ever bought him flowers either." Shawn gave me a smug and proud smile that reminded me so much of Ford it made *me* smile back at him. "I bet he would be flattered."

"I don't even know what kind of flowers he likes."

"That doesn't matter yet," he said. "This is your first date."

Shawn checked his watch and shoved his chair back. "Get your shit on, come on."

"Where are we going?" I stood and slipped my jacket on and wound my scarf back around my neck. It was so soft and so warm, one of my favorite things my parents had ever sent me. I made a note to see if they had any spare ones they wanted to donate so I could take them to the kitchen next time I brought some vegetables over.

"There's a little local florist a few blocks down. Let's go get your man something nice."

Shawn hooked his arm through mine and dragged me out of the cafe before I could protest. Not that I wanted to argue, because he was right. Getting on my knees wasn't the only way to show Ford how I felt about him, and if we were going to date, I was going to give it everything I had.

"I bet he likes peonies," I said, hiking my scarf up to cover my mouth.

"I'm sure he will, Boston. He'll like them because they're from you."

Beamer had laughed at me until I hung up on him, then he called me back to laugh some more. I hadn't gone so far as to tell him *who* I was dating, but the fact I was going on a date at all was apparently the highlight of his life. And that was saying something, considering he'd recently gotten re-married to his husband of nearly two decades and moved across the country to be with him.

"If it's meant to be, Ford, it's going to be," he'd said to me, which didn't feel like the magical and eye-opening kind of advice I'd been hoping for, but he didn't have anything else to offer.

I knew better than to call Brooks about it, and there was no way I was going to ask Kale, so I was unfortunately on my own. It wasn't the first time, though, and I was confident that even though I was new to dating, I could wing it.

It would have been easy enough for us to walk to dinner, but the nights were beyond cold, and I liked the idea of cozying up next to Boston in the back of a town car, so I'd dialed one up while I studied myself one last time in the full-length mirror in my bedroom. Milo purred like a freight train, winding his way around my ankles in a figure eight, swishing his tail up toward my knees before he plopped down on the toe of my shoe. We both looked at ourselves in the mirror, and I would have paid a decent sum of money for my cat to be able to talk and share me his thoughts on what I was doing.

"Now or never, Milo," I said, giving my foot a shake and divesting him of his seat.

He made an unimpressed harrumphing kind of meow, then flicked his tail at me one more time as he sauntered out of my bedroom like he owned the place. My phone vibrated, and I didn't need to look to know it was the car. I fished it out of my pocket and texted Boston to let him know I was on the way, then locked up and headed down to the street.

The ride to his apartment was a short one, and I was shocked to find he'd given my name to his doorman instead of meeting me down in the lobby. I didn't know why it surprised me, but on the elevator ride up to his unit, I couldn't stop myself from remembering it was an elevator ride that had gotten us into this mess. On Boston's floor, I found his front door cracked open, but I rapped my knuckles against the door frame to announce myself anyway.

"You ready, sweetheart?" I called out.

From behind the door I heard rustling and clattering, and then the door swung open with a rush of floral and linen scent that was definitely not anything I'd ever associated with Boston before. But I was quick to search out his mop of dark hair and the black frame of his glasses, his entire face half obscured behind a Kraft paper-wrapped bouquet of pink and white peonies.

"Am I too late?" I asked. "Did someone beat me to you?"

He lowered the flowers down, then awkwardly thrust them toward me.

"They're for you..." he trailed off, and I could have *sworn* he murmured a quiet Sir at the end, but it had been lost on my ears.

Without thinking, I took the flowers out of his hand, the Kraft paper sharp and rough against my palm, a violent contrast to the soft smell and look of the flowers inside of it. Dipping my nose down, I sucked in a deep breath of the fragrant blooms, keeping my eyes open and trained on Boston's nervous expression. His cheeks were darker than the darkest flower he'd given me, and the fine lines around the corners of his eyes only served to demonstrate his uncertainty over the act.

"No one has ever gotten me flowers before." I lowered them after a second smell, giving him the sincerest smile of my life.

Boston was a master at making me feel things without trying, but the emotions that swelled and wrapped around my ribs from the simple gesture were a whole new level of complicated that made it far too hard to breathe.

"Then I'm your first here too." His voice cracked, and he pushed his glasses up with the pad of his middle finger.

I licked my lips, already itching to lay him down and take him apart.

Suddenly, dating felt impossibly hard. Not because I didn't want to, or because I didn't care to know Boston beyond the bedroom, but because his mere presence overwhelmed me to the point of mindlessness.

"You are." I glanced down again at the flowers, such a small and also massive gesture at the same time. "These are beautiful, Boston. Can I put them in some water before we go?"

"Right." He cleared his throat and took a step back. "I wasn't thinking, didn't…"

"Boston." I shifted the flowers to my side, leaving nothing between us, and I slid my hand around the back of his neck, yanking our bodies together. I came close to kissing him without committing, but smiled against his mouth just the same. "This is the sweetest thing anyone has ever done for me. Thank you."

"I'm glad you like them."

"I like you." I kissed the corner of his mouth.

He let out the softest whimper, leaning into me before swaying backward, almost stumbling. "Let me get some water and we can go. I don't want to be late."

I followed him into his apartment, closing the door behind me. "Late isn't for people like us, sweetheart."

Boston blinked at me, taking another step backward before turning and heading down the long parquet-floored hallway.

"The kitchen is this way," he said.

I went after him, doing my best to get a look at his apartment without making it obvious I was trying to get a look at his apartment. From what I could see, it was furnished more like a rustic farmhouse than a multi-million dollar listing, with an overstuffed and upholstered couch facing a bricked fireplace with a low wood table between the two. There were at least three crocheted blankets slung over the back of the couch, and a stack of magazines on the table, one open to a half-finished crossword. There were some picture frames on the mantle, but the view out the tall windows on the far wall wasn't anything to shake a stick at either.

The sound of a faucet turning on pulled me through a narrow doorway into his kitchen, which was as unremarkable as most New York City kitchens. Bigger than most, but still considerably smaller than mine. Boston was at the sink, pouring water into a crystal vase that probably cost five figures on its own. The dichotomy of this man was forever going to keep me on my toes.

I joined him in the small and narrow space, unwrapping the paper and dropping the stems into the waiting container. He took the paper out of my hands like we'd rehearsed the transition a thousand times before, and I worked my fingers through the stems, giving the flowers room to settle and breathe. I set the filled vase on his counter and turned to find him watching me expectantly, cheeks colored with an entirely different kind of flush than before.

I crooked my finger and beckoned him, and he came like there was a string connecting us. Boston fitted himself between my legs and my entire life flashed before my eyes. The depth of promise took my breath away, and before I could try to get it back, Boston's mouth was on mine, his tongue diving eagerly into my mouth. Cradling both of my hands around his neck, I kissed him back until my cock ached. With a gentle shove, Boston groaned, his chin tilted up and his eyes still closed.

"We have to get going or we'll be late," I whispered, pressing a kiss against the tip of his nose.

"I thought late didn't exist for people like us."

"It doesn't." I pressed another kiss against his forehead, then let my hands slide off his neck and over his shoulders.

"But tonight is supposed to be a date and if I kiss you any longer, it's not going to be."

"Would it hurt if I told you I was a sure thing?" He blinked his eyes open, a sly smile flashing across his face before he took a step away from me of his own accord.

"Eventually," I muttered, grabbing his hand and threading our fingers together.

I liked the way his palm felt against mine, clammy and cool, his grip a little tighter than necessary around my fingers, like he wasn't sure if it would be the only time he got to hold me like that.

"Let's go," I said, pulling him back through his house and toward the front door. "Do you have everything?"

"I have you."

"Boston." I groaned, backing him into the wall and burying my face into the crook of his neck. There was the familiar smell of him that I'd already gotten so used to. "You can't say things like that."

"Why not?" His hips bucked against me, drawing another groan from the back of my throat. He was like a pubescent teenager, and he was going to be the absolute death of me.

"Let's go," I said again, kicking the side of his shoe with mine.

"Yes, Sir." With his free hand, he gave me a pretend salute, and I had to put enough space between us to breathe.

While he locked the door, I pressed the button of the elevator, spine stiffening when I felt the heat of his body come up behind me. Instead of fighting it, I tilted my head back and bumped against him. There was no denying that it felt *good* to be with him that way. Much in the same way Boston's attraction to men hadn't manifested until he was focused on me, I didn't think I'd feel the same about dating someone who wasn't him. There was nothing easy about him, but being with him wasn't hard either. Being with Boston made sense in all the ways nothing else ever had before.

The elevator let out a soft chime as it arrived on his floor, and he shuffled behind me into the small space. When the doors closed, he pushed the button for the lobby, but otherwise kept as much of his body pressed against mine as he could manage. I shoved my hand into the pocket of his pants, keeping him close. We didn't say a word, but I didn't think we needed to. On the street, I took his hand and walked him to the waiting town car, closing the door behind us both.

"Where are we going for dinner?" he asked, settling back against the heated leather seat.

"It's a bit of a drive," I said. "Westchester."

"What's in Westchester?" Boston laughed and smiled, glancing out the window as we began to make our way out of the city.

"A restaurant I think you'll like."

Boston rolled his head toward me, looking at me from the corner of his eye. "Are you not going to tell me?"

"I want it to be a surprise."

I knew Boston was a central California boy at heart, from the way he always spoke fondly of his childhood on the farm to the way he wasn't scared of the immense amounts of produce his parents always shipped to him and Kale. He missed that life, missed his family, and I knew he was planning a trip back home sooner rather than later. I'd be lying if I didn't say I hated the idea of him leaving. I was just starting to get used to him, only for him to pack up and ship out for God knew how long. And even though Boston said he wanted more dominance out of me, I knew better than to tell him not to take the trip back to California. It just so happened I'd heard about the farmstead restaurant at Blue Hill in passing months before, but I'd never imagined myself going there, let alone taking a date there. But I'd never imagined a lot of things for myself before Boston wrapped his hand around my thigh and asked me to teach him how to fuck.

The restaurant was booked out for months, but much in the way people like us could never be late, reservations also meant little. Money talked, for better or worse, and I'd secured a last minute, end of night, private dining room for the two of us. It cost me the same as if we'd brought ten of our closest friends, but it was worth it. Getting out of the city offered two incentives, the first being there was zero chance of running into Kale or anyone who knew him, the second that I could get Boston back to the farms he loved so much.

Even if just for a night.

# CHAPTER 21
# BOSTON

NO ONE HAD EVER PUT AS MUCH THOUGHT INTO A DATE AS FORD PUT into ours. I wasn't sure what to make of him at first, from the unexpected and unrestrained smile that flashed across his face when he realized I'd gotten him flowers to the casual way he buried his face in the back of my neck while we waited for the elevator. Everything about how he was acting seemed contrary to how he acted before. It was almost like a switch had flipped after our last conversation and he went from treading water in the shallow end to diving in head first.

Not that I was going to complain.

I was learning to love everything about what it meant to be with a man…to be with him.

Everything about the sprawling farm he'd picked for dinner was perfect. The furnishings, the wine, the service and, most of all, the company. Making conversation with Ford was easier than ever, the confident and sure way he rattled off question after question on his quest to get to know me, all of it fairly interspersed with my own questions as ideas popped into my head.

I learned that Ford had no siblings and had only left New York for college before returning immediately after graduation. He told me his parents had died when he was twenty-five, which had served to quadruple the number of zeroes in his bank account. Ford didn't need to work, but it was obvious to me he was a restless kind of man who would get bored without something to keep him busy. He worked because he enjoyed it and I knew if he ever got tired of his job, he would walk away from it entirely.

Over our main course, I told him more about my memories of growing up on the farm and he was eager to ask me all about what Kale had been like as a pre-teen. I didn't want to give him too much ammunition, lest it become clear he had an inside source, but sharing stories from back home had me feeling a whole new kind of warmth in the stomach. Between that and the butterflies every time Ford touched my hand or brushed the toe of his shoe against my ankle, it was like spring had taken bloom in the center of my chest.

By the time we finished off a pumpkin soufflé with some kind of apple and cream sauce, I was bursting out of my skin with anticipation. Hours of thoughtful and discerning touches had put the physicality of our relationship on the back burner, but it was still doing much more than simmering. Close to boiling over, I was beyond ready to get out of the restaurant and back into the city.

The hour-long ride back to Manhattan was agony, and Ford held my hand in his like we had all the time in the world to waste. I admired the way he was able to act like our relationship wasn't a ticking time bomb, but when he leaned close and brushed his mouth across the shell of my ear, I almost forgot.

When the car pulled up along the curb in front of my building, my legs flopped around like I was some kind of awkward baby deer who'd never walked a day in its life. Ford stepped out of the car after me and stayed close behind, one arm wrapped around my waist and his face inches from my neck.

"Did you have a good night, Boston?"

The question was a whisper, but so loud at the same time.

"Very much." Again I found myself wanting to call him Sir for no other reason than it felt right for the honorific to roll of my tongue, much in the same way he called me sweetheart.

"I've never had a date like this before," he went on, "not as a proper adult and not with someone I truly cared about."

That butterfly garden that had exploded in my chest was out of control, his words as much of an aphrodisiac as the rest of him.

"Did you enjoy it?"

"So much," he murmured, swiveling so our faces were aligned and his nose wasn't more than two inches from mine.

"Come upstairs," I whispered.

"I'm trying to be a gentleman." Ford brushed his lips against mine, sending sparks flying into the crisp night air.

"Don't try to tell me gentlemen don't fuck, Ford."

He groaned into my mouth, snaking a hand around the bank of my neck and changing the angle of my head to get a better press of his mouth on mine. I parted my lips for his tongue, my cock thickening hot and hard as he deepened the kiss.

"I don't want to rush you," he said.

"You're not," I assured him, taking his hand and moving it down to cover my erection. "You never have and I don't think you ever will. If anything, I'm the one being too demanding."

"There's no harm in asking for the things you need, sweetheart."

"Then come upstairs with me."

Both our hands were still between my legs and I tangled our fingers together so I could lead him inside. There was a brief moment where Ford dug his heels in, stare shifting unsteadily between the door to my building and the still open door to the town car.

"You're thinking too hard," I said to him, nodding toward the building.

A thousand emotions flashed across his face, none of them sticking long enough for me to make sense of, but I saw enough doubt to let go of his hand and put a foot of space between us.

"I don't want to rush *you*," I repeated his statement back to him.

Ford licked his lips at that, pulling the bottom one in between his teeth. He chewed on it, his jaw working the entire time. "I'm just wondering the odds," he finally said.

"Of?"

"Of this ending horribly for everyone." Ford scrubbed a hand down his face and took a step away from me, not toward the car, but not toward the building either. "It was one thing when this was just sex, but now..."

He didn't need to say the rest, because I knew exactly what he was thinking. But now, it was more than our bodies involved. Whether we had planned it or not, there were feelings developing, interest, dedication, and those were things that could only stay hidden for so long. That was why he'd said "horribly for everyone" and not just us. His best friend was my brother; the balance of their friend group and my relationship with Kale were all on the line.

"We don't have to do this if you don't want to."

"Are you out of your mind?" Indignation flashed in his eyes and he closed the space between us with one long and sure step. He had one hand around the back of my neck and the other around my waist before I even realized he'd moved, and he was back in space, back breathing my air. "I've never wanted anything more than I want you, Boston."

Slowly, I reached up and curled my fingers around his wrist, holding on to his arm while he held on to me. His eyes were dark and frenzied, searching my face for an answer I wasn't sure I knew how to give him.

"Then who cares about the rest?" I asked.

"You're making it hard to hold back."

"Then don't." I kissed the corner of his mouth, the underside of his jaw. "Stop treating me like a kid who doesn't know better."

"You don't know better." He scoffed. "That's what got us in this situation in the first place."

"I don't know *how*," I corrected, "and I've spent my whole life making my own decisions. I'm fairly certain that the way you kiss me hasn't erased a lifetime of competence."

The corner of his mouth quirked up into a smug smile and I kissed him there next.

"How do I kiss?" he asked.

"Like you want to take me apart with your teeth."

I nipped his jaw with mine to demonstrate exactly what I meant. His fingers flexed against the back of my neck, his other hand splaying out against the small of my back and pulling me closer.

"I do, sweetheart," he rasped, finally tearing himself away from me long enough to slam the car door closed.

We practically ran into the lobby, excitement for the unknown surging up my spine like a tidal wave. In the elevator, Ford backed me into the corner as soon as the doors closed, shoving one of his legs between mine. His thigh pressed hard against my cock and balls, like kindling on an already out-of-control fire. He shoved his face into the crook of my neck and sucked at the skin behind my ear, one hand pressed against the mirrored back wall of the elevator, the other already busying itself with my belt.

We stumbled out of the elevator and down the hall, and then Ford had his front pressed against my back while I struggled to get the door unlocked. His erection throbbed hot and hard against the small of my back, and the deadbolt finally disengaged. Without the door in front of me, we fell into my apartment, and Ford kicked the door closed, not bothering to lock it.

Both of us busied our hands with belts and zippers and buttons, and by the time we made it into my bedroom, we were both naked, save for our underwear. My dick pressed so persistently at the already soaked material, I didn't even see the point in keeping them on. Ford must have agreed because he gave me a rough shove toward the bed, gripping the waistband of my briefs and yanking them down my legs and off.

He didn't bother with his, crawling onto the bed between my spread thighs and peppering kisses up my stomach toward my chest. He paused there long enough to suck each nipple into his mouth, one at a time, and then his lips were at the hollow of my throat, my Adam's apple, the underside of my chin. I tilted my head back, giving him more room to explore.

I was a disaster beneath him, half arousal and half anxiety over having another man on top of me the way he was. When he pressed his mouth against mine, the hot line of his cock seared itself against my hip, and I hooked my ankles around the backs of his thighs.

Ford groaned, pumping his hips against me, holding the top of my head with one hand and my hip with the other. Like he was trying to pin me down and stretch me out, Ford explored my mouth like a man who was meant to make maps from touch and taste alone.

"I want you more than I've ever wanted anyone in my life," he whispered against my lips, sucking the bottom one into his mouth until I arched off the bed and pressed all the hot contact points of my body against him.

"I know I said this before, but I really do bet you say that to all the boys."

At my comment, he went still, lifting up enough for me to blink him into focus. I still had my glasses on, even though they'd been knocked about from the rough kisses. He searched my face with those impossibly breathtaking eyes of his, then slowly shook his head.

"Not a single one, Boston," he said, every word enunciated and punctuated clearly as to deliver the seriousness of his intent.

I swallowed, the intensity of his declaration stirring more feelings in me than the first time Colette had said she loved me. What had I been doing my entire life? Settling for lackluster and less than, when what I should have been doing was chasing after a love like this with every ounce of focus I possessed.

Wait, no.

Not a love...

This was infatuation, this was passion, but there was no way it was anything more than new lust. Even as I tried to convince myself of that, the warmth in my chest blossomed further, spreading to my stomach, down my legs, into my throat making it hard to speak.

I don't know what Ford saw in my face, but he leaned back in and left a soft, chaste kiss against the corner of my mouth. My legs, which had been hooked around his, relaxed and fell against the sheets. I wrapped my arms around his back, testing the way the broad expanse of his shoulders felt beneath my hands, and Ford licked into my mouth, taking the kiss back toward the tumultuous pools of desire we'd just stopped ourselves from drowning in.

I was in love with Boston Sheffield.

I rolled him on top of me, knowing I was in love with him.

I helped him strip me out of my underwear, knowing I was in love with him.

I kissed him, knowing I was in love with him.

I watched when he reached over to his nightstand for lube and a condom, already helplessly in love with him.

"Tell me what to do," he said softly, holding the gold foil packet and the bottle of clear liquid in his hands.

"Put some lube on your fingers," I told him. "If you think it's too much, you still need more."

He moved onto his knees and cracked open the bottle, squirting a liberal amount onto his fingers. He used his other hand to slick it up and down the length of his first two digits, bottom lip pulled between his teeth in a show of adorable concentration.

"What now?"

"I have a sneaking suspicion you can figure it out, sweetheart." I covered my eyes with my forearm, unable to look at him a second longer.

How long had it been since I'd bottomed?

My erection flagged at the thought, and I covered it with my palm, pulling my shaft and balls up toward my stomach so he could see what he was working with. There was still part of me that expected him to absolutely freak out and beg off from what we'd gotten ourselves into. I wouldn't have been able to blame him. There were plenty of things different about having a man beneath you than a woman, and everything we'd done up until this point was nothing more than foreplay.

"I don't want to hurt you," he said softly.

"You won't." I desperately hoped that wasn't a lie. "Just go slow. One finger first, then the other."

The cold and wet press of his finger against my asshole was enough to almost send me into orbit. I gritted my teeth and spread my legs for him, digging my heels into the bed and lifting up enough for him to see.

"Put a pillow under my hips," I whispered, lifting my hips off the bed to make room. "It'll be easier."

At least, that's what I always told everyone else. I hoped I wasn't getting ready to make a liar out of myself.

Boston slid one of his pillows underneath me and I relaxed against it. His finger was back against my hole, and his other hand grabbed my wrist, tugging my arm away from my face.

"I want to see you," he said,

Didn't he understand he saw me better than anyone else ever had? Wasn't that enough for him? How foolish I'd been going into this with him, thinking that Boston deserved anything less than everything.

Sucking in a breath, I stared down my nose at him as he

pushed the tip of his finger into my body. He caught my reaction and immediately went still, but I shook my head.

"Don't stop," I told him. "All the way in. Just like that, sweetheart."

His pointer finger bottomed out, the knuckle pressed against my rim, his slick second finger curled and ready.

"Don't stop, Boston," I said again, and with an agonizing slowness that unfurled a ripple of goose flesh up both of my arms, he pulled his finger all the way out of me, then pushed it back in.

Letting him get used to having his finger inside of an asshole was going to be the death of me, so I told him to add another one. If I was going to die, it might as well be with his cock inside of me, not something as simple as fingers. He struggled to get his second finger into me, but it was nothing a little lube and a little willpower couldn't get done, and with both of them inside of me, Boston fell forward, bracing his hand beside my head. His chest heaved as he breathed, the position shifting one of my knees toward my ear to make room for the spread of his body.

"Does it feel okay?" He asked, brow knit together, but pupils shot.

"Feels like I need more of you," I admitted, lifting my head from the pillow so I could chase after another kiss.

Boston teased the full length of his fingers in and out of me until a cold sweat broke out against my temple. He moved to the side and licked the sweat off me, sending a shiver through us both.

"This is amazing," he said, more to himself than to me, I thought. "This is more than I ever expected."

"I know."

Boston kissed down the side of my face and the curve of my neck. I lifted my arm, reaching above me for his headboard. I needed to ground myself, but when he took the opportunity to bury his face in the sweaty crook of my armpit, I almost came on the spot.

"I need more, sweetheart," I said again, voice cracking on the endearment.

"Right. Right."

He quickly pulled his fingers out of me, and I groaned at the absence. The condom had gotten lost on the bed somewhere, and while he searched around for it with a curse under his breath, I made the decision to hammer the final nail into my coffin.

"Don't use the condom," I rasped, shaking my head when he looked sharply at me with hooded, yet confused eyes.

"What?"

"Don't use the condom," I repeated. "We're exclusive, right?"

His mouth twitched at the statement.

"We've been tested, we don't..." My throat was dry as the desert, so I stopped trying to find words. I know I told him I always used condoms, and it had been the truth, but the thought of using one with him was unfathomable.

At my silence, Boston stopped trying to find the condom.

"Are you sure?" he asked.

*No.*

"Very."

He opened the lube again and smeared it over his cock, just like he had with his fingers. His brow was furrowed in a look of single-minded focus and as he used more than enough lube to get himself ready. I was thankful for the prep, thankful for the wet slide that his attention was going to give us both, thankful for the opportunity to—at thirty-something—find out for the first time in my life what it meant to make love with another person.

With the same look of determination, Boston pressed the swollen head of his cock against my lube-slicked hole. His mouth pulled down into a frown, and I knew he was struggling with that first, hard push required to get past the resistant barrier of muscle.

"You feel good," I promised, bearing down to help him out.

The head of his dick slid into me and Boston shouted out a surprised cry over the curse I loosed under my breath. My heart slammed against my ribs, pulse beating like mad in my ears as he went still with the first inch of his cock inside of me.

"Don't stop, Boston," I encouraged him. "Come kiss me."

The bend to bring our mouths together brought another few inches of his cock into me, and I rose up enough to kiss the stuttered and surprised gasp out of his mouth. Hooking my legs around the backs of his thighs, I pulled the rest of his length into me, slamming my eyes closed when he bottomed out.

"Holy shit," he murmured against my mouth.

Over and over again.

Holy shit.

Holy shit.

*Holy shit.*

"How do *I* feel, sweetheart?" I nudged my nose against his, reaching up with a trembling hand to take off his glasses and toss them toward his nightstand.

"Like home," he croaked, pushing his hips forward once again and chasing any extra inch of depth he could find.

The weight of his words landed on the center of my chest like an anvil, making it near impossible to breathe. Even when he started to move, easing out of me and then back in, my lungs refused to fill. The sight of him above me, the burning swell of him inside of me...

I reached between our sweaty and tense bodies, grabbing my dick and giving it a rough stroke. My field of vision was already blurred, and the friction around my cock brought my orgasm up faster than I'd expected. Less than five minutes after Boston first started to pump in and out of me, I shot searing hot ribbons of cum across my stomach and chest, knowing all the while I was in love. When he cursed at the way my body gripped and sucked at him, drawing his own orgasm out, I still knew I was in love.

He gritted his teeth, lip curling into a feral and ferocious scowl. The pace of his hips turned frenetic, and he shook his head, cursing and whimpering like either of us had any control over anything between us anymore.

"Can I come now?" He begged the question in my ear, his temple pressed against mine and his forehead buried in the pillow.

The only sounds in the room were the harsh pant of our breaths, mine exhausted from the orgasm and his fraught with the restraint of fighting his off, layered under the loud and sharp slap of skin against skin as he fucked my legs wide, fucked me into the headboard.

I didn't answer him because I wasn't ready for it to end.

I wanted to be in love with him like this for another

minute longer because I didn't think my heart was a truth I could hide from him.

"Ford." He groaned, hips thrusting and going still. "Please. Sir. Please, please, please."

I'd never had someone beg to get off with their cock inside of me. I had never felt dominance from my back, but it was headier than any high from any play session I'd ever had before. I flexed my muscles around him, relishing the way his pleases turned into unintelligible mumbles. He was all but still inside of me, the muscles in his stomach and back pulled tight from his restraint.

"Sir," he pleaded one last time, shaking his head. He sounded like he might be crying. Boston pressed his mouth against mine, lips moving in what was either a curse or a promise over and over until I finally relented and gave him what he needed the most.

"Come inside of me, sweetheart. Let me feel you."

Not even a full second later, half a breath at best, his cock thickened and swelled, testing my already swollen and well-fucked hole. Boston's mouth opened, no sound coming out, and then he spilled inside of me, hot jets of cum painting the deepest parts of me...places no one had ever touched before him. A shiver wracked through his whole body and I wrapped him up with my arms and my legs, holding him tight against me in every possible way I could while he rode out the intense waves of his orgasm.

Finally, long after the cum and the sweat between our stomachs had gone cool, Boston relaxed against me. His cock slipped out of me and he tucked himself into my side, nose once again buried deep in my armpit. He curled himself alongside my ribs and my legs, molding his body to the shape of mine in a way that felt righter than anything else ever had before. I kissed the top of his sweaty head, sighing and turning my attention to his ceiling.

His bedroom had long windows, and the lights of the city street down below played off the stark white paint, a kaleidoscope of everyone else's life moving on while mine had irreparably stopped in time.

"Boston," I whispered, drawing gentle spirals against his spine.

He hummed, scrunching his nose against my skin. "Ford."

The ache of his penetration was still warm and throbbing between my legs, my dick still half hard and ready to go a second round with him. A thousand words and futures raced through my mind, all of them conflicting with the only future I knew I would ever dream of again. I wanted to tell Boston that I loved him, but I wasn't ready to give him up yet.

Everything was the same, but everything was different.

I hadn't been wrong in saying Ford had changed the way he treated me after we'd made the decision to be together for real, but after we had sex for the first time, he was even more focused. Ford was demanding, but he was thoughtful, dominant, but gentle. I'd admittedly never fantasized about what it would be like to have a boyfriend, but if I had, it would have been just like this.

The morning after we had sex for the first time, I woke up embarrassed to find myself wrapped around him like an overzealous octopus. With one arm strapped over his chest and a leg hitched over his thigh, my face was buried in his armpit again, the rich and musky smell of his sweat and skin ripe in my nostrils.

The scent of him alone was enough to make my cock twitch back to life, which impressed me because, after the night before, I didn't think I had it in me to ever get hard again. Being with a man—being with Ford—was more than

I'd ever expected, but as the soft rays of the morning sun streaked across the floor of my bedroom, previously unconnected pieces of my life slotted together in a brand new way.

I had always thought I loved Colette. That I had wanted her too. But after being with Ford, parts of my past were called into doubt. I didn't think I wanted to take it as far as to say that I favored men over women, but I favored Ford over almost anyone. It was impossible to ignore the specter of my brother, though, the hovering fear of him finding out about us forever hanging over our heads. Thankfully, Kale wasn't in my bed. He wasn't in my apartment. He wasn't even on my street.

"I can hear you thinking from here," Ford grumbled, slinging his arm over my shoulders and pushing my face deeper into his armpit.

I groaned, sucking in a deep breath of him. "And what am I thinking about?"

"You're thinking you want to fuck me again," he said, kissing the top of my head.

That was much better than what I was actually thinking about, so I decided not to argue with him about it. There was already enough of my brother between us, I didn't want more.

"I wouldn't mind," I admitted. "But are you up for that?"

Ford hummed thoughtfully, shifting out from underneath me. He flipped me onto my back and straddled me, hands braced against the middle of my chest,

"I'm not," he said, squinting at me with a smile in his eyes. "But I am up to suck your dick until you come in my mouth."

"Sounds like a well-balanced breakfast, but I think I'm late for work."

"Tell your brother you're sick," he suggested.

I didn't think Kale would buy it, but I reached blindly for my phone on the nightstand and did what I'd been told. Ford waited until I tossed my phone away before sliding down between my legs and dropping kisses on my stomach and hips while he worked his way down to the quickly thickening erection between my legs.

Together, we kicked the sheets down to our feet and, with his mouth inches from my cock, Ford said, "I expect you to at least buy me a coffee after this."

Before I could say one way or the other, he sealed his mouth around the tip of my cock and sucked. Oh, the way he fucking sucked. With his stare trained on me and his tongue hot against the underside of my shaft, Ford hollowed out his cheeks and sucked me into his mouth. Inch after agonizing inch, Ford used his tongue, his cheeks, the roof of his mouth, even his teeth to work me into an absolute frenzy.

Still high on him from the night before, Ford was able to make quick work of me. He used his shoulders to spread my legs apart, took my balls into his hand, and he stretched one exploratory finger toward my asshole. He barely grazed over my hair-covered hole, but my body reacted like it had been an electric shock. I arched off the bed, grasping blindly at his hair, his shoulders, whatever parts of him I could reach.

Ford made a thoughtful sound around my cock, sliding his finger into his mouth alongside my shaft. The sensation was unreal, and then his finger was back between my legs, teasing against my hole with soft and slow circles. He pulled his hot mouth away from my dick with a wet pop, and with his stare still focused on me, he licked his lips and pushed his finger harder against my hole.

"If you don't stop that, you're gonna be the one buying me a coffee," I murmured, forcing myself to untangle my fingers from his hair.

"I'll buy you anything you want," he said, dragging his tongue up the entire length of my erection. Ford tapped his finger against my hole and tilted his head to the side. "Is this okay?"

"I think so."

"Is it a lot?"

I nodded and dropped my head against the pillows with a groan.

"Do you want me to make it easier for you?" he asked.

"How?"

Much to my disappointment, Ford righted himself, coming up onto his knees and taking his mouth and hand regrettably out of reach.

"Boston." He gave a small shake of his head, a war of emotions on his face before he settled on determination.

"How?"

"Let me tie you to the bed so you can't fight it," he whispered, crooking his finger until I gave him my hand. He curled his fingers around my wrist, kissing just below the place where he held me, with such a gentle touch I thought I would break from it. "Just your wrists and then I'll make you come so hard you'll beg for me to put something inside of you, then I'll make you come again."

"And then?" I arched a brow.

"Greedy little thing."

"I don't have rope," I said.

Ford released my arm and angled his head toward my closet. "You have ties."

"Alright." Adrenaline coursed through me, making it hard to stay still. The promise of restraint would be a blessing...the only way I would be strong enough to take what he wanted to give me.

"Alright?"

"Ties in the closet," I told him.

My cock jerked, smearing a trail of spit and precum against my stomach.

Ford moved quickly, crawling off the bed and making his way to my closet. He was back in under a minute, three ties clutched in his hands, and he was back on top of me, silk looped around my wrists and fastened to the headboard before I could second-guess myself. His fingers worked steady and sure with the material and the knots, grazing against my skin with a gentle intent that caused more precum to drip from my dick.

"What's the third one for?" I asked as he settled back between my legs.

Ford smirked at me, looking more like the familiar and arrogant version of himself than he ever had. Immediately, I was a virgin again, not sure of myself or anyone else, and Ford was there, confident in all of it.

"Now would be an impeccable time to call me Sir, sweetheart."

He wrapped his hand—and the third tie—around my aching cock and stroked from the root toward the tip.

"What's the...what's the third tie for, Sir?"

"This," he said, stroking me again. "Or it could be a gag. Or a blindfold."

I shivered.

"Do you like the idea of those things?"

"Yes, Sir," I rasped.

"Are you a slut, Boston?" Ford tightened his grip around the soaking wet head of my dick. "No, that's not it. Are you *my* slut, Boston?"

My body arched off the bed, silk cutting into my wrists as I pulled against the restraints.

"Yes, Sir. I think I might be."

"Let's find out for sure."

Ford was buried between my legs before I could say a single word, the entire length of my erection sealed in the wet heat of his mouth and throat. The hand that held the tie dragged over my stomach toward my chest, fingers tangled with the satin, all of it pushing and pulling against my skin.

He sucked cock like he'd spent years practicing it, and when I was so close to coming I saw stars, he released me from his mouth. I cried out, thrashing against the binds. My protests turned to pleas as he slid lower, spreading my ass cheeks apart and burrowing his face in between them. Where earlier he'd used his finger, this time he used his tongue, licking and sucking around my hole like my body was an oasis in the middle of a desert.

I'd never felt anything in my life that compared to how intrusive yet wonderful it felt to have a tongue inside of me down there, and when he once again wrapped his hand around my dick to stroke, I added another indescribable feeling to the list.

"One day I'll suck my cum out of your asshole and feed it back to you, Boston." He murmured the dirty words against my wet hole. "I'll fuck you with my cock and my tongue, sweetheart. I'll be the best lover you've ever had."

"You already are," I promised him.

I knew it to be true without a single doubt, and I knew no one after him would ever compare. The way Ford knew his body and applied the knowledge to learn mine was a master class, and he had barely gotten started.

My first orgasm came on quickly. Something about the smooth silk of the tie and the rough drag of his skin against mine was the perfect mix of sensation. Ford's mouth was sealed against my asshole, sucking and nipping against the tenderest skin, and my cock throbbed in his hand, pulsing in time with my heart as cum spurted out of me.

I cried out again, ties biting into my wrists and the headboard creaking as I pulled against it to get free. Ford looked up at me, smile clear in his eyes even as he kept his mouth busy between my ass cheeks. Cum continued to trickle out of my cock, but Ford didn't let up. He stroked and licked and sucked, using his body weight to pin me to the bed so I couldn't get away from his attention.

"Ford," I whimpered his name, and he pulled back enough for me to see the spit-slicked lower half of his face. His lips were rosy and covered in saliva, hungry for more.

"Sweetheart."

The way the endearment scratched its way from his throat was almost enough to send me headlong into the second orgasm he'd promised me. It also took his mouth away from my asshole long enough for me to register that I really didn't want him to move. I wanted his tongue back inside of me like I wanted my next breath.

"What do you need?" he asked.

"You."

His mouth quirked into a self-satisfied smirk and I pictured myself back at my desk, fingers spread against his thigh as he looked down at me and made me use words to ask for exactly what I wanted from him.

"More."

"More teasing?" He bit his lower lip, fighting off a knowing smile.

Good lord, in his element, Ford Carlisle was a deadly weapon. He had no right being as handsome and talented as he was, in bed and out of it. A threat of the worst variety, Ford was going to ruin my life whether he intended to or not.

"Please put your finger inside of me, Sir," I begged, yanking at the ties around my wrists.

"Just a finger?" He reached between his legs and curled his hand around the base of his own long and hard erection.

My lips fell open and the breath left my lungs in a whoosh of fear.

He stroked himself, scooting forward and dragging the tip of his cock up the length of my ass crack. Electricity sizzled through my spine as he pressed against my hole, but he pulled away with a satisfied look on his face.

"Another day for that," he suggested, sucking his finger into his mouth.

He fellated his finger like he'd earlier done to my cock, and I had to look away from him so I didn't come again. My body was so primed, I wasn't sure I had even finished coming the first time, and the sight of him sucking on his finger like he could draw cum out of the tip had no right being as hot was it was. In retrospect, I wondered how I'd been so ignorant toward my attraction to men before because it was near impossible for me to take my eyes off of Ford.

"Please," I begged again, tilting my head back and screwing my eyes closed. My body trembled, vibrating from want and need and anxiety all at the same time. "Please put your finger up my ass and my balls in your mouth, Sir. Please make me come. Please let me come. Oh, God."

"I love it when you use your words, sweetheart," he said, diving back between my legs and giving me exactly what I'd asked for.

TIME BEGAN TO PASS IN A BLUR OF LATE NIGHTS AND EARLY MORNINGS, with Boston's body pressed against mine until the sunrise. After I tied him to his bed for the first time, Boston wasn't scared to ask to try new things, whether it was a blindfold or a different type of restraint. One night, I'd looked up from my knees, his cock stretching my mouth wide, only to find his head thrown back in pleasure and his fingertips twisting his nipples away from his chest as he shot down my throat.

Being intimate with Boston was more play than I'd ever had, but more than that...being with Boston was *fun*. Guiding him through the explorations of his sexuality, while also dabbling in the kinds of kink I enjoyed, had led to some of the most fulfilling sex of my life. Unfortunately, it only solidified my feelings for him, which I was still determined to keep to myself.

One thing at a time, and all that.

I woke up two weeks later on Saturday with his mouth wet and hot against the back of my neck, his cock hard between my ass cheeks. He rutted against me, one arm wrapped over my chest and the other braced against my hip. Closing my eyes, I leaned back into him with a quiet sigh, enjoying the way he moved against me.

"Is there something you need, sweetheart?" I asked softly, my voice still rough with sleep.

His fingers flexed around my hip and he went still.

"Did you not realize you were humping me like a lovesick teenager?" I asked next, rolling over to face him. I slotted one of my legs between his and hauled him closer.

Boston's eyes were half-closed, his entire face sleepy as he shook his head and gave me a soft smile.

"Even in my sleep," he murmured, lashes fluttering as his eyes fell closed.

I brushed the tips of our noses together and smiled against his lips, licking my way into his mouth. He groaned, trying to pull away from me for only a second before giving up and letting me inside. He'd complained once about not wanting me to taste his morning breath, which I told him was absurd. For as much time as he spent with his face buried in my armpit, a sour mouth was the least of *my* concerns.

Reaching down between us, I curled my fist around both of our erections and gave a slow and loose stroke from root to tip. He shivered and arched his back, pushing his chest against mine and opening his mouth wider for me.

"I love when you submit," I whispered, tracing the shape of his lips with my tongue. I dragged my way across his teeth and deeper into his mouth, hand still working our cocks with all the lazy tenderness the morning deserved.

"I love submitting to you," he said back, breath skipping out of his mouth and against my cheek. "I..."

"What else?" I leaned back enough for us both to slow

down and breathe. My hand continued to work our shafts with a torturously slow pace. "There was something else you were going to say."

An unanticipated flare of hope exploded in the center of my chest, my brain assuring me that Boston was ready to confess *his* love to me. My grip faltered, and I tightened my squeeze around the base of our cocks before going still. I didn't want to miss whatever came next, especially if it was him.

With an agonizing slowness, Boston blinked his eyes open, squinting until he was able to bring me into focus. I smiled at him and pressed a soft kiss against the corner of his mouth.

"I want to submit *more*," he said.

Of all the things I'd expected, that was the last of them. "What do you mean?"

Boston groaned and rolled onto his back, effectively taking his cock away from mine and out of my hand. I turned so I could keep an eye on him, bending my arm at the elbow and propping myself up on my hand to stare down at him while he tried to find the words.

"My brother thinks I'm some naive little child, but I know about The Black Door." Boston dragged the tip of his tongue back and forth against his canine tooth while he squinted up at my ceiling. The sheets pooled low around his hips, the long stretch of his chest and torso looking like a slab of gold in the early morning sunlight.

"What do you think you know about it?"

"It's a kink club."

"It is," I confirmed.

"You go there," he said.

"Often."

Boston licked his lips and angled his head toward me. "Still?"

"No," I answered.

"It's something you like," he said carefully.

"You're something I like."

Boston groaned, rolling away from me entirely and flinging his legs off the side of the bed. He bent over, back bowed as he rested his elbows on his knees. I shifted my way toward what had become his side of the bed, resting my cheek against the top of his back in the space between his shoulder blades.

"What are you asking me, Boston?" I kissed him at the place on his neck where his hairline faded away. "You know I can't take you there."

"Why not?"

"Everyone knows us." I wrapped an arm around his front. "Me, and your brother, and Brooks, and Alex...Beamer."

"They don't know me."

"You think I'll be able to get away with taking someone new there with me and have it not get back to him?" I asked.

"From what I remember, Ford, that wouldn't be terribly out of character for you."

The barb ached, lodged firmly between my ribs, and I was careful when I untangled myself from Boston's hunched over body.

"I need coffee for this," I told him, climbing out of bed and grabbing my discarded pajama pants from the floor. "Come to the kitchen when you're ready to talk and not argue."

I left him alone in my bedroom, his stare steadily focused at his feet, which served him right. We both knew we were in over our heads with whatever we were doing together, and he had to know what he was implying with the unspoken ask. Taking Boston to The Black Door would threaten the foundation we'd started to build behind closed doors. I didn't want to keep our relationship a secret forever, but I wanted us both to feel a little steadier with each other before we faced what it meant to tell his brother about us.

It was muscle memory to put the coffee on, and I stared at the empty carafe while I waited for the brew to start percolating its way down. Boston had yet to make his appearance, and the longer he waited, the more I convinced myself that taking him to The Black Door was a terrible idea. Letting him submit in general was already risky enough. The way my blood burned when he called me Sir was life-threatening on its own. I was already halfway through my first cup of coffee by the time I heard the shuffle of his feet behind me. His drink was already turning cold, but I'd made a decision in his absence.

"Get on your knees, Boston," I said, not even turning to face him.

He exhaled softly, and I listened to his pajamas rustle as he went to his knees.

"Ass on your heels," I said, my morning erection quickly returning. "Palms hands up on your thighs."

I gave him time to adjust before turning.

I should have given myself time to prepare, had I understood the magnitude of what I'd asked and how it would change me far more than it would change him. Boston was in a pair of navy sleep pants and nothing else besides his glasses. His face was still relaxed from sleep, hair mussed from all the places I'd yanked and tugged on it the night before. From his place on the floor, he gazed up at me through the fan of his lashes, fingers spread and relaxed against the tops of his legs, just like I'd commanded.

"I don't need to take you to a club for you to see what it's like to submit," I finally managed to say, rinsing the tension out of my throat with a drink of coffee.

"It's different, though, isn't it?" he asked.

"Sir."

Boston's jaw worked, a flash of movement just below his ear. "It's different though, isn't it, Sir?" he repeated.

"Very."

"I want to see it, Sir."

I blinked slowly, dropping my chin against my chest because it hurt to look at him. I wanted him so fucking much. Maybe Kale had always known his brother was perfect for me, long before either of us had even begun to seriously entertain the idea. Maybe that was why he'd been so insistent that I didn't flirt or tease the way I always liked to do.

"Why?" I asked. "Why do you want to see it? What do you think you're missing?"

His fingers flexed, the slightest curl before straightening back out, ready to receive.

"I want to know that part of you," he said softly, dropping his stare to a spot on the floor between us. "Those parts of us."

"I don't feel like anything is missing," I told him honestly. "You have the most important parts of me, Boston."

My soul.

My heart.

He angled his head back and to the side, somehow looking up and down at me at the same time. "It's not all about you... Sir."

I scoffed at the audacity, my cock leaking against my pajamas from how hard his attitude made me. I crossed my legs at the ankle and raised my mug for another drink.

"Do explain," I prompted.

He lifted his hands from his thighs and curled his fingers around the waistband of his pajama pants, shoving them down behind his balls. They were heavy and lifted, his cock hard and swollen, a bead of precum leaking out of the tip.

"I like it too," he said quietly, almost like he was ashamed of it. "I don't understand it the way you do, but I want to. I'm trying to."

I had to close my eyes, rub the bridge of my nose, but it was too late. The visual of Boston on his knees with his thick erection jutting toward the ceiling was emblazoned on my brain for the rest of my life. The earnest and desperate look on his face, the way he was chasing after completion and under-standing without any fear was one of the sexiest things I'd ever seen in my life.

Boston faced himself head on, whether it was his quest to understand his attraction to men...his attraction to *me*, or now his sudden interest in why his cock got hard while his knees got bruised. His bravery was commendable, if not stupid. His bold need to understand himself was going to be the end of us both.

In a way, it was my fault.

I'd danced around the basics for long enough to give him a taste and now he was here, on his knees in my kitchen with an erection he didn't know what to do with. I'd brought this curse on myself, but I didn't want to do anything besides damn us both and indulge him.

For so many years, I'd used the guise of kink to keep

people at arm's length. I craved the impersonality of submission because it meant I didn't have to hear men whisper my name when they came. It was always Sir, sometimes Master. I could get them off, get myself off, and keep a tight grip on the privacy and control that meant so much to me.

I knew, of course, that submissive partners held most of the control in many scenarios, but as a once-off at The Black Door, it wasn't that simple. People searched out partners there to fulfill base needs, and that exchange only came into play when there was more established trust and long-term understanding. It was what Boston and I were quickly working toward, and my nights with him were also changing my understanding of my own kinks, my own fetishes.

I'd always been about pleasure, chasing the most for myself and for my partners. Pleasure to the point of pain until it wrapped back around again to pleasure. I'd made people come so many times they lost count of the orgasms, until men were shooting blanks into the palm of their hand. But it had been simple, basic. Pleasure was orgasm after orgasm after orgasm. It was straightforward and easy for all of us. We knew what to expect.

When it came to Boston, I had already come up with at least a dozen new ways to chase that same kind of end for us both. Whether it was letting him kneel for me on a Saturday morning in my kitchen while I drank my coffee or me getting on my back for him so he could see what it was like to fuck a man for the first time. My new kink, it seemed, was giving Boston anything and everything he asked for.

With a tired sigh, I set my coffee down on the counter next to his untouched mug and crooked a finger for him to come closer. He didn't stand. He didn't hesitate, instead falling forward onto his hands and crawling across my kitchen to close the space between us. When he reached me, Boston nuzzled my leg like a cat, and I knew I'd never tell him no for the rest of our time together.

"You really want to go to The Black Door?" I asked, gesturing for him to stand.

He rubbed his body against mine as he straightened to his full height, eyes glinting with trouble. He'd always had me wrapped around his finger, from the very first time he touched me and he knew it. I slid my arms around him and pressed our foreheads together, ready to kiss him as soon as he opened his mouth.

"Yes, Sir."

I had bruises on my knees from Ford's kitchen floor, and my joints ached as I stood at the security desk for The Black Door later that night. The girl at the desk looked at my ID and raised a delicately arched brow in Ford's direction. He schooled his features, doing his best to appear unaffected by her silent question, but I understood the weight of what I'd asked him to do.

With both of our IDs returned, Ford tightened his grip on my hand and led me into the front room of the club which, save for the amount of skin on display, looked like any other upscale bar in Manhattan. There was a decent amount of seating, lots of exposed brick and frosted glass, and dim and moody lighting washing over the whole space except for the dark hallways that stretched toward the back of the building.

"Don't talk to anyone," Ford said, the words sharp and almost angry against my ear. "You're here with me. Do you understand? You're *mine.*"

The insistence in his voice was beyond hot and I told him so, which earned me a flush on his cheeks and a tick in his jaw as he led me to the middle of the room toward the bar. Ford held my hand tighter than a vise grip, and I didn't think I'd ever been as turned on in my whole life. It didn't matter that the room was full of men, it was something about the unbridled possession in his tone and his movement that had me ready to crumble at his feet and beg for...

I didn't even know what.

For anything, at that point.

Everything. All of it.

All at once.

"We don't have to stay," I whispered, partially because I didn't want him to have a heart attack from the stress of it and partially because I would have been content to go home and have sex with him again.

"I want to." Ford's eyes were wide, and he pulled us together until I could smell the mint of his toothpaste between us. "I never want you to wonder about things. I want you to have everything you've ever wanted, sweetheart."

His lip quivered and he snapped his mouth closed, almost like he hadn't meant for the words he'd just said to come out. My breath caught somewhere in the middle of my chest, and I answered him with a silent nod. He led me to the bar, ordered both of us a drink, never letting go of my hand.

"Do you want to stay here or see the upstairs?" he asked, passing me my cocktail.

"I don't know. You tell me."

He traced his tongue across the front of his teeth, weighing his options. "The upstairs is more private, but also more...open."

"Both of those things sound nice," I said.

He studied my face, dark eyes scanning me from chin to

hairline, undoubtedly searching for any doubt or lie. But he would find none. Ford had woken something inside of me that had been long dormant, and it wasn't just my attraction to men. I might not have as much experience with kink as my brother and his friends did, but I'd seen enough on the internet to understand the logistics, and Ford had already began to fill in the blanks with his instructions.

Kneeling for Ford was right in a way I couldn't explain, whether it was as a resting place or to put his cock in my mouth didn't matter. I enjoyed letting him take the lead in things. It made me hard, and I hated that he was so nervous about it. We'd done so much talking about the growing dynamic in our relationship, but I couldn't shake the feeling he was still handling me with kid gloves. I didn't just want him to choose where we ate or when, I wanted more, but I also had no interest in changing. I wasn't going to be scared to ask for what I wanted, just because I was leaving it up to him to give it to me.

We found ourselves alone in the elevator, and I pressed him against the corner of the small space, needing him to understand.

"I'm not scared of this," I swore against his mouth. Ford's hands carefully settled themselves on my hips and he dropped his head against the wall. "You're not going to do or say something that's going to scare me off."

"What if I hurt you?" he asked.

The elevator reached the top floor and the doors slid open with a smooth and silent glide. Before I could answer him, he used his hips to bump me off of him, then took my hand and walked me into the new space. It was a lot like the main floor, but I immediately understood what he meant when he'd said it was more private and also more *open*. The lights were dimmer and if I thought there was a lot of skin downstairs...

Ford weaved his way through the maze of people and tables, finding a quiet space in the corner for us to stand. We could both still see everything around us, but a shadow from one of the walls cast a dark veil of secrecy over half the corner.

"If you hurt me, I'll tell you to stop," I promised. "It's not any different from sex. If you were doing something I didn't like, I would tell you. Why do you think I wouldn't when it comes to this?"

"People haven't," he answered, lifting his drink and taking a swallow.

"I'm not people."

The corner of his mouth quirked into a smile. "No, you're not."

"It turns me on to do this," I said to him, not for the first time as I lowered myself to my knees. I nuzzled my face against his fly and inhaled the musky scent of him. Mixed with the crisp smell of his detergent and sandalwood soap, Ford smelled like a dream. He stared down at me, doubt warring in the back of his eyes, and I took a sip of my drink before setting it on the ground beside his shoe. The black leather toe shined under the barely there light and my cock ached in my pants. "Can I kiss your feet?"

"Pardon me?" Ford's eyes went wide, and he bent halfway over to bring himself closer to where I was on my knees.

"Can I kiss your feet, Sir?" I corrected myself, but Ford shook his head with a surprised laugh.

"I wasn't asking you to repeat yourself for the Sir, sweetheart. I just didn't think I'd heard you right." He pulled his lips between his teeth, stare flickering from my face to his foot. "You can do it if you tell me why you want to."

If there was one thing about Ford, he wasn't afraid to make me use my words, even if there were times when I would have rather not. But it was his insistence that I give life to my thoughts that had brought us to where we were, and I understood the importance of explaining myself to him. Not only did it turn me on to say some of my fantasies out loud, it helped him believe I wanted them for myself and not just for him.

"I like how it feels to be here, and I want to thank you for bringing me," I said.

Ford gave me a jerky nod, and I shifted my body lower, shoving my ass into the air in front of him so I could get my mouth closer to his shoe. A voice in the back of my head told me I should have been embarrassed to be kissing another man's feet, let alone doing it in public, but all I found in response to the worry was an overwhelming sense of rightness. When my lips pressed against the leather for the first time, precum spurted from the slit in my cock, smearing across my underwear as if to demonstrate my body's approval of the action.

Curling one hand around the back of his knee, I parted my lips enough for my tongue to drag across the leather of Ford's shoe. My fingers dug into his leg as I dragged my mouth toward the waxed black laces and back to the toe again. I hadn't meant to slobber all over his feet, but a simple peck didn't seem like thanks enough for everything the man above me had brought into my life.

In those brief moments, I knew without a doubt I'd fallen in love with Ford. Those feelings opened up an entire new host of problems that I didn't think either of us was ready to deal with. Things had moved so quickly, but they were also so right neither of us had fought terribly long or hard against them. Love, though...love was another complication entirely.

"Boston." Ford's voice sounded like sandpaper.

With a great deal of reluctance, I pulled my mouth off his shoe. Transfixed by the outline of my lips and the trails of spit I'd left on the already shiny leather, it was Ford's hand around my wrist pulling me to my feet that finally forced me to turn my attention from his feet to his face. His lips were parted and his nostrils flared with every heaving breath, and again he scanned my face for some answer that I think he found... whether he wanted it or not.

Without another word, he spun us, shoving my body into the corner and crashing our mouths together. My shoe knocked into my cocktail on the floor, spilling it beneath out feet, but Ford's knee was pressed hard and insistent between my legs and his hand worked furiously at my pants to get my fly down. His tongue dove deep into my mouth and I had no choice but to yield completely. Going pliant beneath him, it was heaven to let Ford use my body in whatever way he needed.

He kissed me until I couldn't breathe, and then his fingers were wrapped around my achingly hard erection. He stroked me with short and tight pulls of his wrist. I came like that, with my shoulders digging into the brick behind me and his mouth half on mine, half on my chin. Ford kissed me like a man possessed, and I knew in that moment it was a gift. It was a treasure to be wanted in the way Ford wanted me.

His name fell out of my mouth on a whimper as my cum spilled over his fingers, and he growled, that same possessive sound he'd made when we first got to the club and he said I was his. It hurt to move, hurt to breathe, but Ford's fingers around my cock were tight and steady, still stroking, even though he'd already wrung all the cum out of me with the first orgasm.

He choked out my name again, bringing his sticky fingers up between us and smearing my cum across my lips and my face.

"Open," he demanded, and I did.

He shoved his fingers into my mouth.

"Suck," he told me, and again I did.

I thought he'd worked all the cum out of me with his hand, but with his fingers halfway down my throat, pressing down hard against my tongue, more found its way out the tender slit of my dick. I choked around his fingers, and he raised his other hand to the back of my head, cradling me away from the wall but also making sure his fingers stayed right where he wanted them. Tears leaked from the corners of my eyes as I swirled my tongue around his fingers, licking him clean.

After another gasp for air, he tore his hand out of my mouth and then leaned in. His eyes were fraught with some emotion that had to have been more than arousal, and for the very first time, I let myself wonder if it was possible for Ford to love me in return. A man like Ford didn't do love, and I didn't want to set myself up for heartbreak by thinking him possible of it.

He dragged his tongue across my face, flat and hot. I closed my eyes, tilting my head back against his hand so he could reach where he wanted, and after he'd licked all of the cum off my chin and my cheeks, he crashed our mouths together, licking the rest of it out of my mouth.

Everything about the way he handled me was frantic, and when he shoved me back to my knees, I was already half drunk from his kisses. My cock was still out, half hard and stuck to my pants, and Ford freed his own erection with a practiced ease. He tapped himself against my lips, swollen and already parted for him. With a rough grunt, he shoved his cock into my mouth, fucking my face with as much urgency as he'd just used during our kisses.

There were no slow movements, no explanations of what was coming next, just the sharp and almost angry snaps of his hips while he used my mouth to get himself off. It should have been demoralizing, but kissing his feet should have been the same. All it did was make me harder. Pride swelled in my chest. I was the one who had turned him this way. I was the one who'd made him so dizzy with need that he'd forgotten himself around me until he had no option but to give into the base needs of his body.

Ford threaded his fingers into my hair and buried his dick into the back of my throat with one last thrust. It wasn't the first time he'd been that deep inside of me, but it was the first time he came that far, jets of his spend painting the back of my throat as he spilled. Half bowed over me, Ford's entire body trembled, and I obediently sucked and lapped at his cock until he was well and truly finished.

With a full body shiver, Ford pulled me back to my feet and took my face into his hands. His fingers were still wet with my cum and my spit, and they shook as he dug them into my cheeks.

"I'm good," I promised him, knowing it was the answer he was after even before he asked the question.

"I'm sorry," he said softly, eyes doing another rapid scan of my face. "I shouldn't have—"

"I'm not sorry." I covered his hands with mine, our cocks warm and sticky against each other, still out of our pants. There was something indecent about being fully dressed but having the most private parts of our bodies out in the open. "I'm not sorry, Ford. I loved all of that. I loved it so much, I lo—"

Before I could finish the thought, Ford slammed his mouth back into mine, using his skilled tongue to push whatever declaration I'd been about to give him back into my throat where it belonged. I slid my hands around his waist and situated him against me. Taking my cock back into his hand, he gave it a squeeze.

"I need you to come again, sweetheart," he said, and the tone of his voice let me know it wasn't a request.

Every part of me was on fire, from my cock to my heart. I wanted to tell him I loved him, wanted to show him. I needed him to know before I left that everything between us was so much more than what I'd meant for it to be, but I wouldn't change any of it for the world. Ford had opened my eyes in more ways than one, and I loved every second of it.

I loved him.

"I don't know if I have another one in me right now."

"Don't worry about that, sweetheart." He kissed the corner of my mouth, the underside of my jaw, then he licked a hot stripe up to my ear where he bit my lobe so hard I whimpered and went weak in the knees. "If I want it, I'll find a way to get it."

THE NEXT WEEK, AT WORK, I FOUND MYSELF FACE TO FACE WITH Kale.

It wasn't so much that I'd been trying to avoid him, but I actually had avoided him, so of course he made his way upstairs to my office with a hickey behind his ear and an amused expression on his face.

"Come get lunch with me," he said, tugging at the cuffs of his dress shirt. He wore a pair of crown-shaped cufflinks, which I imagined were a gift from his prince of a boyfriend.

I have plans with Boston was what I wanted to say. I have plans with your brother and I'm in love with him. I took him to The Black Door and he kissed my feet and let me make him come four times before we went home. Your brother is every-thing I never even realized I wanted and we're together now.

That was what I wanted to say.

"I'm busy," I said instead, not able to look him in the eye.

"You're always busy. You never come out and play, always holed up in your house with your cat."

"I'm terribly sorry that I'm not interested in watching you

making Christian come in his pants every night," I countered, rolling my eyes. "And I've gotten exceedingly good at Sudoku."

"I find that hard to believe. Come eat. Brooks is meeting us."

"What about Alex?" I asked, resigned that if the gang was together, there was no way I was getting out of it.

"He's still brooding a bit, but he'll come around soon. Brooks said he bought a motorcycle."

I had known Kale for years and knew there was no way I was wiggling out of lunch. Boston would have to wait, which was one of the greatest tragedies of my life. I stood up and checked my clothes to make sure everything was as in order as it could be, then grabbed my phone and fired off a quick apology text to Boston, promising to make it up to him later.

As it was, his trip back to California was less than a week away and to say I wasn't looking forward to the separation would have been an understatement. It hadn't been more than a few weeks we'd been together, but I'd already grown extremely accustomed to his presence in my house and his fingers on my skin.

Things had only gotten worse—or better—after I took him to The Black Door for the first time. Seeing him on his hands and knees, tongue dragging lazily across the top of my shoe to *thank me* had caused something inside of me to snap. I took him after that like a man possessed, and Boston had loved every second of it. I wondered if I'd unleashed a monster when I'd agreed to his *teach me how to fuck* ruse, but he'd awakened something just as dangerous inside of me. Something just as hopeful...

The eager and exploratory ways Boston touched me had led to some of the most exhilarating sex I'd ever had. And that was completely aside from the penetration. We'd still only been together like that once, with me bottoming for him, but all the other times—the blow jobs, the hand jobs, the making out...Around him, I found myself feeling like a teenager again, all spiked hormones and bad decisions.

Speaking of...

"A motorcycle sounds like a death wish." I slid my phone into my pocket and kicked the back of Kale's knee, trying to pretend I wasn't already half hard thinking about fucking his brother. Kale's leg buckled, and he cursed at me on his way to the door of my office.

"I didn't know he had it so hard for Beamer," Kale said.

Our friend Carter Royce IV, affectionately nicknamed Beamer, had recently absconded to California with his husband, leaving all of us more than caught off-guard over the whole thing. First, watching Beamer submit to a man none of us knew. Second, to watch the way his very new relationship with Alex unraveled in front of our eyes. I knew the thing between them wasn't serious. The group of us had been friends for years, but Alex had found something in Beamer and then Beamer found Dalton, and all of our lives changed.

It was beyond weird to have our group of five cut down to four, and Alex had practically turned into a recluse since the shift. Hearing that he'd bought a motorcycle was beyond concerning, but Alex wasn't the kind of man who could get pushed into submission with words.

I'd spoken to Beamer most recently when I'd needed advice about Boston. I'd tried to catch up and see how life in California was for him, but when I tried to see if he had any suggestions as to how we could get through to Alex, he clammed up immediately. "I think there's more to it, but Beamer's a vault."

"Obviously."

We rode the elevator down to the lobby, and as soon as we were through the revolving door onto the sidewalk, Kale made a sharp left turn and started off. I jogged to catch up, falling in stride beside him as we turned a corner and found Brooks waiting for us against the façade of the building, one leg bent at the knee and his arms folded in front of his chest. He was bundled up, a black beanie on his head and a pink scarf wound tight around his throat.

"I'm so glad you guys are here," he said, yanking the scarf up over his mouth. "I have a story to tell you, but it's freezing cold."

"Maybe Boston has the right idea," Kale said, shoving his hands into the pocket of his coat. "Wintering in California."

"He's not going to be gone that long," I said without thinking. Even though we hadn't really talked about his trip beyond his departure date. It was a bit of a sore subject because I was a greedy man and didn't want him to leave, but I also wasn't about to flex my muscles and demand that he stay. I'd already made him that promise a hundred times over.

Kale's head whipped toward me, one brow raised. "What are you talking about? He hasn't even booked a return flight."

A knot wrapped itself tight around my throat, and I swallowed, thankful for the cold wind and the bundled clothes, hoping I could excuse my burning cheeks on the brisk city air. What was Kale talking about? Boston hadn't booked a return flight? That was absurd. We were together now. We were in a relationship and he'd booked a one-way flight across the country and not even bothered to tell me about it? After everything we'd used our bodies to say to each other...

"I just assumed," I said weakly, covering my mouth with my scarf and folding my arms in front of my chest as we continued our walk down the street.

I should have known better.

I was a fool.

Falling for a man who didn't know better, who'd only wanted me for sex in the first place. I'd gotten stupid ideas in my head and talked us both into more when all he'd wanted was to learn what it felt like to suck a cock. This was why I never let myself get tied down with people or with feelings. This was why I did hookups and nothing more. Because I knew myself well enough to know how easy it was for me to get interested, to get obsessed. I tried to shake it off, ignoring the way Brooks eyed me speculatively from Kale's other side.

"He's always favored farm life over city life," Kale went on, completely unfazed by the way his words sounded to my ears.

He might as well have been saying *you're the biggest idiot in the world to think you had a future with a man like my brother, Ford. He's too good for you, too good for this life.*

"I knew it was coming, but I'd hoped giving him the job would keep him here a little longer."

"Has he said he's not coming back?" Brooks asked.

We reached some restaurant that looked like every other restaurant in the city, and I followed the two of them inside, beginning the tedious work of stripping out of my scarf and coat. The host walked us toward a white tablecloth-covered table, and for some reason, I pictured Boston sitting there with dirt under his nails from another box of vegetables he didn't know what to do with.

"No, but he was talking that way before I hired him," Kale said.

"Has nothing else changed for him?" Brooks asked, stare focused on me and my stare focused on the crisp iron lines in the tablecloth. "Since you gave him the job?"

"Maybe Ford's incessant flirting was the last straw." Kale laughed, and I was painfully aware of the weight of my phone against my leg and the way it hadn't buzzed with a return message since I apologized for missing our lunch plans.

"Could be," Brooks agreed.

I swallowed back the knot and forced myself to play the whole conversation off like it meant nothing. Leaning back in my seat, I slung one arm over the back of Brooks' chair, giving Kale what I hoped was a flirtatious and casual grin that would have lived on my face the month before.

"I think I should be insulted that you're implying your brother is moving across the country to get away from me," I said, every word tasting like razor blades.

It was impossible.

Kale must have misunderstood. There was no way *I'd* been the one who misread all of Boston's signals.

"I told you not to flirt with him."

"You told me not to fuck him," I corrected, knowing that even though we'd done plenty, the one thing we hadn't done was *that*.

Brooks cleared his throat like he was ready to call me a liar. I bumped the side of my shoe into his beneath the table and pasted a fake smile on my face.

"Tell me the story you wanted to start on the street," I said.

Brooks studied my face carefully before a mask slipped in

place over his features and he shifted away from me so he was more fully facing Kale.

"I met this bartender named—"

Kale cut him off, "Axel?"

"Of course you know him." Brooks laughed.

I swallowed, still finding it hard to breathe.

I *loved* Boston, and he was seriously making plans to leave for California with no return date in sight. It had to have been a misunderstanding with his brother because Boston would have told me if he wasn't planning on coming home. I replayed the conversations we'd had about his trip, which had been admittedly few and far between, and I was horrified to realize at no point had we ever talked about a return date. It was all about when he was leaving and what he would do when he was there, all about the things he loved and missed about the farm.

The quiet hours in the morning with coffee on the porch and the way the sun looked like cotton candy when it crested the horizon. I could hear his voice in my ears, clear as day, and I cursed myself for letting my guard down and not even both-ering to read between the lines. I'd been so hung up on the idea of him, my best friend's very off-limits little brother, and the way he touched me with so much fucking intent.

I thought things could have been different with him.

I thought they already were.

Beside me, Kale and Brooks rattled on about some bartender named Axel, and I tried my hardest to focus on them, but I was too busy going back through every conversa-tion I'd ever had with Boston to really hear them. And not just the conversations about his trip home, but every conversation ever.

Was Kale right about me?

Had I—in some way—coerced Boston into bed, into doing things he didn't want to do? I didn't think so. Honestly, in almost all of our encounters, Boston had been the aggressor. Sure, I'd taken over in the middle and gotten us to the end, but Boston was the one who was always loud and clear about what he wanted with me. He wanted to learn what it was like to be with a man, and I'd taken the bait—hook, line, and sinker. Boston saw me for who and what I was...a player of a man with enough experience to show him the ropes and send him on his way. The submission wasn't an exception; it was an addition.

"What do you think, Ford?" Kale asked, and I blinked at him.

"Sorry." I cleared my throat and gave him a grin. "Didn't catch that. I was busy thinking about your brother."

Kale lobbed his napkin at me across the table, and I deflected it with a quick flip of my wrist.

"Christian is making a trip home this weekend, and I was telling Brooks I think it would be a great opportunity for the four of us to get together and coax Alex out of hiding."

"A night at The Black Door," Brooks said beside me, choosing his next words carefully, "just like old times."

Just like old times meant a decent amount of liquor and even more skin. There'd been plenty of nights we'd found ourselves at the club with mouths around our cocks and our handprints bruised onto strangers' asses. It felt like a lifetime ago, when in reality it hadn't been more than a handful of months since the last time I'd picked out a play date for myself from the unsuspecting herd of guests who managed to find their way onto the elusive guest list of my favorite club.

"Not exactly like old times," Kale said with a shrug. "Christian and I are monogamous, so…"

"The three of us then." Brooks glanced at me from the corner of his eye. "You, me, and Alex."

Both of them watched me, and I was desperate to get my head out of my ass. The four of us all had our roles to play in the friend group, the five of us if I counted Beamer. Kale was the ringleader, the one who'd always been up to get the lot of us into the most amount of trouble. Beamer had been the most reserved and level-headed of us, the anchor. Alex had always been a brooder, long before whatever transpired with him and Beamer, and Brooks was the mother hen of us all, the secret keeper and the protector, a sharp counterbalance to Kale's troublemaking.

And me?

I was the fuck boy.

The player.

The fool.

I raised my glass in a mock toast to no one. "Perfect. Let's make it a date."

THE CLOSER IT GOT TO MY TRIP HOME, THE LESS I WANTED TO GO, but I'd committed myself to the visit. If for nothing else, to confirm the suspicions that had started to take root since things had gotten serious with Ford.

I no longer missed the farm because everything that used to feel like home now felt like him. He'd ingrained himself in my days and nights, whether it was sly text messages or coffee in bed. Ford was so much more than I imagined and I also thought he was more than he'd ever let himself believe. I found myself falling in love with him, but the trip to California would either confirm or deny those feelings one way or another.

The space would do us good, I figured. It was impossible to think around him because it was so easy to let him think for me. From where we ate to what we did to when we went to bed, Ford took care of me in ways I never knew I wanted—or needed. On my knees for him at The Black Door, I'd learned a thing or two, not just about myself but also about him.

Staring at the clothes thrown across my bed and the open

suitcase on the floor, I frowned down at the entire scene. I hadn't booked a return flight because I feared if I gave myself a week, I wouldn't make it more than two days. I didn't want to be stuck there longer than necessary...only long enough to know. The problem with that, though, was I had no idea how much to pack.

An unexpected knock on my door pulled me out of the haze, and I found myself smiling as I headed to the front door. Ford had texted around lunch and said he was working late, which was why I'd taken advantage of the downtime to pack for my trip. The thought of him coming after a long day had all sorts of ideas racing through my head for the rest of the night. I wanted to care for him in the same ways he tended me. I wanted to make sure he ate and drank and then take him into the shower after our orgasms and let him press me against a wall and kiss his way up my neck. I wanted to feel the weight of his cock in my mouth again, the way he'd fucked my throat like he was desperate for the heat of it.

But it wasn't Ford at my door. It was my brother.

Thankfully, the sight of him was like a bucket of cold water on what had been a quickly thickening erection. Clearing my throat and hoping I didn't look too surprised to see him, I stepped out of the way to let him into the narrow entryway.

"Am I interrupting something?" he asked, shrugging out of his pea coat and hanging it on the rack behind my door.

"Why would you say that?" I turned away from him quickly and went for my bedroom. Kale detoured into the kitchen to get himself a drink, and then he was pushing my clothes out of the way to sit down at the foot of my bed. I wondered if my bedroom smelled like sex, if we'd left lube or tangled ties out, if there were any signs that would give our secret away prematurely.

"You're flushed." Kale surveyed the mess in my room and the half-empty suitcase at my feet. "Like you ran a mile."

"I'm just here packing." I pulled my cellphone out of my pocket and checked in with Ford, sending a quick message to let him know my brother had shown up unannounced so he didn't do the same.

"Boston." My brother sighed, shifting so one of his legs bent at the knee and rested on the comforter and an old t-shirt I'd stolen from him after college. Worry knit together between his brows, and my breath caught in my throat.

"Kale," I said back to him.

"You're coming home, aren't you?"

The breath that had twisted itself into a knot unwound as fast as if it had been shot out of a cannon, falling out of my mouth in a strangled-sounding gasp. I coughed and pounded my fist against my chest, clearing my throat to bring myself back to normal before sitting on my bed and mirroring my brother's pose.

"Of course I'm coming home," I said, tilting my head to the side. "Why wouldn't I?"

He shook his head, trying to play off his earlier concern, but he was my brother, my *twin*, and I knew him as well as I knew myself sometimes. I could see the doubt and the worry etched deep into his features. I reached out and patted the side of his knee with my hand, and he slammed his down over mine, holding it against the rich fabric of his slacks.

"Before I hired you on at my office, you were definitely talking like you didn't want to stay in the city."

"I know you only gave me the job to keep me here longer," I said.

"I thought I had more time." Kale frowned.

"I'm coming home, Kale," I said to him again.

"Then why did you book a one-way flight?" he asked, shoving my hand off his leg and standing up so abruptly the stolen t-shirt stuck to his leg and fell onto the floor. With a muttered apology, he bent down to pick it up off the floor, eyes narrowing when he recognized the faded USC logo. "This is mine."

"It was." I snatched it back from him and dropped it into the open suitcase before he could take it back.

"Why didn't you book a return flight?" he asked, bracing his hands against his hips and glaring at me, the same look he always affected when he wanted to try and flaunt his four minutes of seniority over me.

"I didn't know how long I wanted to stay for," I answered.

"A week or two, tops."

"I don't even know if I want to be gone that long."

I tugged on the cuff of a pair of black joggers, folding them haphazardly before dropping them into the suitcase and moving on to a pair of jeans. They were the cheapest ones I owned and they'd still cost me a few hundred dollars. After one morning on the farm, they'd be ruined beyond repair, and I found myself wondering when I'd morphed from being cut out for farm life to a cookie cutter city boy. I folded them anyway, dropping them onto the joggers.

"You miss it there," he said carefully.

I bit the inside of my cheek, thinking very carefully about what I wanted to say next so I didn't incriminate myself. But for as much as I knew Kale's tells, he also knew mine.

Kale raised a brow and smacked his lips, pointing at me with one well-manicured, judgmental finger. "Is this about the man you're seeing? The one who works in our building?"

"No," I said quickly, shaking my head and walking out of the bedroom before I even had time to realize I'd lost track of the half-truth I told my brother the last time we had lunch together in his office.

He caught up to me in the kitchen before I even had a chance to get a drink poured out, and he snatched the bottle out of my hand, holding it above my head like it was a video game controller and we were seven all over again.

"Don't lie to me," he said.

I smacked him and wrestled his arm back down, stealing the bottle out of his grip and turning away at the same time as I jutted my leg out with the intent to kick his kneecap out. Kale dodged, laughing at me.

"You're predictable and you're a bad liar."

I poured two fingers of whiskey into a glass and rolled my eyes at him.

"I'm not lying to you," I said, washing the lie down with a mouthful of the spicy, amber-colored liquor.

Kale stole the glass out of my hand and took a drink for himself, glancing sideways at the bottle I'd set safely back on the counter.

"I didn't know you liked Pappy Van Winkle." He made a show of smacking his lips before taking another sip, and I turned away because I knew what was coming next. "It's Ford's favorite."

"What does that have to do with me?" I asked, screwing my eyes closed and waiting for him to redirect his line of questioning back to the mystery man in our office.

"Something is going on with you," he said, tapping my shoulder.

I groaned, turning back toward him and stealing back the drink out of his hands. I took a sip to buy myself time, not realizing what a bad idea it was because he wasn't wrong. It was Ford's favorite whiskey. That's how a bottle of it had ended up in my kitchen, and I definitely wasn't having a Pavlovian response to the taste of it because my brain already associated the rich flavor with kisses from the man I was falling in love with.

"I'm just re-thinking this trip," I admitted.

"Because of that man."

I let out a long breath. "Because of that man."

"What's his name, Boston?" my brother pressed, bumping his shoulder into me and walking us out of the kitchen and into my living room.

I sat down on the couch without prompting, making silent note of the way Ford had stacked my magazines into a neat pile against the far edge.

"Doesn't matter," I said, taking a drink before passing the glass back to him. "It's still new and I don't know if it's going to last. I'd rather...rather wait before you get invested in my relationship on my behalf."

"I don't want to get invested. I want to run a background check."

"I'm not a child, Kale." I held out my hand and he passed the whiskey back to me. "I'm not making bad decisions."

"Have you slept with him?" he asked.

"Would you ask me that if he was a woman?"

Kale scrunched his nose a little at the question, then

huffed out a breath indicating I'd bested him at his current line of questioning.

My brother was a skilled negotiator, though, and quick on his feet. It didn't take him more than five seconds to redirect. "You've been missing home for years, Boston." He turned toward me, face a little sad and a lot serious. "I've honestly just been waiting for you to decide you wanted to leave New York and go back there for good."

I'd been waiting for myself to make the same decision for as long as my brother, but everything was different now. It was complicated and wonderful and messy, and I wanted to be right in the middle of it. But our parents were excited to see me, and I still needed to test the theory for myself.

I needed to be sure.

"I know I have, but lately I've been wondering if what I missed was a place or a feeling."

"And your trip is going to help determine that?" he asked.

"Stop worrying about him," I said. "Things with him are very new and before I tell you anything about him, I want to make sure it lasts. The two things are not entirely related."

"Don't let this new man cloud your vision, Boston," he warned.

"Isn't that what happened for you and Christian?"

"Christian had a slew of obligations he needed to get in line. That's why he had to go home. Otherwise, I never would have let him out of my house," Kale said with a smirk that danced right up into the dark pools of his eyes. "There was nothing cloudy about it."

I fidgeted with my glasses, the weight of the lie to my brother beginning to wear on me as much as the rest of it. Hopefully after I returned home from California, Ford and I would be better positioned to decide how to come clean to him about what we'd been doing.

"I don't like being away from him," Kale went on. "He has to go back for a few days to visit his nephews and I'm not looking forward to it."

"Love has made you a sap." I handed off the glass with the remaining whiskey because he looked like he needed it more than me. "How long is he gone for?"

"Ten days."

I swallowed, the thought of being away from Ford for ten days was enough to draw out a cold sweat on the back of my neck.

"You look like you want to die," Kale said, finishing off the whiskey and carrying the glass into my kitchen. I heard him run the water and then the familiar clink of crystal against marble as he set it on the counter beside the bottle. "When do you leave again?"

"Tomorrow night," I called out to him.

"I give you three days, tops."

I blinked quickly, wondering if I was even going to make it two.

Kale came out from the kitchen, head cocked to the side as he gave me a knowing look, then he shook his head and laughed.

"What's funny now?" I forced myself up from the couch to follow Kale to the front door. Apparently, he decided he'd had enough of me and was ready to go home and bury himself balls deep into his prince. I couldn't blame him for that, because it was definitely the same thing I wanted to do to his best friend as soon as our schedules allowed.

Kale slipped his coat on and fastened the buttons, then

shoved his hands into the pockets with a quick jerk of his wrists. "It's just that Ford's gonna cry when he finds out you're in love with someone else."

I bit my lips between my teeth, cheeks immediately burning red, but not for the reason my brother would have suspected.

"I doubt that," I murmured, reaching around Kale to open the door for him. "I'll see you at work in the morning, Kale."

"Make sure you spend some quality time with your mystery man before your trip, if you know what I mean," he said, backing out into the hallway.

"I need you to make up your mind about if you want me to sleep with men or not."

"I want you to sleep with whomever you want," he said with a lopsided smile. "Just not Ford. See you tomorrow, Boston."

I HATED SNEAKING AROUND.

At first, it was fun because I was being seduced by my best friend's straight brother, but I should have known that fantasy wasn't going to last. The worst part was, I wasn't even mad about it. Whatever my relationship with Boston had turned into was so much better than what it had started as, what either of us had intended for it to be. I wanted to tell him I was in love with him. I wanted the whole world to know—his brother included—that I'd finally met my match.

But that wasn't allowed, and I spent an extra hour at work killing time because Kale had showed up unexpectedly and neither of us was ready for that conversation yet. So I sent strongly worded emails, set meetings, reviewed contracts, and did all of the things that I used to love the most about my job while I waited for Boston to text me and tell me it was okay to come over. I finished my to-do list and the text hadn't come through, so I shut down my computer and sent a text message of my own. After hailing a cab so I didn't have to walk across town, I found myself on Brooks' front stoop with a bottle of wine tucked under my arm and no common sense in my brain.

He opened the door and raised an eyebrow at me, but didn't stop me from pushing past him into the warmth of his house. He closed the door behind me, hand already extended to catch my coat. It was a joke to call him the mom of our friend group, but he probably paid more attention to the care of us than anyone else had before. At least until Kale met Christian and then I'd found myself involved with Boston...

Brooks followed me into his kitchen and took a seat at his kitchen island while I busied myself with opening the wine and pouring two glasses' worth. Then he waited quietly while I poured half the contents of my glass down my throat, trying to find the words.

"I know you don't want to hear about this," I finally said.

"It's fine, Ford."

I rested my ass against his kitchen sink and folded my arms in front of my chest, still not sure where to start. Thankfully, Brooks took pity on me.

"Why are you here and not with Kale's brother?"

"Because I'm mad that he didn't tell me he wasn't coming back."

"Are you really mad?" he asked.

I sucked my tongue against the roof of my mouth and stared up at the stark white coving of Brooks' ceiling.

"I'm hurt," I grumbled, not caring if he heard me or not. I took another drink of my wine, but a more reasonably sized one this time.

"This is new for you. The feelings, I mean. You don't know how to communicate them."

I opened my mouth to protest, but he wasn't wrong in the

assertion. I'd been in over my head from the first time Boston put his hand on my thigh.

"You're not going out this weekend to pick up a stranger, I'll tell you that much," he said to me softly.

"Why not?" I asked, an unfamiliar heat pricking at the corners of my eyes. "Why shouldn't I?"

"You're not a cheater."

"I'm not a boyfriend either," I snapped. Boston and I had agreed we were in a relationship, but he'd never called me his *boyfriend*. That wasn't something I'd gotten to experience or to embrace. Even though we'd had a date, the foundation of our relationship was built behind closed doors. That wasn't any different from everything I'd had before him, which felt patently unfair because Boston was more than everyone who'd come before him put together. I was in love with him and he didn't even know.

"Semantics."

With a foul glare in Brooks' direction, I set the wine glass down on the counter with a little more force than was necessary. It was the wrong angle, the right frequency, and the glass shattered in my hand, Chablis spilling over my wrist and down to the floor.

"You're a fucking child," he said, not bothering to get up from his seat.

I grabbed a dish towel off the counter and dropped it at my feet, using my shoe to push it around and mop up the spilled wine. I dared a glance at my palm, finding my skin intact, and myself a little drunker than before.

Brooks wasn't finished insulting me. "If you come out to the club this weekend and even look at another man the wrong way, I'm telling Boston as soon as he gets back from California."

"If he even comes back," I grumbled, bending over to pick up the sopping wet towel. The wine was cleaned off the floor and I threw the towel into the sink.

"You owe me a hundred dollars for that glass," Brooks said, ignoring my protest.

I pulled my wallet out of my pocket and dug all the cash from my billfold, throwing no less than five hundred dollars across the island at him. He smirked, folding it all neatly and tucking it into the pocket of his joggers.

"Boston is coming back," Brooks said, sounding surer of it than Kale had when he brought it up before. "Which you would know if you talked to him about it, but I don't imagine the two of you do much talking."

"How do you know?"

"That he's coming back or that you're too much of a fool to have a real conversation?"

"We have conversations," I snapped, slapping my hands down on the edge of his white marble kitchen counter. "We talked about what it meant for him to be with me, to be with a fucking man. We talked about being together. We talked about..."

The heat in my eyes was unbearable and I stopped, squeezing them closed so I didn't do something ridiculous like cry in front of him.

"Did you talk about telling Kale?" Brooks asked.

"We talked about *not* telling him." I swallowed, rubbing the center of my chest. "It wasn't supposed to be anything. He just wanted me for sex."

Brooks chuckled. "How the tables have turned."

I rolled my eyes, rubbing them furiously as if enough pressure from my fingers could push the unshed tears back into their respective ducts. It was futile, so I turned my back to Brooks and wiped them away with one lone sniffle.

"I'm out of my element," I admitted.

"I can tell."

"I don't want him to go."

"I can tell that too," he said again. "Have you told *him* that?"

I shook my head and frowned.

"Don't you think you should?"

"It's just a vacation," I mumbled.

"Well, which is it, Ford? You can't have it both ways." Brooks took a drink of his wine, smirking at me like the arrogant prick he was. "He's either leaving you forever or he'll be home before you realize he's gone."

"Fuck you."

"If you don't like what I have to say, you're more than welcome to leave." He climbed off the barstool and left me alone in his kitchen.

With a loud exhale that I hoped he heard, I squatted down and picked up all the broken glass, collecting the shards in the palm of my hand. Carefully, I dumped them into his trash can, using an old takeout container to house them, then headed upstairs toward Brooks' office.

I didn't know that was where he went, but Brooks was as predictable as the rest of us, and so I found him sitting on one of the matching wingbacks that flanked the bay window on the far wall of the room. There was a fireplace a few feet away, a brick mantelpiece that dated to the 1800s framing the small fire he'd just turned on.

"I don't want to scare him," I said reluctantly, settling into the chair beside him.

"If your incessant and unwanted flirting didn't run him off, I can't imagine your sincerity will."

"He's the one driving this whole thing." Brooks arched a doubtful brow at me and I answered with a helpless shrug. "He propositioned me. He's been making all the calls."

"Are you trying to tell me you got on your knees for Kale's baby brother?" Brooks asked.

"No, but I definitely got on my back."

Brooks huffed out a surprised-sounding laugh, and I glared at the dancing flames in his fireplace instead of looking at him. I didn't want to see how he was looking at me, didn't want to read the judgement or the scorn on his face.

"Are you expecting me to be horrified that you bottomed or something, Ford?" He reached over and flicked my earlobe. "There's nothing wrong with how you like to fuck."

"I don't like to bottom," I countered, "or at least, I didn't."

"Knowing that I'm going to regret asking this…" Brooks paused and took a tentative drink. "Does he submit?"

"Do you want the answer?"

"I want to understand why you're failing to grasp every straw you reach for with him."

I wanted to have an answer for him, and I wished it was as easy as saying yes, he submits or no, he doesn't. My relationship with Boston was built on so much more than the hierarchy of who said what and who went where. That was the problem because I didn't have a playbook for how that sort of thing was meant to work. With one-night stands and people who knew their place, I was confident of what to expect. With Boston, everything was a crapshoot.

"He submits," I answered, "but in the way that works for us."

"And how is that?"

"Sometimes. Less than he'd like, I think. But also *very* fucking well."

Brooks heaved a sigh and pushed the wine glass toward me. I took a grateful sip before setting it back down on the table between our chairs.

"You're in love with him," Brooks said. "And you don't think he's on the same page."

"I don't want to scare him off," I said again, frowning. "This wasn't supposed to be anything that it is, Brooks. It was supposed to be some lessons in sex and then he was going to be on his way."

"So, it's more than he expected too?"

"Yeah."

"Do you think he's maybe feeling as overwhelmed as you are by the whole thing?" he asked.

"If he is, he hasn't said anything about it."

Brooks rolled his eyes so hard, I worried they were going to get stuck staring at the inside of his skull. "And have you said anything about it? To him?"

I scrubbed a hand down my face.

"I know you haven't had a relationship like this before, but you're both setting yourselves up to fail if you aren't talking about anything besides what brand of lube to use," he said.

"We never even talked about that," I muttered.

"Don't be obtuse." Brooks stole the wine glass back to his side of the table and took a decent drink of it. "I think this trip is going to be good for the two of you, as long as you can keep your dick in your pants when we're out this weekend."

"How is him leaving me good for us?" I asked.

"He's leaving New York," Brooks corrected, shaking his head like he was scolding a five-year-old for not eating all their vegetables. "He is coming back to you."

"When?"

He pursed his lips, and I found myself feeling more and more like the petulant child he was treating me as, but it was impossible to react any other way. Boston had be beyond fucked up and out of my depth, and I couldn't have the conversation with him without scaring him off and ruining everything entirely.

I shoved up out of the chair and paced across Brooks' office, making it to the far wall before I turned back and repeated the journey four more times. Eventually, I stopped in front of his fireplace and bracketed my hands on my hips, staring down at the fire like all of my answers—and my problems—were burning away in the flames.

"I cannot have these conversations for you," Brooks said from his seat. "But if you don't have them for yourself..." He trailed off, the rest of his sentence not even needing to be spoken out loud.

If I didn't have them myself, Boston would be gone, one way or the other. Either because he didn't come home to New York or he didn't come home to me. Neither of those were acceptable choices, but the fear in my bones was too embedded, too thick. I would have rather taken scraps from Boston than nothing at all, and I wasn't ready to lose him when I was barely learning what it meant to love him.

More than anything, I wanted to see Ford before I left for California.

Kale's visit the night before had sidelined that, and trying to get our schedules aligned before my flight had proven to be more of a struggle than expected. Ford had back-to-back meetings that were near impossible for him to get out of, but at lunch he texted and promised, if nothing else, to take me to the airport. We had barely had any time together since he'd taken me to The Black Door, but maybe that was for the better.

Every time I thought about the things we'd done that night, my brain spun out of control, leaving me dangerously dizzy over the whole thing. Six months ago, if someone had told me I would get on my hands and knees in a public place to kiss another man's feet, I would have served them with a cease and desist. But now there was no denying the throbbing ache that took up permanent residence between my legs whenever I thought about doing just that.

But maybe the break would do us good because it was

getting hard for me to keep track of which way was up when it came to Ford. Things were getting so serious, so fast, and we were going to come up with a way to tell my brother sooner rather than later. It was one thing neither of us had dared to talk about, the threat of him acting as more of a looming disaster and not something we had any control over. I think we were both waiting to make sure we hadn't overestimated the other before getting ready to have that conversation.

Ford picked me up at the curb, another sleek black town car coming to a stop a few feet away from me. He climbed out of the back seat at the same time the trunk popped open, and then I was in his arms, face buried against the front of his shirt. It shoved my glasses at a crooked angle up my nose, but it was so nice to see him again, to feel him, I let the hard plastic dig into my face. The driver slammed the trunk closed after depositing my bag and, reluctantly, I untangled myself from Ford's hello hug to get into the car.

It was easily an hour to the airport, so I settled in against him, staring at the city outside the window as the driver headed toward JFK.

"Sorry this is all we get before you go," he said, kissing the top of my head.

"It's okay. You're busy."

I hadn't let my brain convince me that Ford had been avoiding me, but he also wasn't going out of his way to see me either, which I had sort of expected after everything we'd done. I didn't know how to explain it, but I thought things had changed between us after I had kissed his shoes that night, but maybe I was being foolish and making something out of nothing. Maybe my brother was right to worry about me. Maybe it was why Ford hadn't brought up the need to come clean to Kale about us being together.

Ten minutes went by in silence until Ford finally cracked, bumping the side of my face with his shoulder until I looked up.

"When are you coming back, Boston?" he asked.

"I don't know."

"Were you going to tell me?" Ford leaned away from me, brushing his hand through his hair.

"I wasn't not telling you." I shifted away from him too, a little offended by the tone of his question. "I've spent most of my free time with you and the rest of it thinking about being with you."

I'd been spending so much time with Ford that Shawn was feeling rather neglected, especially considering I was ready to get on a plane and head out of town. He hadn't bothered to ask when I would be back because I suspected he didn't doubt my return. Ford, on the other hand, was questioning me like I was ready to fly to California and never come back again.

"It seems weird you have a one-way ticket then. I thought that would be discussed since we're supposed to be in a relationship."

"And you're an expert in those?" As soon as the snappy question left my mouth, I regretted it. Sighing, I thumped my head against the seat rest and scrubbed a hand down my face. Ford gently kicked the toe of his shoe against mine and I let my hand fall limp in my lap.

"That wasn't fair. I'm sorry," I said.

"It was honest." Ford licked the corner of his mouth, worrying his tongue back and forth for a breath before his shoulders sagged and he notched himself against the window and the seat.

"I didn't book a return flight because I didn't want to be stuck there longer than I had to be," I said.

Ford pursed his lips. "Your brother says you love California. You've always told me you love it too."

"My brother knows I'm seeing someone and he thinks I'll be back in three days or less." My cheeks burned with the admission and I stared at my hands, folded neatly in my lap.

"That's not long at all," Ford murmured.

"No." I shook my head. "It's not. But I miss my mom and…"

"You miss the farm," he said.

"I miss the way the farm made me feel," I corrected.

Ford reached over and took my hand into his, lifting it to his mouth and dusting a kiss across my knuckles that felt a lot like an apology.

"Tell me about it." He angled his head toward the window and I slid back to my original seat, tucked against his side. With our hands joined together on top of his thigh, I traced my finger over the places our skin touched, marveling at the connection.

Ford didn't understand what he was asking of me, the weight of a thousand confessions I wasn't quite ready to make hanging in space between my ribs. How could I tell him the farm was home, my knees and hands in the dirt giving me the same satisfaction I found when I was in the same position, but at his feet? What words could I string together to tell him that seeing the sun lift over the horizon in California gave me the sense of being part of something bigger than myself, just like how I knew it to be true when he dragged his mouth across the back of my neck? All the things I'd been missing since Kale and I came back to New York as teenagers had shown up sevenfold in Ford, and that was a daunting reality to try and balance.

As long as I'd known him, Ford had been a player, a one-night stand kind of guy. His reputation preceded him, even in the most expensive parts of the city, and with one touch of my hand against his leg, he'd crumbled. Ford had gone from different men every night to the same man every morning, and that was no small change of heart for him. And for myself? A half-baked idea and a proposition I never should have been brave enough to ask found my entire world turned upside down.

"It's familiar," I said instead. "It's easy."

Ford smiled into my hair, huffing out an amused breath. "I thought *I* was easy."

"Getting you into bed was one of the easiest things I've ever done." I gave his hand a squeeze and then kissed his knuckles just like he'd kissed mine minutes before. "Once I got over how scared I was to ask you about it."

"You were scared?"

"Nervous, at least." I tipped my head back to gaze up at him. Ford brushed his thumb across my cheekbone, and my lashes fluttered closed. "I didn't know what to expect."

"Are you disappointed?"

My eyes flew open and I turned halfway around, grabbing him by the shoulders and bringing us face to face. Ford's eyes went wide with shock, then he chuckled, looking down at the spot on his arm where my fingers were curled right around his muscle. I loosened my grip, but otherwise held steady.

"Are *you*?"

"I'm surprised." He leaned forward and brushed a kiss across my lips. "Pleasantly."

The breath left my lungs in a rush and I sagged against him, gooseflesh prickling its way down my arms. My brain hadn't realized how much my body needed to hear that, how badly I'd been searching for confirmation this wasn't as one-sided as I feared. I pressed my hand over my mouth to stop myself from confessing that I was in love with him.

"I was so upset, Boston." He pushed my hand off my mouth, his own lips twisted downward into a frown. "When I found out you didn't know when you were coming back, I thought..."

He went quiet, sucking his tongue across the front of his teeth and turning his stare toward the window to his left.

"I thought I was worth more to you," he said softly.

"Ford." I pressed our foreheads together, moving my hands to his shoulders, to the back of his neck. I wove my fingers together and pulled his head against mine, our noses smashed. He huffed a breath against my lips, smile curling up at the sides of his mouth.

"You're so demanding, sweetheart." He tangled a hand into my hair, his other one pressed against the middle of my back, fingers spread wide. "So bold."

"Are you sure about me?" I whispered.

"Sure as I've ever been about anything."

"When I get home..."

"We'll figure out how to tell your brother," he finished the thought, and I gently pressed our lips together.

The kiss was unlike any we'd shared before. Ford's hands roamed their way around my back, fingers scrabbling at my shirt, trying to get underneath it. He reached down and rucked up the bottom of my t-shirt, groaning when his skin landed against mine. I'd never been more unhappy to be in a car, more miserable about going to California, less ready to leave New York.

Ford peppered kisses against all the space around my mouth, cursing under his breath when the car jerked to a stop. I pried one of my eyes open, seeing the gridlocked traffic of JFK on all sides of us.

"We're here," I grumbled, moving away from Ford's exploring hands and mouth so I could get myself in order before we reached the departure gate.

"Next time use your brother's plane," he suggested.

"He's never been good about sharing his toys, and I don't mind flying commercial."

"You still fly first class?"

"Of course I do."

Ford reached up and adjusted my glasses, smoothing back a chunk of hair that had fallen into my face.

"I'll buy you a plane if you want one," he said, scrunching his nose like he was embarrassed at the offer. "If you plan on spending a lot of time going back and forth."

"Ford."

"I know it means a lot to you. The farm, I mean."

"Ford." I sealed my palm over his mouth and felt his jaw clench beneath my fingers. "It's a feeling, not a place."

He wiggled his lips against my hand until I took it away.

"I'm just saying."

"I hear you." I took his face into my hands and kissed him.

I dropped a peck against his lips and he leaned into me, mouth half open and trying to chase after more. Outside the car, horns honked and a siren blared somewhere behind us. I could see the terminal coming into view.

"Three days then?" he asked when the car finally pulled to a stop against the curb.

"Tops, so I'm told."

My door opened from the outside, the driver busying himself with getting my luggage from the trunk while Ford looked at me, green in the face like he was ready to throw up all over my lap. The feeling was beyond mutual, as most of ours had turned out to be.

I climbed out of the car, pleased to find the somber mood of my departure had done enough to soften my cock so I didn't get charged with public indecency on my way through security. Ford followed me out, rolling my suitcase from the asphalt onto the sidewalk, then he pulled me into a tight and unexpected hug. I sucked in a deep breath, burrowing my face into the crook of his neck and kissing just beneath his ear.

"I have to tell you something, Ford," I said when I broke away from the hug.

A car honked behind us, and Ford flipped him off without even looking back.

"Tell me."

"The most unexpected part of all of this was you."

He bit his lips between his teeth, even as they tried to tug up into a smile. His mouth moved like he was ready to speak, but no words came out until he said, "Let me know you get there safe, sweetheart."

"I will," I promised.

"And come home as soon as you can."

I swallowed and blinked hard, burning tears ready to spill.

"I will."

I SHOULD HAVE TOLD BOSTON I LOVED HIM.

It was the only thought that replayed through my head as the car left JFK and drove me back home.

I should have told Boston I loved him.

Kicking my shoes off in the middle of my living room and swatting Milo's tail out of my face, I told my cat, "I should have told him I loved him."

After getting restless and heading to the kitchen for a drink, I knew in my bones I should have told Boston Sheffield I loved him. I was stupid to let him walk away and get on a plane, with no return flight booked, without making sure he understood without a shadow of a doubt how I felt for him.

It was going to be hours before he landed in California and longer still before he made it from the airport to his parents' farm. I had nothing to do but wait and brood and dwell. Milo wrapped himself around my ankles and mewed up at me, so I gave him some wet food from the fridge and went back to my whiskey. I dropped my phone onto the kitchen counter, tapping it awake in case Boston had logged on to the Wi-Fi and decided to text me.

That train of thought felt more than a little bit desperate, and I let the screen go black while I fought to call up memories of the man I'd been before him. Pre-Boston Ford would *never* be moping about being home alone. Pre-Boston Ford would have already had someone on their way over, ready to get naked and on their knees.

Pre-Boston Ford wasn't me anymore.

I grabbed my drink and my phone, padding unhappily back into the living room. My bedroom had Boston all over it already, and I hated to think about what kind of sniffling mess I would turn into once I laid my head against a pillow that smelled like his skin. The couch seemed like a safer bet, even though it was the exact place we'd been when we had that first kissing lesson.

There was no place in my home where I could escape him, so I narrowed as much of my attention onto my phone as I could manage. Pulling up the MLS app, I busied myself with applying filters that included acreage and farm properties in the tri-state area. I focused on upstate, finding more than a few pieces of land that I had a sneaking suspicion Boston would love. I didn't know the first thing about what would make a good farm and what wouldn't, so I bookmarked all of them for a discussion when he came back from his trip.

I'd take a weekend and drive him to all of them, let him look around and even get his hands in the dirt if he wanted. Maybe it would snow. Maybe we could kiss in the snow. It would be cold outside, but the thought of fucking Boston on a hay bale ignited a whole slew of rural fantasies I'd never even dreamed of before. Though, that was another thing for us to talk about when he got home...

First up, his brother.

Second, a farm.

Third...

I wanted to top.

It wasn't that sex with Boston was unfulfilling, because it could never be, but even though I'd found myself versatile for the first time in decades, I was much more aligned with the sexual preferences of a top. Letting Boston do the driving for his first couple of times felt like the right choice to make because, even with my experience, taking a dick up the ass had the potential to be emotionally—and physically—overwhelming. I'd walk the line for him, but I hoped he would at least be okay to *try* it.

With the to-do list out of the way, I finished off my drink and realized I still didn't know what to do with myself. Now that I was in love, was I going to have to find hobbies that didn't involve spanking strangers until their asses turned purple? That sounded horrible and wonderful all at the same time because that meant I had an ass at my beck and call and that ass was Boston's, and I just *knew* he would love that little dose of pain in the mix. He'd taken to every other part of our roles so perfectly, I wasn't worried about the pain. I'd seen him tweaking his nipples when I sucked his cock, and after all, it wasn't like I was a proper sadist.

Not like Alex.

Sighing, I set my empty glass down on the side table, thinking about Alex and the absolute one-eighty he'd pulled since Beamer hooked up with Dalton. I think it had been just as surprising for Kale, who'd been beyond caught off-guard at just how deep Beamer's submissive tendencies ran, but Alex... He'd gotten a taste of someone who could keep up with him for the first time in five years and then lost it in the blink of an eye.

I called him and, much to my surprise, he answered.

"Hi, Ford," he said after picking up on the third ring.

"Alex."

He laughed. "I bet you didn't think I'd answer."

"I didn't," I admitted, "but I was hoping you would."

There was a short silence.

"What's up? You all right?"

"I was just thinking about you. Wanted to check on you."

"I'm being herded out tomorrow night," he said. "Proof of life and all that."

"Kale is just worried about you."

"I feel a lot better now."

"That's good." Another pause, because I didn't think either of us knew what to say.

"Did you want to come over or get a drink or something?" Alex finally asked.

"I'm not really feeling being alone right now, so that sounds great."

"That sounds like there's a story," Alex teased.

"Not sure I can share it yet," I said.

"Is this about your mystery man?"

"How do you know about him?" I asked, before I realized the answer. "What did Brooks tell you?"

"That you were going to be the next to fall, but he didn't say much else."

I scrubbed a hand down my face, cursing Brooks under my breath.

"You'll find out sooner or later," I said, "might as well tell you the truth now. Would you rather go out or stay in?"

"Honestly." I could hear Alex stretching as he talked to me. "I would love to get out of the house."

"I'll hop in the shower," I told him. "Just text me where to meet you and I'll be there."

"Lazy Dom." He huffed out what sounded like it wanted to be a laugh, but fell short. "I'll see you in a bit, Ford."

The phone beeped in my ear, signaling the disconnect. Leaving it on the table, I headed upstairs to the bedroom, ready to face the memories of Boston so I could get ready to go. The shower was boring, getting dressed was boring...

How had one man changed me so fully in such a short amount of time?

When I made it back downstairs, I plugged the address of the bar Alex had picked into my maps, then decided it was too cold to walk. I didn't have to go far outside to find a cab, and twenty minutes later, we'd emerged from traffic to a neon-lit bar that looked entirely out of place for as close to Manhattan as it was. As soon as I met my friend on the sidewalk, I wrapped him in a hug so tight it threw both of us off-balance. My shoulder bumped into the brick wall to my left, and Alex shoved me off of him with a laugh.

"You're clingy," he said with a smile.

I couldn't argue because it was just so nice to see him smile again.

"You're a recluse," I said, tipping my head back to search for a business name or a sign on the wall. "Where is this place?"

"Just a new spot I found."

"What's it called?" I asked.

Alex gave me a shove toward the front door. "*Tryst.*"

I snorted, rolling my eyes and undoing the buttons on my coat as I followed him inside. The bar, Tryst, was dimly lit with swaths of neon light coming out from behind cut-outs in the walls. The entire room was cast in a bright purple and blue neon that would have given the place a pretty seedy vibe were it located in any other part of town. Beyond the questionable lighting, it looked safe enough, with a mixture of high-top tables and low level seating arrangements with comfortable chairs and some couches in the mix. On the far wall was what looked to be a glass bar top, though I imagined, for safety sake, it was probably acrylic, and it also offered up some of that moody neon glow.

"Respectfully, Alex…how did you find this place?"

"Do you want the truth?"

"Of course."

We reached the bar, taking the last two stools down the entire length, all the way at the far end by the little tray where they kept the cherries and the lime slices.

"I met a kid on an app after Beamer moved," he said, raising his hand to flag down the bartender.

"A kid?"

"Obviously not a kid, you prick." He slapped my chest with the back of his hand. "He was legal, but young. He knew what he was doing with me."

Before I could open my mouth to question that comment, the bartender was there, a warm smile on her face for my friend as she greeted him by name.

"Back so soon, Alex?" she asked, tucking a bleached dread-lock behind one of her ears.

"Brought a friend." He pointed at me with a grin. "This is Ford."

"Like the car?" she asked.

"Like the..." I clenched my jaw together, deciding to not even waste my time correcting her.

"I'll have the usual," Alex said, thankfully making it so I didn't have to speak again. "And he'll have the same as me."

"What's the usual?" I asked after the bartender walked away. She looked like her name would be something like Flora or Fauna. I bet she smelled like patchouli, and I was suddenly glad Brooks had taken the initiative to arrange a trip to The Black Door tomorrow, because if this was where Alex had been spending his time, God help us all.

"Marigold makes a great dirty martini," he said.

Marigold was close enough to Flora for my tastes.

I wanted to get up and leave and drag Alex out of that place with me, but it was honestly so nice to see him again, I decided I could endure the ambiance—or lack thereof—for at least one round before I started to try and talk him into going somewhere else.

"Anyway, back to our earlier conversation. What do you mean he knew what he was doing with you? That feels like a weird thing to say about a hook-up."

Alex gave me a deadpan look that I wanted to smack off his face. "It was his job, Ford."

My eyes had to have gone a little wide at that, one of them twitching in the corner. But Marigold was back with our drinks and a casual smile for Alex that had me wondering if she was a prostitute too. I pulled a fifty out of my billfold and dropped it on the bar for her.

I leaned in closer to him, lowering my voice before asking, "Are you saying he was a sex worker?"

"Don't make it sound like it's not a respectable profession," Alex snapped, rolling his eyes and swirling an olive skewer around his glass.

I'd never been a judgmental man, and I was definitely not going to start with Alex. Though it was easy to judge his new choice of hangout, I'd never knock him down as a person. I understood as much as the next man in our friend group what it meant to have unique preferences and tastes in the bedroom, but I'd never imagined Alex so desperate for that kind of connection that he would have to resort to paying someone to play them out.

"I'm just surprised," I said, popping one of the stuffed olives into my mouth so I didn't say something regrettable.

"Anyway, this was where he wanted to meet up before we…"

"I can figure it out," I said.

"I know this place isn't our usual vibe, but the change of scenery has been nice," Alex said, taking a sip from his martini. The way his mouth twisted into a sour pucker led me to believe there was a reason a dirty martini at a neon dive bar on the outskirts of Manhattan had become his new favorite hangout.

"Are you still seeing that guy?"

"No. It was good while it lasted, but it wasn't a long-term thing for me."

"Not interested in playing for keeps?" I asked.

"I just needed to get some pent-up energy out of my system," he said. "But I'm looking forward to tomorrow."

"Back on the market, then?"

"I'm always down for a good time, Ford. You know that."

He *had* always been down for a good time, at least until things went south with Beamer. But I was happy to see him again, and even though Alex had a little bit more of an edge about him than he used to, I was fairly sure he was ready to come back around.

"Now." He bit into one of his olives, smiling at me with the green orb between his teeth. "What's been up with you?"

Days before, I never would have offered him the truth, but Boston and I had agreed that once he was home, we were going to tell Kale about us, we were going to find a way to have our relationship in the open. Hell, I had four properties bookmarked that I'd be ready to buy him at the drop of a hat if that was what he wanted. I'd have honestly bought him a plane if he didn't want to fly commercial anymore, would have bought him a house to get him out of his apartment. I knew he had his own money, but the edge of my obsession with Boston was far from wearing off. I wanted to own him in every way possible, and I was not above using my money to endear myself to him.

Anything to make him love me back.

"Well, if I tell you, you have to keep it between us."

"Brooks has already told me you're seeing someone," he interrupted, looking like he'd gotten the best of me.

"I know, but he didn't say who, did he?"

Alex shook his head.

"It's a secret," I said.

"Tell me."

"It won't be a secret forever," I tried to explain, my nerves suddenly getting the best of me. But if I couldn't tell my friend, someone who had no skin in the game, that Boston and I were involved, there was absolutely no way in hell I'd ever be able to tell Kale the truth about us.

"Out with it, Ford."

I took a healthy swallow of the strongest martini of my life, hoping the vodka and olive juice would offer enough lubrication for the truth to get out.

"I'm sleeping with Boston Sheffield."

MY FLIGHT GOT IN LATE, BUT THE SMELL OF CENTRAL CALIFORNIA WAS unmistakable, even in the dark of night. It was all dirt and garlic and a little bit of smog, and by the time I made from the airport in Fresno to my parents' farm, I was already almost used to it again. My parents had offered to pick me up, but with my flight not landing until eleven, I told them it wasn't a hardship to take a taxi. The ride alone in the car gave me time to check in with Ford and do everything I could to steady my racing heart.

**Me**: Made it to CA.

It took Ford a few minutes to text me back.

**Ford**: Proof of life.

I sent him a tired looking photo of myself, head resting against the window of the taxi, farmland rolling by in the background.

**Ford**: I didn't know California looked like that.
**Me**: Most people don't.
**Me**: How are you still awake?
**Ford**: Went out for drinks with Alex.
**Ford**: Told him about you.

My already frantic heart went into overdrive, and I almost dropped my phone trying to tap out a concerned message in response to him.

**Me**: Why? What did he say?
**Ford**: If we're telling your brother when you're home, we have to tell our friends.
**Ford**: I figured it would be easier to get them out of the way so I don't get ganged up on when Kale finds out.
**Me**: How did he take it?
**Ford**: Less surprised than I expected. He's more concerned about my welfare after we've told Kale.
**Me**: My brother will be fine.

I wasn't so sure, but I needed to convince myself it was the truth. If I was serious about Ford, which I was, then Kale was just going to have to get his head out of his ass and deal with it.

**Ford**: Alex says good luck with me. Apparently I'm the worst.
**Me**: I don't think so, but tell him thank you.
**Me**: I won't keep you if you're out.
**Ford**: We're back at his place. I'm tucked in for the night.

Another message came through, a photo of Ford in a bed I

didn't recognize, his hair messy and tangled around his face like he'd been asleep when I texted.

**Me**: Did I wake you up?
**Ford**: I don't mind. I wanted to talk to you.

I swallowed, pushing the call button on the screen of my phone. Ford answered on the first ring and I kept it on speaker so I could look at the picture and match the image of him up with his voice.

"Hey, sweetheart," he said, voice rough and drawn out with the laziness of sleep.

I screwed my eyes shut, angry at myself for all the things I'd left unsaid with Ford on the way to the airport. I had half a mind to turn around and go back to the airport, fly home so I could tell him face to face that I was falling for him. That I'd *fallen*. But if the feelings were real, they could wait. They'd still feel as urgent on my tongue in three days if they were the truth.

"Ford," I whispered his name, blinking my eyes open to stare at his face. "Sir."

He hummed, and the sheets rustled. "I don't want to get greedy, but I do like the idea of you trying that out more."

"I'll keep that in mind," I said.

"How long until you're at your parents'?" he asked.

"Five minutes probably. The airport isn't far."

Ford let out another low hum that turned into a yawn.

"I didn't mean to wake you up. I'm sorry."

"I wanted it," he said quickly. "I asked you to and you did what you were told. Don't apologize for that."

I took the phone off speaker and pressed it against my ear.

"I'm sorry," I said again, choking off a laugh. "You know what I mean."

"Be a good boy while you're gone, Boston," he murmured.

I pressed the heel of my hand against the base of my cock, urging it to go back to sleep the way I wanted to.

"Yes, Sir."

Ford cursed under his breath.

"Enjoy your time with your family," he said. "I have big plans for us when you're back."

"Telling my brother doesn't sound like my idea of a good time," I said.

"More than that," he promised. Another yawn.

"Go back to sleep, Ford. I'll be at the farm in no time and we can talk tomorrow."

"So bossy." Another yawn, this one longer, drawing his tease out into one long, drawling syllable.

"Goodnight," I said quietly, a confession of love burning on the tip of my tongue.

"Goodnight, sweetheart."

I disconnected the call as soon as the cab made a left up the winding gravel of my parents' driveway. The farm was on hundreds of acres, and the road that led to the main house was almost a mile off the main road. Dust kicked up all around the taxi and then it settled, giving me a look at the farm I'd spent the first thirteen years of my life in.

"Right place?" the driver asked after I hadn't moved.

The front screen door swung open and I recognized the looming silhouette of my father in the shadows. Kale and I were both built like him, even if we didn't have all his facial features. Tall and slender with muscles that most people wouldn't notice, bodies made of sharp angles and lines made more for tailored suits than patchwork jeans.

"The right place," I confirmed, pulling cash out of my wallet and handing it over the back of the front seat. "Keep the change."

The driver popped the trunk, and I used my shoulder to open the door. I had my carryon, a slender satchel with a book and my iPad, and not much else. I slung it over my shoulder then went for the trunk. My mom's smaller, rounder figure appeared in the doorway beside my dad, but neither of them moved toward me. I closed the trunk and stepped up onto the first wooden stair, then up, up, up, onto the long wraparound porch that had become a permanent fixture in my dreams.

"Boston," my mom finally said, brushing past my dad and meeting me in the middle of the porch. She wrapped her arms around my waist and pressed her cheek against the middle of my chest. I kissed the top of her head and tried to shuffle us both toward the door. My father met us halfway, wrapping his arms around the two of us, but pulling back enough to let his stare roam unbidden over my face. I wasn't sure what he would see there, and even less certain he'd like what he found.

"Let's get inside," he said, ushering us both inside.

The house was everything you'd expect from a typical farmhouse but with a little bit of flair. A hot pink blanket was thrown half off the couch and whatever movie had been on the TV was paused in the middle of an action scene.

My parents had waited up for me.

"You must be tired," I said to my mom.

She laughed and untangled her arms from around my middle. "*You* must be tired," she said with a yawn.

"I am," I confirmed. "My body says it's time for the bars to close."

My father laughed and took my suitcase out of my hand.

"Your old room is set up," my dad said, always practical even in light of the circumstances. "Let's get to sleep and we can catch up in the morning."

"I know the way."

I took my bag out of his hand, gave them both a kiss on the cheek, then made my way over the creaking floorboards in front of the bathroom, toward the stairs. My parents' room had always been on the main floor, an office or library space they'd converted to avoid the stairs. Kale and I had shared a room on the second level, a sprawling attic-style room with two twin beds and matching nightstands between them.

The stairs groaned more under my weight than they had before, but I weighed well over a hundred pounds more than I had at thirteen. This was far from my first trip back home after we'd left, but everything felt foreign in a way I didn't know how to articulate. Making my way up the familiar stairs the times before had always felt like a homecoming. This time, it was a reckoning.

I didn't even bother to flip on the lights. I knew my mom hadn't moved anything around. I dropped both my bags, closed my eyes, and counted the steps to my bed. I was asleep before my head hit the freshly washed pillow.

———

Growing up on a farm had meant it was in my blood to be an early riser, but I slept so long and hard that first night back home, the sun had already cleared the small attic window before I managed to pry my eyes open. Sleep crusted together in the corners and I wiped at my eyes with fingers, rolling onto my back with a pained grunt. The mattress had always been shit, but the room was bright now and I realized the sheets were the same pale blue they were when Kale and I walked away for the very first time.

Stretching, I finally bothered to toe off my sneakers, but it took a valiant effort to crawl out of bed to get my bags. I fished out my charger and plugged it in, then found my phone and put it on charge. I didn't have any more messages from Ford, but I did have one from my brother telling me not to worry about letting him know I'd gotten in safe because he'd tracked my flight and already knew.

If that wasn't typical Kale, I didn't know what was.

My brother was diligent and meticulous, busying himself with everyone else's business as much as his own. I wouldn't have been surprised if he already knew about Ford and me, but that thought was enough to make my blood run cold. Kale had made it a life goal to leverage his four minutes of seniority over me, but the thought of him knowing the whole time and being content to let Ford and I wallow in secrecy was too much for me to entertain.

Sitting up on the ancient oak bed, I stretched my arms over my head and cracked my back, then dug out some fresh clothes and my leather toiletries bag. Kale and I had grown up sharing a decent-sized bathroom across the hall, but as a six-foot tall adult, the shower was smaller than I remembered. The water pressure was as shit as it had always been, but after some muttered cursing and some beginner contortionism, I was freshly washed and ready for the day.

I hadn't quite been able to wash the flight off of me, my

head still fuzzy in the way that jetlag had about it, even though I knew in a day or two my equilibrium would be level set. Downstairs, the house sounded quiet, but I wasn't surprised to find my mom in the kitchen, sandwich supplies spread out across the counter.

"Hey, Mom," I said, shuffling toward her.

She turned, eyes warm and smile wide, then quickly enveloped me in another hug. I closed my eyes, leaning into her and trying to separate out the feelings that came from being with her and the ones that were ingrained with being in the farm. The property was in their blood as much as the crown belonged to Christian, and I let that thought be enough to make me stop trying. This place was her and the city was me, and I didn't know when the farm had stopped being mine.

I didn't mean that in the way of saying I wasn't welcome here, but as I separated myself from my mom's welcome home hug so I could sit at the kitchen table, I found myself a visitor, an interloper. She made me a sandwich and brought me coffee, and told me it was nearly eleven in the morning. She and my dad had been up for hours.

Sliding my hands up the sides of my nose, I rubbed the bridge where my glasses sat against my skin, wondering if New York had turned me more into Kale than I'd ever intended. As a teenager, when I thought of home, I'd thought about digging vegetables out of the garden. Even in the city, my upbringing had been rooted as deep inside me as the massive oak tree out back of the house. And sitting at the place that had always felt like home to me, I didn't think of my brother, didn't think of his ridiculous jet or my job or apartment.

When I thought of home, I thought of Ford Carlisle.

WHILE I WAS GETTING READY TO GO MEET ALEX, BROOKS, AND KALE at The Black Door, Boston texted me a picture of his erection. The thick swell of his shaft and the precum pooled at the tip were enough to stop me in my tracks, and I braced myself against the edge of the bathroom counter to stare harder at my phone.

**Boston:** It hurts.

I groaned, cracking my neck before typing out a reply.

**Me:** Is there a question there, sweetheart? Because I'm not hearing it.
**Boston:** Can I come?
**Me:** I've seen you do it more than once.
**Boston:** MAY I come?

I huffed, a smile flashing across my face because I could hear the sarcasm in his voice, even through text.

**Me**: No

**Boston**: Are you serious?

**Me**: Want to test me and see?

**Boston**: How would you know?

**Me**: Are you implying you would lie to me about it?

I dug some pomade out of the small tub beside my sink and rubbed it together until it was warm, then ran my fingers back into my hair to style the strands away from my face. It wasn't that I didn't want Boston to come—I very much enjoyed Boston coming. I even enjoyed it if we weren't together. But the night ahead of me felt like something to endure and I selfishly didn't want to be alone in my misery.

**Boston**: I've never lied to you.

I rinsed my hands in the sink and dried them on my hand towel, then snatched my phone off the counter and flipped off the lights. I was already behind schedule on account of the fact I didn't want to go, but I hoped that with Brooks and Alex both knowing the truth about my relationship status, they'd help run interference so Kale didn't notice I wasn't as eager as usual.

**Me**: Don't come until you're with me.

**Me**: Why are you even hard right now?

**Boston**: I took a nap after dinner and woke up with it.

**Me**: What did you dream about?

There was a knock at my front door, and I hopped toward it, phone in one hand, shoes in the other. I unlocked the door to let Brooks inside, then leaned against the wall beside him and laced up my shoes. He held his hand out for my phone.

"Not a chance in hell," I said, holding the device between my teeth so I could finish with my shoes.

"The last thing I want is to read your dirty messages to Kale's baby brother."

"They're four minutes apart." I finished off the last lace and swiped the screen on to see what Boston had said in answer to my question. "They're the same age."

**Boston**: You tied me up again, spanked me, then you... fucked me.

I swallowed hard, rubbing my eyes. I would have woken up with an erection too.

**Me**: Save it for when you're home.

**Me**: I'm going out with the guys. I'll be with your brother, so I won't be able to text much. Sorry.

**Boston**: It's not forever. I miss you.

**Me**: I miss you.

"Are you done?" Brooks asked with a sigh.

I took one last look at my phone before sliding it back into my pocket.

"I'm done," I told him, checking my other pockets for my wallet and my keys. "I told you I would have met you there."

"Didn't want you to bail."

I shoved Brooks back out of the house and locked the door behind me. The Black Door was walkable from my house, but I was very happy to find a town car idling alongside the curb and a driver standing with his hand on the back door handle at the ready.

"I'm not bailing," I said, pushing him out of the way to climb into the car first. "I want you to know, by the way, Alex knows about Boston."

The car door closed as Brooks settled onto the seat beside me, one brow arched toward his hairline. "How did that happen?"

"I told him."

"When?" he asked.

"The night Boston left for California," I said. "I called him up and he answered. We went for drinks and I crashed at his place."

"I'm just glad he's alive," Brooks said.

"I think he's almost back to normal."

The car pulled away from the curb and shot down the street until it reached a red light and jerked to a stop.

"Beamer really did a number on him."

"I think Beamer opened his eyes to some things that were maybe more important to him than he thought," I said.

I didn't want to go into details about the late night conversation Alex and I had shared, but it was safe to say Marigold's dirty martinis were some of the best social lubricant I'd ever had.

"I'm sure he'll tell me when he's ready," Brooks said.

The car lurched away from the light and made a right turn toward the club. I sighed and dropped my head against the headrest.

"You're really serious about him, aren't you?" Brooks asked a moment later.

I didn't bother looking at him. I just nodded in agreement.

"Alright," he said, like my answer had helped him make some decision for himself I hadn't even been aware of.

"Alright?"

The car stopped in front of The Black Door.

"Alright," he said again, not bothering to wait for the driver to come around and open the door. I crawled out after him, tilting my head to the side.

"Don't worry about everything," Brooks said, reaching up and flicking the collar of my shirt. "Just worry about how you're going to tell Kale that you're sticking it to his precious baby brother."

"They're the same age!"

Brooks laughed, then raised a shoulder and cleared his throat, stare flickering to a distant point over my shoulder. I schooled my features and glanced behind me, finding Kale coming down the street with Alex beside him. With his broad shoulders and thick-rimmed glasses, Alex looked the polar opposite of Kale, and I wondered what the group of us looked like to outsides. Beamer had been a brick wall of a man himself, Kale and Brooks were on the smaller side of things. I was slender, but taller than them both, and I imagined us to look like some sort of mismatched circus troupe.

"I hope you fuckers are ready for a good time," Kale said, ushering all three of us toward the door. "I'm ready to live vicariously through you."

"Don't act like you're bored of monogamy," Brooks drawled.

"It suits you," I said.

Kale grinned, and the four of us showed our IDs at the desk and then headed for the bar. Still thinking of my outing with Alex, I ordered a dirty martini to start, but it came nowhere near to the one we'd had at Tryst. He offered a similar reaction to his drink, but didn't say anything about it.

If I hadn't just spent the night with him, I would have been worried about the mood, but I knew Alex was slowly but surely making his way back to us.

"Down here or upstairs?" Kale asked, taking a look around.

I'd always favored the downstairs for the start of the night because something about seeing people disappear down the dark hallways toward the private rooms always got me going. I worried, though, that with the visual of Boston's hard and leaking cock in the forefront of my mind, the proximity would only put me on edge.

"Let's go upstairs," I said.

Kale had always favored the top floor, finding the guests less inhibited. Just one of the many ways the two of us differed.

The elevator was open and waiting when we got there, so the four of us crowded in. A couple who'd been trailing behind us from the bar managed to get in at the same time, the scent of the arousal between them immediately filling and then overpowering the space. I patted my cellphone against my leg, staring at the seam in the doors and willing them to open for some air. As soon as they parted, I was out of the elevator and sucking in as much fresh air as I could breathe.

"You all right?" Kale asked, clapping his hand against my back a couple of times.

"Fine," I said quickly, scrubbing a hand down my face. "Just got a little claustrophobic in there for a second."

"I didn't know you were."

"Neither did I."

Alex and Brooks headed past us toward the main room, no doubt either looking for seats or looking for partners. Probably both. I knew Alex had been looking to get back into the swing of things, but until I saw the predatory way his eyes scanned the crowd, I hadn't realized just how much he'd meant it.

"Surprised you're not off prowling with them," Kale said, weaving around a table and taking a seat on a small couch fit for two. I sat down beside him and moved the olive skewer out of the way so I could get a drink of my martini.

"The night is young, Sheffield. Relax."

"It's been a while since you pulled," Kale went on.

"Been awhile since you came up for air," I countered, chomping down on an olive. "There's plenty that you've missed."

"You'll have to enlighten me."

I spied an awkward-looking twenty-something across the room and raised my finger to shut Kale up.

"You'll have to wait."

I sucked down another olive and headed to the other side of the room. The man I'd set my sights on was alone as far as I could tell and attractive enough, but nowhere near as good looking as Boston. He appeared a little nervous and a lot out of place, like if someone threw him a life preserver, he'd thank them for it for the rest of his life.

"You look like you want to be anywhere but here," I said when I approached him, flicking the last olive off the skewer and into the bottom of my drink.

"What?" His voice cracked a little and he blinked up at me with wild eyes.

"You look miserable."

"My friends ditched me," he said. "I don't know anyone."

In another life, I would have probably taken him into a

back room and found a way for him to pass the time until his friends reappeared. But I knew the old Ford was already long dead and buried.

"What were you looking to get into tonight?" I asked.

"Just…" He trailed off and looked around with a frown. "All of it, I think. I honestly wouldn't mind getting into you."

"You're bold." I tsked my tongue against the roof of my mouth. "And I'm taken."

"Shit. Sorry."

I held up my hand and gave him a quick shake of my head. "You're fine. I'm taken, but nobody knows and that puts me in a bit of a bind."

"How so?" he asked.

"Because my friends *haven't* ditched me yet." I glanced over my shoulder at where I'd left Kale, finding a smirk playing across his mouth while I talked to the decent-looking stranger. "I need a decoy."

"A what?"

Knowing Kale was watching, I took a step closer, resting my forearm against the wall beside the man's head. I should ask his name, but I really didn't even care what it was. I never would have asked before.

"Decoy," I said, angling my head like I was going to kiss his neck. He smelled like drug store soap. He couldn't have been more different from Boston, and the rouse had me wanting to throw up all over my shoes. "I'll give you all the cash in my billfold if you come sit at my feet for a while and do what you're told."

"Sexually?" The question was far breathier than it had any right being.

"Maybe for you, but not for me. I just want you to pretend

you're being a good little boy waiting for me to get tired of talking with my friends so I'll take you home and fuck you silly."

"But you won't take me home?" he asked.

"I'll walk you out front and give you all the cash I have on me," I promised him.

"And you'll buy my drinks?"

That wildness in his eyes had sparked into something a little more knowing than I'd initially read it as. I narrowed my eyes, wondering if I was getting played. Though, I supposed it didn't matter. I wasn't going to spend any substantial time with the man. I wanted him to pretend he was biding his time and nothing more.

"I'll buy your drinks," I said. "But that's all this is. A transaction."

"Understood," he whispered.

"No touching," I told him. "Nothing sexual at all."

"What about with your friend?" His stare flickered toward Kale behind me.

"He's married to a prince."

It was an exaggeration, but I didn't want the little actor to get any ideas.

"No, the other one."

I turned to look toward the couch, finding Brooks sitting in the seat I'd been ready to occupy before hatching my brilliant plan. His eyes were focused in on me like laser beams, mouth pulled into a tight line.

"You're welcome to have at it with him," I said, turning back. "Do we have a deal?"

"We have a deal," he said, pushing off the wall.

I downed the rest of my martini and then pulled a

hundred out of my billfold. "Go get me another dirty martini and get whatever you want for yourself. Then come back and get on your knees at my feet."

There'd been a time when the action alone would have done something for me, but now it wasn't anything more than a lifesaving measure. I wondered if Boston would be mad over it, knowing how much he liked being at my feet. I'd tell him in the morning and hope for the best.

"Aren't you going to tell me your name?" the man called after I took a step back toward the couch.

"My name doesn't matter," I said, "but the one you're eye-fucking over my shoulder is named Astor Brooks."

"My name is Tate," he said with a brief smile at the bill in his hand. At a certain angle, I could see the appeal of a man like him, but there was only one man for me and it definitely wasn't him.

"That's great." I shrugged, mouth quirked up in the corner. "But I really don't care at all. Now, I thought we had a deal?"

Tate swallowed, cheeks flushing pink. "We do."

"Then you best keep up your end of it." I jerked my head toward the bar. "Go get us drinks and then do what you've been told."

# CHAPTER 33
# BOSTON

THE DISTANCE BETWEEN CALIFORNIA AND NEW YORK DIDN'T BEGIN to wear on me until my third morning at my parents' farm. I was sure the incessant ache that had taken up permanent residence between my legs as a result of not being allowed to come hadn't helped matters any, but Ford seemed content to let me wallow in that misery until my return.

I'd woken earlier than my parents, with a cock so hard it could have sawed enough lumber to build a new barn, then I'd shuffled downstairs to the kitchen to make myself some coffee to enjoy on the porch. My mom found me an hour later in an old white rocking chair with my feet propped up on the porch rail. The sun was just starting to crest over the horizon, shooting a wash of pink and orange in announcement.

"Didn't take you long to adjust back to farm hours," she said, sitting down in the empty chair to my right. She had a mug of her own coffee, which she sipped while looking out at the sky before us.

"I haven't," I admitted. "I'm just missing home that much."

"What's her name?" she asked me, and I instinctively clenched my jaw, back molars grinding together.

I slurped a lukewarm swallow of coffee. "His name is Ford," I said.

She made a surprised noise, wood slats of her chair creaking as she started to rock.

"I can't imagine there's many men in that city named Ford," she murmured.

"Yes, it's Kale's friend."

"How has your brother taken that?" she asked.

I took another drink my coffee. "He doesn't know yet."

"Boston."

"I know, I know." I dropped my feet off the railing and let them thump against the wide planks of the porch.

"And a man?"

"You're just as surprised as I was," I told her, casting a sideways glance at her. She studied me with a worried brow, that typical mom expression when she knew something was out of her control but a potential problem for either of her boys, just the same. "It's very new."

"Does he make you happy?"

I reached over toward her and she took my hand, giving it a squeeze.

"Very much."

"Then your brother will bear it."

I snorted a laugh, and caught her smirking. "Kale is not going to be happy."

"That you're with a man?" she asked.

"That I'm with Ford."

"Boston." She let go of my hand in favor of cradling her mug with both hands. "Why would you say that?"

I debated the merits of coming entirely clean with my mother about all of the reasons Kale was going to be furious that Ford and I were together, eventually deciding that I could give her the CliffsNotes version without divulging all of the sordid and unnecessary details.

"Ford isn't the kind of man who has relationships," I explained. "He's a shameless flirt and even before Kale knew I was interested in men, he warned me away from Ford."

"This man flirted with you even knowing you were straight? Or that you weren't interested in him?"

"It was harmless," I said, knowing her well enough to know where the train of thought was getting ready to take her. There was no coercion to be found between Ford and me, at least not from his side. It was entirely possible that I'd tricked him into the whole thing, but if that was true, he didn't seem to have a problem with it anymore.

"Oh." She made a knowing noise in the back of her throat. "He's a playboy."

That was a far nicer thing to call him than the current vernacular, so I answered her with a short nod.

"Is he still?" she asked. "Now that he's with you?"

"No."

"Your brother will be fine with it," she said, matter of fact.

I chuckled, not convinced. "If you say so."

"Your brother wouldn't be close friends with people who lacked moral character, Boston. Even if this Ford was a reckless flirt before you, the core of him has to be good. And I know you wouldn't be with him if it wasn't."

I swallowed, thinking about Ford's ridiculous offer to buy me an airplane. The ways he'd been so nervous about going too far or too fast with me. The way he was always so willing to let me explore...

"He's a good man," I said.

"Then bring him home to meet us," she said, squinting and tilting her head back as the sun itself finally crested from behind the low, rolling hills.

"You've already met him."

"But not as the man you love," she said thoughtfully, making a sound of maternal displeasure I'd never be able to duplicate. "And while you're at it, have your brother bring that prince of his."

I laughed, setting my coffee on the porch rail. It was too cold to drink and I didn't want to get up and go back inside. I leaned back and pushed my weight on the balls of my feet to start the chair rocking.

"Christian gives Kale a run for his money," I said, "I think you'll like him."

"I'm sure I will, and I'm sure I'll like Ford too. The men who make my boys so happy." A soft smile danced across her face and she closed her eyes.

My first night away, Ford had texted me late to let me know that Brooks and Alex both knew about us. They'd taken it well, considering they were friends with Kale. Ford had asked them to keep the secret until we'd had a chance to come clean, and I wondered briefly what it would be like to be with Ford out in the open, without worrying about hiding from my brother.

I'd always been social enough with Kale's friends, but they'd never been *my* friends. I had Shawn and others who'd come and go, but I'd never had a close-knit friend group like the one my brother and my boyfriend found themselves in the middle of. While I used to be jealous of their tight relation-ships, now that Ford and I were navigating the limits of secrecy, I was glad to not have the same constraints for myself.

Behind us, dishes clanked and clattered in the kitchen, and my mom let out a quiet huff of a laugh. "It sounds like your father is up."

"What was it like for you before?" I asked her, rocking my head against the back of the chair to face her. "When you and Dad met and all of that?"

"You mean when he told your grandparents that we wanted to own a farm and not a firm?"

"Yeah," I rasped, "but before too."

"Oh." She chuckled, rolling her eyes like the memory was fond and not horrible. "You mean when that ancient hippie from California stole your dad out from under their piles of money and ruined his life forever?"

"That doesn't sound like how you two tell the story."

"It's how your grandparents used to," she said. "At least at first. They weren't happy I was older than him, and they hated the way he loved me."

"Why?" I asked, nose scrunching up at the thought so violently it displaced my glasses. "You just want Kale and me to be happy. Didn't they want that for him?"

"They wanted him happy *there*," she clarified. "Just like I wanted you two happy here."

"Mom."

Being a snappy teenager had been a horrible time for me and for Kale. We'd both struggled to balance the obligations of rural farm living with the expectations of public school. Even though we were still better off than most, kids were cruel and in the absence of knowing any better, we'd thought money would fix it all. When our grandparents proposed that Kale and I finish school in New York, it had felt like a win...for all of us.

Kale and I would get away from the farm and into a more comfortable life. But I learned quickly that money didn't make people any nicer and there were just new things to get teased and tormented about. There'd been a time, two months in maybe, when I thought I'd made a horrible mistake and wanted to come back to California. My grandparents hadn't been too keen on the idea, and neither had my father. Even though he'd walked away from his life to be with Mom, the lessons that had been hammered into his head through school hadn't gone away. I'd made my decision and I had to live with it. If I still felt the same way in a year, we could revisit the conversation.

For as much as our parents loved us, I wondered sometimes if they wanted more for my brother and me. If that was why they'd been so willing to let us go. Even though the farm had always done well enough to keep us clothed and fed *and* turn a profit, the comfort and the money my grandparents were offering was far more than they ever could.

"I'm not mad the two of you chose to move with them," my mom said, reaching over and patting my hand before I could let that worry take me too far down a dark road. "I never have been. I missed you both terribly when you left, but just like now, I've wanted the two of you to have the best of everything and I've wanted you to be happy. If New York made you happy, if the money and the rest of it...I wanted that for you."

"I love you."

"I love you too, honey."

The screen door swung open behind us and my father

stood in the doorway, half-full carafe of coffee in his hand. He bent down and kissed the top of my mom's head, then ruffled my hair.

"Does anybody need a refill?"

I snatched my mug from the rail and held it up for him to top off. The warm scent of fresh coffee drifted around the three of us, and I took a slow sip while he refilled my mom's cup.

"Thanks, Dad," I said.

He grunted an affirmative noise, never good with feelings, just like his parents before him. My grandparents had given Kale and me a good life, if not a cold one. They weren't as affectionate or as friendly as my mom and dad, and there was only so much money could buy.

For so long, even though I'd built a happy life for myself in New York, I'd longed for the comforts of home, the kindness of my parents. It was amazing to be back with them again, but even after barely two full days, I'd realized the feelings I was missing weren't so closely tied to a place, as I'd so long believed. Ford had stirred all of them up inside of me without even meaning to.

With Ford, I found sanctuary.

"You should tell your father all the things we just talked about," she said, pushing up from her chair.

"About how you stole him from grandma and grandpa?" I asked with a chuckle.

"The rest of it, Boston," she said, smacking the back of my head.

"Is the porch a confessional, then?" Dad asked.

The sun was working its way higher into the sky by that point, and I knew the chores of the day weren't going to hold for long. I took another drink of my coffee and stood, turning to face them both.

"The farm," I corrected. "Did you want help with the eggs?"

My mom patted her hand against my dad's chest and slipped past him into the house. I rolled my head around to crack my neck, and my dad shook his head, expression feigning judgment.

"You can't collect eggs in your pajamas."

"Of course I can." I took another drink of my coffee and scooted around him toward the door. "Just let me borrow your boots so I don't get my sneakers dirty."

He laughed at that, smacking the back of my head in the exact same spot my mom had.

"And here I thought there was a chance you'd be moving back for good."

The quiet statement stopped me in my tracks, and I spun back toward my dad, mouth half-open in shock. The corner of his mouth was quirked into a self-deprecating smile, and one eye was squinted closed. He looked so much like my brother, the comparison was shocking.

"Dad, I..."

He wiped the look off his face, expression turning softer and far more honest.

"Let's go get the eggs, Boston," he said, ushering me back inside the house. "And then you can tell me all about the things you've found for yourself in New York."

I'D MANAGED TO MAKE IT THROUGH THE BLACK DOOR UNSCATHED, even if Kale did raise a doubtful eye when I let my hired guest go home with Brooks. I slept like shit that night and the night after, finding that the conversations and texts with Boston weren't enough. How had I gone from being a man who was terrified of commitment to being one who couldn't even function when the man I loved was away from me? It was sickening.

For his part, Boston had stayed in as much contact with me as he could manage. Between working on the farm with his dad and spending time in the kitchen with his mom, hopefully he was getting what he needed from his visit back to California. I hadn't dared ask him when he was going to come home because I didn't want to appear too eager, nor did I want to rush him back. I didn't know what appeal the farm held for him, and I didn't want him to resent me for pushing him to come home before he was ready.

I spent most of the day Sunday browsing more property listings upstate, ready to show Boston the list whenever he returned, but our now normal goodnight phone call ended without a date and a time. It took well over an hour, but I managed to fall into a fitful sleep, not ready to face the night or the day that would follow. Kale's boyfriend Christian was on a visit back to his family as well, but Kale had gone mad with the absence and caught a flight after breakfast to go bring Christian home. The urge to do the same was barely manageable for me, but I wanted to trust Boston would have invited me if he wanted me there.

While I slept, winter rolled into the city full force in the shape of a massive storm with some of the loudest thunder I'd ever heard. It woke me just shy of midnight, the vibrations shaking the windows. The rainfall was so insistent and constant, I barely heard the frantic knocking on my door. Flinging my legs out of bed, I checked my phone and saw it was right after one in the morning. I had no idea who would be at my door that late at night, and the last person I expected to see standing there was Boston, looking like a cross between my salvation and a drowned rat.

I grabbed him by the lapels of his coat and yanked him inside. He brought the weather with him, puddles of rain-water immediately pooling in my entryway. His dark hair was plastered to his face and his glasses were so wet they looked polka-dotted. More drops ran off the cuffs of his jacket, and I shoved his bag off his shoulder and onto the floor so he could get out of his coat before he caught a cold.

"What are you doing here?" I asked, fingers working at the buttons on his pea coat. He shivered a little, nose scrunched up into the cutest smile I'd ever seen.

"Wanted to surprise you," he said, giving his shoulders a shake after his coat hit the floor. His shirt beneath was soaking wet too, and I tugged the hem of it up and over his head, adding it to the growing pile on the floor.

"Shoes," I said, and he toed off his sneakers and cast them to the side.

I was still in shock to find him in front of me, tall and warm and real as if I'd dreamed him to life.

"You should have called when you left the airport." I fussed with his belt next, getting it open so I could get to his zipper. The heat from his cock was a contrast to the rest of him, half hard and pressing against his underwear, wet like the rest of him.

"That's not very surprising."

"Neither is pneumonia."

"That's not a real thing," he grumbled. "That's not how people get sick."

He balanced himself with one hand on my shoulder so he could lift his legs and step out of his pants. My entryway was a disaster, but once I stripped Boston out of his clothes, I pulled him right into my arms. He smelled the same as he always had, the normal undertones of earth and grass a little more in the forefront than usual

"You're here," I rasped.

Boston buried his face into the crook of my neck, sliding his arms around my waist and pulling me as close to him as his damp fingers could manage.

"I wanted to surprise you," he said again, lips moving against my collarbone. "I missed you so much."

"I missed you." I kissed the side of his head, ready to tell him the rest, ready to let him know I was in love with him, but he stole the words right out of my mouth when he said, "It's so good to be home."

For as long as I'd known Boston and his brother, home for Kale had always been the city and home for Boston had always been the farm. Even though the two of them were made of the same DNA, they couldn't have been more different when it came to the things that meant the most to them. It was probably the only thing that helped me rationalize why I loved Kale as a friend, but Boston as so much more. I often thought that if Boston considered New York home, it would change his personality entirely, but he had never sounded as relieved or sure as when he whispered those six words against my skin.

"So good to be back to you," he mumbled, shifting his head and pressing a kiss against the side of my neck. It wasn't a casual kiss or a welcome home kiss by any stretch of the imagination. His mouth was wet and hot, insistent as he dragged his tongue up toward the underside of my jaw.

His cock jerked, tapping against my thigh and reminding me of his nakedness. I wasn't much more dressed, only in a pair of low-hanging pajama pants, my own dick eagerly trying to find an escape route.

"I've got you," I promised, grabbing the back of his neck and tugging his face upward so I could slant our mouths together and kiss him. "You're right where you belong, sweetheart."

He whimpered and I kissed him harder, using my tongue to search out any new flavors that might have lingered in his mouth since I saw him last. Boston groaned into my mouth, tongue swirling around mine as his hands came to the waistband of my pajamas. He didn't ask, and I didn't care. He reached behind the waistband and took a hold of my dick like he had any right to it, which...he had all of them.

"I'm so fucking horny, Ford," he whined, knees buckling as he stroked me. "It's been days. I need you. Need this."

"What do you need?"

"Want to come. Want you to come," he said, words slurred with sleep and arousal.

Using my body, I pushed him back against the closed front door, both of our bare feet squelching in the piles of his discarded and soaking wet clothes. His breath huffed out into my mouth when his shoulders hit the door, his grip on my cock remaining unchanged. I matched him, taking his thick and hard cock into my fist and giving him a slow and tight stroke from root to tip. Boston's entire body trembled and he blinked rapidly at me from behind the lenses of his fogged-up glasses.

"I'm not going to last," he whispered, shaking his head. "Please tell me I can come."

I loved that even back in my house with my hands on his body, he asked for permission. The way he'd taken that instruction—and all the ones before it—to heart with such a serious level of dedication and interest meant more to me than I'd ever be able to explain. Boston truly wanted to please me, trusting that by giving that up to me, I'd give him every-thing back—and then some.

"Ford."

My name fell out of his mouth like a prayer.

"Sir, please. I need you so much."

His desperate little pleas were the best kind of lube, and my own orgasm crashed into me as another crack of thunder rumbled through the city. Slamming my free hand against the door beside his head, my dick shot hot and sticky jets of cum over his hand and his bare stomach. My own hand on his cock went still, tightening as I emptied into the space between us. I didn't realize how hard of a hold I had on him until the aftershocks of my release died down and I felt the way he trembled beneath me. I dragged my fingers through the mess I'd made on his stomach, then traced them across his lips.

"Come then, sweetheart" I said softly, dragging my tongue over his mouth, shivering at the taste of myself there. "Come for the man who loves you."

Boston's eyes went wide—and so did my own—at the unplanned confession, then his entire body went still. Outside the house, lightning lit up the sky and Boston's mouth parted on a silent cry. Cum streaked out of his dick, smearing between my fingers, my wrist still moving over his length long after his balls had emptied. Boston was a quivering mess, falling away from the door and against my body as if I could offer him more support than the sturdy beams of my hundred-and-fifty year-old home.

With one hand still steady around his burning erection, I wrapped the other around his back. Any other time, I like to think I could have held him up, but it was the middle of the night, we were both tired and spent from the orgasms, so with as much grace as I could manage, I took us both down to the floor. Boston curled up against me, turning so his back was pressed against my chest. I leaned against the wall and bent my legs at the knee, and he matched the pose, resting his hands on my knees while he caught his breath.

I kissed the side of his head, the top, his temple, everywhere I could reach, all the while still giving soft and slow pulls up and down his cock. He would occasionally grunt and whimper, body twitching with the kind of spasms brought on by an overwhelm of pleasure, but beyond that he was limp and pliant in my arms.

My dick hurt as my erection waned, the quickly drying stickiness of my cum making it painful for the skin to retract, but there was no way I was going to move either of us from the position we'd found ourselves in. I held him and stroked him until he found his words again, swiveling halfway around to look me in the eye.

"Did you mean what you said?" he asked.

I knew what he meant, what he was really asking. But there was something so vulnerable and scary about having him naked in my arms and covered in cum, being half naked myself but somehow fully exposed. It was almost two in the morning and we were in the hallway covered in it like we were teenagers who'd stolen an hour together with our parents not knowing. It felt less than and more than all at the same time, and even though I'd been in love with Boston for a while now, admitting it out loud was another thing entirely.

"Yes, I meant it when I said you should have called. Meant it when I said I didn't want you to get sick."

He made an unhappy sound, shifting from one side to the other. The air in the house was cool, and I watched how the puddles of water from his clothes had started to inch their way toward us as they spread. That was the way of love, I realized. A crash through the door when you least expect it and then a slow progression until you're drowning in it and there's no real turning back.

"Yes," I said again, clearing my throat to make sure he heard me clearly. I'd spent the last four days missing him like crazy, ready to crawl out of my fucking skin to have him back in my bed. The time for being coy was long gone. Whatever

Boston and I had was very serious and very real. Now that he was back from California, we had to face reality, and he deserved to know the truth before we decided how to do that. "Yes, sweetheart. Boston. *My* Boston. I missed you beyond measure and I've fallen in love with you."

He screwed his eyes shut, turning to face me and straddling my lap in the process. Boston tore his glasses off and blinked me into focus, then grabbed my face between his hands and studied me thoughtfully with a furrowed brow and a small frown on his mouth. I worried, for the first time, that my confession had been ill-timed or would be unrequited, and I was ready to make light of it when the biggest and brightest smile spread across his face.

"I love you too," he swore, fingers pressed hard into my cheeks. He leaned in close and kissed me on the lips, nothing deep or needy, just a soft and simple kiss that tasted like knowing.

I curled my fingers around his wrists and held on for dear life.

"Welcome home, sweetheart," I murmured against him, a happy groan rumbling up from the middle of my chest. I didn't just mean home to New York, I meant home with me, home to the future we were going to build together, home to the rest of our lives.

I woke up with Ford's hot erection pressed against the small of my back and his lips sealed around my earlobe. He reached around the front of me, tugging my cock with loose and sleepy flicks of his wrist.

"Please tell me you're awake now," he whispered after I'd groaned and stretched my legs toward the foot of the bed.

"I'm awake." My voice was rough and tired. "How long have you been at it like this?"

He dragged his lips from my ear to the thin and sensitive patch of skin just below.

"Long enough for this to show up," he whispered after a kiss, pushing his dick against me with more insistence than before.

"I think you always have one of those."

"When I'm around you, yes," he agreed, pumping his hips against me. "Will you let me fuck you one day, sweetheart? Let me bury myself so deep inside of you that it feels like home?"

I groaned, arching against him.

One of the first things I'd thought about when I propositioned Ford to teach me about sex had been what it would be like to get penetrated, but when it came time for us to "go all the way," he'd gotten on his back for me without any question. I absolutely loved topping him. I'd never felt more in control or necessary as I had when I pushed my cock into his body, and I imagined the feeling would have been much the same for him in reverse. But after a whole lifetime of being only with women who were happy to stay as far away from my ass as possible, the promise of that final step was more than a little daunting.

Ford released my cock and slid his hand up my stomach, fingers spreading as he reached for my nipples before settling his hold around my throat. It wasn't a strong grip, and I swallowed, Adam's apple bobbing against his palm.

"You don't have to be scared, Boston." He whispered the words into my ear and they sparked through my body like a firecracker being set off inside its packaging. "You just have to say yes and trust me to do the rest."

I closed my eyes, focusing on the hot press of his erection against my ass, the cool smear of precum against my skin as he slid his body against mine. I loved this man, loved him more than reason and by some stretch of coincidence, he loved me in return. I had put his cock in my mouth, swallowed his cum, I'd gotten on my knees for him more than once and I loved it. I really fucking loved it, and there was no reason for me to doubt that he'd make sure I loved the next piece of our relationship.

"Yes," I whispered, nodding to double up on my consent. "Yes, I want you to."

Ford growled in my ear, using his weight to roll me onto my stomach and notch himself between my spread thighs. His dick pushed against the tight, virgin ring of my ass, and I fisted the sheets to stop myself from fighting against him.

"I've got you, sweetheart."

He kissed the back of my neck, running his hands down the length of my arms and intertwining our fingers. I let go of the sheets and held on to him instead. Ford rutted against me until I started to fuck my own erection into the tangle of sheets beneath me, then he slowly released my hands and slid down my body. With his shoulders spreading my thighs wide, he grabbed my ass cheeks and pulled me open. It was exhilarating to be so exposed, and I breathed into the trust that Ford wasn't going to take things too far or too fast.

He blew out a soft breath and then licked a hot stripe from my hole to my balls. It was almost enough to make me come on the spot, and were it not for his hand bracketing hard against my hip to hold me down, I would have flown off the bed. His lips curved against the sensitive and untouched skin down there, and then he licked me again, applying a little more pressure against my hole.

There weren't words that existed in my understanding of the English language for me to describe how good it felt to have his mouth down there, so instead of trying, I closed my eyes and decided instead to let the sensations wash over me and sweep me away. Precum poured out of my cock, almost an orgasm's worth slicking a wet spot against Ford's sheets, and I arched my back, pressing my hole against his mouth, using my body to beg him for more.

Ford puckered his mouth against my asshole and speared his tongue inside of me. My balls lifted, high and tight against my body, and a burst of cum spurted out of my cock. The orgasm caught me off-guard, and Ford too, judging by the surprised noise he hummed that vibrated right up my spine. He shoved his tongue deeper into me, swirling it around as he French kissed my asshole until my cock had emptied itself and hung limp once again between my legs.

Pulling back the breath he exhaled, it sounded like a growl as his fingers still gripped hard into my ass.

"That felt so fucking good." I gasped for air, shoving my face into the pillow and groaning through the aftershocks of pleasure that rolled over me. "Holy shit."

"I didn't even get a finger inside of you," he said, voice thick with arousal. "I hope you have another one in you. Or two more at this rate."

My knees trembled, and I glanced over my shoulder in time to see him slide his middle finger out of his mouth with a wet pop. His eyes were nearly black, pupils wider and darker than I'd ever seen before.

"I'll find them for you," I whispered.

He grinned, returning to his place between my ass cheeks, this time adding his finger to the mix as he licked and sucked his way around my pucker. He traced his fingertip around my rim and then teased my entrance, pressing just the tip past the resistant ring of muscle that had already parted so readily for his tongue.

"Relax, sweetheart," Ford whispered, mouth still hot against my hole. "Let me make it good for you."

He eased his finger another inch deeper into me and, for the first time, my body reacted in agreement. Relaxing to make room for him, he slid another inch and another until his whole finger was inside me, his tongue and lips still kissing and licking and nibbling against my rim. A loud commotion from the main floor of the house startled me, my muscles clamping hard around him. Ford cursed under his breath and pulled away from me, taking his finger out entirely and tearing his mouth away. I whined, rolling onto my side to follow his stare out the bedroom door. My heart hammered against my ribs, and I already missed the feel of him between my ass cheeks.

"Is it Milo?" I asked, dropping my face into the pillows, the soft material wet with drool and sweat.

"If it was, I'm going to kill him." Ford climbed off the bed, grabbing his pajamas from the night before and sliding them up his legs to go investigate. "Don't move. I'll be right back."

He padded out of the bedroom barefoot with his cock sticking out of the hole in the front of his pajamas. I imagined it wasn't anything Milo hadn't seen before, and if it wasn't Milo, some intruder was about to get about nine inches more than they bargained for. Ford closed the bedroom door behind him, which felt like the sweetest gesture, but no more than two minutes had passed before I heard raised voices from the downstairs.

Worried, I jumped out of bed and ran to Ford's closet, yanking a pair of basketball shorts out of his dresser and hopping awkwardly into them as I headed for the door. The shorts were tight around my waist, a reminder of how slim he was, and the faded logo of his college team barely reached the middle of my thigh. I didn't think, didn't prepare, I only reacted, coming around the corner and down the stairs so quickly it took me a good thirty seconds to make sense of the sight in front of me.

The front door of Ford's house hung open, my messenger bag and soaking wet clothes from my arrival still piled in puddles in the entry. In the midst of the whole mess stood my brother, my dark pink cashmere scarf in his hand and a murderous look in his eye. He barely glanced my way, his glare beyond focused on Ford, who stood a few feet back with both of his hands raised in surrender.

"I told you not to fuck my brother, Ford." Kale seethed, giving the scarf a violent shake. "So, I would love to know why all his clothes are in your entryway and he's standing behind you in a pair of *your fucking shorts*."

At my brother's indication, I entered the room and Ford's head snapped around toward me. His lips were drawn into a thin, tight line, the erection from minutes before long gone. I tilted my head to the side, intending my sad, half smile to serve as much of an apology as the situation would allow.

"Kale, calm down," I said, slowly closing the space between Ford and me until I was able to rest my hand against the small of his back. Ford's shoulders squared, then quickly softened. He didn't go as far as to lean into me, but the shift was subtle enough to have Kale blowing fire out of his ears. "My clothes are in his entryway because that's where Ford took them off of me."

"Jesus," Ford whispered under his breath. "Rip the bandage off, why don't you?"

"We talked about this," I reminded him.

"But we didn't have a plan."

"Are you..." Kale sputtered and raised his voice, flinging my scarf at Ford like he was a toddler having a tantrum over a broken toy. "Are you serious right now? I'm standing right here."

"Uninvited," Ford said, tilting his head to the side.

"Don't try to whittle me down with semantics."

Ford sighed. "I thought you were off with Christian."

"So you decided to take advantage of my absence and sleep with my brother? And not that it matters, but I hopped on a plane to bring Christian home. We're home now. I'm home and so is my brother apparently."

"I'm also right here," I said, stepping alongside Ford and slicing my hand through the air, ready to cut my brother off at the knee before he got any more out of control. "I'm a whole adult, Kale. And I'm standing right here beside the man I love, feeling like I need to justify that to my brother because he's chosen this moment to come over unannounced and then be upset about the repercussions of his own actions."

"Don't try to turn this around on me, Boston." Kale's eyes were still furious. "How long as this been going on?"

"Long enough," I said.

I wished I'd gotten a shirt, but with Ford's spit running down the inside of my thigh I was reminded we were meant to be in bed, not having a showdown with my brother about the state of my clothes.

"Why are you here, Kale?" Ford sighed, scrubbing a hand down his face.

Behind Kale, the city reflected a pale gray and yellow across the sidewalk, that early morning, after the storm kind of glow. The rain must have stopped overnight, and we'd both slept right through it.

"Because you're my friend and I was worried about you," he snapped.

Ford licked his lips, rolling his eyes at the same time. "Why?"

"You weren't yourself on Friday. You haven't been for a while and..."

My brother trailed off, bracing his hands against his hips

and drawing in a labored breath. He shook his head and turned his stare toward the floor, toward all of my clothes.

"And?" Ford prompted.

"And I went to bring Christian home, but I couldn't stop worrying that something was really wrong with you." Kale shook his head, dragging his tongue across the front of his teeth. "I tried calling you last night and you didn't answer, and I didn't want a repeat of how things went with Alex after Beamer left."

"Kale, come on." Ford took a step toward my brother, shrugging his shoulders helplessly. "Do you really think I'd—"

"I don't know what I think!" Kale threw his arms in the air, letting his palms slap hard against his thighs. "I don't know what I thought. I just...didn't want to lose you and him. We flew back home and I found the spare key you gave me in my junk drawer and came over."

"I don't remember giving you a key."

"I know where you keep the spare, remember?"

Ford sighed. "We'll circle back to that later, but you haven't lost either of us, Kale. Alex was there at the club with us, almost back to his old self."

"But you weren't your normal self," Kale protested. "You didn't even take that guy home with you."

I sucked in a breath, swallowing down any argument my instinct said to throw between my brother and my boyfriend. This conversation now involved me, but it was squarely between the two of them.

"I paid him to sit there and pretend he was interested so you wouldn't harass me about not picking anyone up," Ford explained, throwing a frown over his shoulder in my direction.

"It's fine," I mouthed to him, and he turned back to Kale.

"That man went home with Brooks because I was in love with your brother then and I'm in love with him now. We just weren't ready to tell you yet."

"Why not?"

"Well, this is a good start, Kale." I gestured at the space between the three of us, the soiled clothes and all the hurt feelings.

"I told you anyone but my brother, Ford."

"And it's not up to you," Ford tossed back, shaking his head. "You're not the great fucking decider, Kale. It's not up to you to say where I can and cannot stick my dick."

Kale took a step toward Ford, hands flexing at his sides. "I absolutely do get a say when you're trying to put it inside my brother, you uppity little fuck boy."

"Alright." I sidestepped around Ford, coming between them and flattening my palms against their chests, pushing them apart. "That's enough of that."

"Boston, get out of the way," Kale warned.

I shoved Ford behind me and pivoted, knowing full well he could most likely take my brother in a fight, but my brother was getting mean and personal, and I wasn't going to entertain his attitude any longer.

"Stop it." I poked my finger into his chest, pushing him back toward the still open door. "Ford and I are together on this, and neither of us is going to speak to you until you're ready to act your age."

The venom in my tone must have triggered something because a hurt look flashed across my brother's face and he finally turned his stare away from Ford and onto me. He worked his jaw, swallowing a couple of times before blinking rapidly and shaking his head. If I didn't know better, I might believe he was on the verge of tears.

"You owe both of us an apology," I said.

"Like hell."

"Get out of my house, Kale." Ford's body was hot against my back, and he reached around, holding the door open to make sure there was room for Kale to see himself out. "If you ever speak to Boston like that again, it will be the last time."

"He's my brother," Kale said again, like if he uttered the words enough times, they would take on some new meaning that neither of us understood.

"You're *my* brother," I reminded him, "which is why you're still here and not on the other side of that threshold."

"You both lied to me," he whispered, shaking his head.

"I never lied." I scrubbed a hand down my face, leaning back against Ford's chest. The jetlag from the trip and the late night in bed had caught up to me, the adrenaline from Kale's outburst quickly wearing off and sucking the last of my energy.

"Your brother just got back from California last night," Ford said calmly. "He's tired, I'm tired, you're tired."

Kale opened his mouth to argue, but thought better of it, letting Ford finish his thought. "We can talk about this when we've all had some rest, alright?"

My brother didn't say anything.

"Alright, Kale?" I pressed.

He swallowed again, stare darting between Ford and me, lingering on our bare chests, my messy hair, and the way Ford crowded behind me like a defensive lineman.

"Sure, brother." He took a step backward onto the porch. "Whatever you two say."

BOSTON HANDLED BEING OUTED FAR BETTER THAN I WOULD HAVE, were I in his shoes. It probably had something to do with the fact he wasn't in shoes at all, but instead a pair of my shorts from college that had no right holding his thighs so well. After Kale left, Boston shuffled into the kitchen and made himself a cup of coffee. He appeared at home there, the way he didn't even have to look as he reached into the cabinet because he already knew what height the mugs were at, the way he pressed the button as he turned his back to the counter, focusing on me instead with his arms folded loosely in front of his chest.

"That could have been worse?" I said, voice lilting up into a question at the end.

Boston pursed his lips, reaching down and swiping his hand against the inside of his thigh. "He has impeccable timing."

I realized he was wiping my spit from his leg. Realized less than ten minutes before I'd had my face buried so far into his ass I could have lived there, that I'd been closer than ever to knowing what it would feel like to be inside of the man I loved... and his overbearing, asshole of a brother had ruined it.

"He's just upset that we kept him in the dark."

"His behavior is exactly why we put him there," Boston said.

"You're not wrong."

He turned away from me, filling the two mugs he'd taken out of the cabinet and handing one to me. I was exhausted from the night before and weary from the adrenaline crash after Kale's departure.

"Come sit on the couch," I said, tilting my head toward the living room.

Boston padded behind me, ever the obedient one. We sat down shoulder to shoulder, the outsides of our thighs brushing together as we settled into the cushions.

"He'll get over it." Boston dropped his head back and stared up at the ceiling.

I wanted to kiss him. "I know he will."

"He's been on a power trip since he came out of the womb," he continued. "He can consider this a life lesson."

Boston sighed and curled up against me. I extended my arm around his shoulders and pulled him close, kissing the top of his head. "I think he's really hurt," I murmured.

"He brought it on himself. If he wasn't so much *himself*, we would have told him sooner. We wouldn't have felt the need to hide it in the first place."

He wasn't wrong, but I still felt a sharp stab of guilt over betraying one of my closest friends. I knew from the start it was risky to get involved with Boston, but Kale had been the least of my concerns back then. It was exhilarating to sneak behind his back, to know his little brother wanted me. But as our feelings developed, there was so much more on the line than just Kale knowing about us.

The one thing I did know was that all of it would keep. Kale was too angry for either of us to talk to him, and sitting around worrying about Kale wasn't good for either of us. I also knew that getting Boston back into bed was off the table. Another time, that might have worried me, with the fleeting- ness of life and all that, but Boston loved me and I loved him back and Kale hadn't killed us yet.

There would be time.

"Let's get dressed," I said, taking a big swallow of coffee and doing my best to dislodge us both from the couch.

"I'd rather not," he groaned, falling into the corner of the couch with his arm outstretched to save the coffee.

"I want to hear about your trip, and there are some things I want you to see."

I still had a whole list of properties on my phone that I wanted to get Boston's opinion on. He might think I was moving too fast, but he would have been wrong. For what might have been the first time since I got involved with him, I felt comfortable enough to be myself around him, and this... this was myself. The obsession over Boston had never been manageable and I was finally able to lean into the way my body craved his, the way I wanted to own him and take care of him.

He wouldn't let me buy him a plane—I was going to buy him a farm.

"I'm sure my clothes are soaked through my suitcase," he said, reluctantly unfolding himself from the couch and taking a drink of coffee.

"You can wear mine or we can go to your house first," I said.

He plucked at the tight and worn fabric around his thigh. "Yours aren't going to cut it."

"We can just throw yours in the dryer," I suggested, setting my coffee on the table before heading toward the front door. "And we can shower off while they're getting nice and dry."

Boston trailed behind me, leaving his mug on the floor as he bent over to undo the zipper on his soft-sided suitcase to dig out some clothes.

"And you say there's something you want to show me?"

"More than one something."

He pulled a pair of jeans from the middle of his bag, the knees still dusted with dirt. Then he dug out a clean pair of underwear and a plaid button up.

"They're not wet," he said, tucking them under his arm.

I reached toward him, sliding my arm around his waist and pulling our bodies flush.

"Put them in the dryer anyway," I murmured, kissing the shell of his ear. "I still want to get you into the shower before we go."

———

Two hours later, after flattening Boston against the wall of the shower so I could eat his ass one more time, we were dressed and ready to head upstate. While Boston dug his wallet out of the wet clothes in the entry, I texted my real estate agent—Lisa —the list of properties I wanted to go see. I hadn't told Boston where we were going, and beyond the initial query in the entryway, he didn't ask for more information. It spoke volumes that there was somehow enough trust between us—in and out of the bedroom—that he was content to let me drive…literally.

Having a car in New York was a frustrating and expensive luxury most times. Before Boston, it was rare I bothered to escape the city, but with the heater on and his fingers tangled through mine and resting on top of the center console, I wanted to use it more. There was something so gloriously easy about being with Boston, and I'd never been happier.

"Can I ask you something?"

"Always," he said, giving me a soft smile along with the words.

"Are you going to be happy with me?"

He squeezed my hand, eyebrows tilting together above his nose. "Why wouldn't I be?"

"Just…because I'm your first and—"

He cut me off with a derisive snort. "I'm not like you, Ford. I don't need to sample the buffet to know I picked something I like."

"I think I should be wounded." It would be a lie to say the barb didn't sting, but I knew Boston didn't mean for it to. Neither of us would ever pretend my past had been anything different than it was.

"It's who you are," he said with a shrug. "Who you were. I don't fault you for that. I probably wouldn't have even solicited you in the first place if you weren't that way, so…"

"Are you saying my lack of sexual decency is a blessing?" I chuckled.

"Not exactly, but close enough. And you're not like that now."

I sighed. "I'm the same man I've always been, Boston," I assured him. "But I'm happy with you. I'm more than happy. I'm satisfied. This...this relationship with you, it's been missing my whole life, and I'm grateful for you. For it."

"Okay, Ford. Thank you." Boston squinted, cheeks flushing. He glanced at me quickly like he was embarrassed, then looked out through the windshield. "Are you going to tell me where we're going?"

I'd said everything I needed to say. If he didn't want to acknowledge my truth yet, that was fine. The fenced gravel drive was half a mile ahead on the right anyway, so I answered Boston with a knowing smile, content to let the rest of the conversation slide away.

"We're here."

My tires kicked up loud clouds of dust as I turned up the drive, the wooden entry gate looking like it had come straight out of an old TV show.

"Where is here?" Boston asked, nose scrunched.

We drove about a mile down the road, over a small hill that crested with the most gorgeous flat land view I'd ever seen. Right smack in the center was a white farmhouse with a huge wraparound porch and the sun shone through the windows from behind making the whole house look like it was glowing gold.

"Where is here?" he asked again, eyes darting back and forth between the house and my face.

I rolled to a stop at the end of the driveway, coming alongside Lisa's car. The fact she'd made it upstate faster than us only demonstrated how much money talked. She knew when I wanted to buy something, I moved quickly, and she wanted that commission almost as much as I wanted to see Boston smile.

"It's currently called Rolling Acres," I said, putting the car in park, "but if it was yours, you could rename it whatever you want."

"What do you mean if it was mine?"

Boston scrambled out of the car after me, face flushed pink by the time I introduced him to Lisa. We shook hands, and she walked us onto the porch, unlocking the door with the key box and then taking a seat on one of the white rocking chairs in front of the big bay window.

"I know your parents' farm means a lot to you." I followed him into the house, marveling at the boyish expressions on his face as he looked around the sprawling living room of the farmhouse. "And, honestly, the thought of you moving back to California terrifies me. I told you I'd buy you a plane, I'd buy you a house, a farm...anything within my power to make you happy, Boston, it's yours."

His nostrils flared and he licked his lips, staying silent.

"You don't even have to say the word, you know," I said, taking a step toward him. "You've already said it. You already gave me that control. Remember?"

"I do remember, "and I'm not moving back to California." He said it simply, then disappeared into the kitchen.

I liked the house because it wasn't open floor plan. I appreciated the sanctity of each room being contained by itself, even if that wasn't what was considered popular anymore. It was also one of the things I enjoyed about New York. With houses going up instead of out, the rooms were far more segregated than homes that weren't limited by the constraints of the city.

I joined him in the kitchen, coming to stand beside him as he stared out the window over the sink. It offered a gorgeous view of a large back yard, and beyond that, fenced-in fields and a barn in the distance.

"Tell me about your trip," I said softly.

"It was good to be back," he answered, leaning against me. "Nice to see my parents, but I missed you."

"I missed you too."

"I've never really felt like I belonged in New York, not the way Kale does." He sucked in a breath, letting it out in a long and slow exhale. "When we moved here as kids, I just wanted to impress him, you know?"

"He really leverages those four minutes over you, doesn't he?"

Boston chuckled. "I have a great life because of my grandparents, but I've always missed the comforts of home."

Something twisted in my stomach, and I slid my arm around his waist to pull our bodies closer together. Even before Boston and I got involved, Kale had always told me the ways he and his brother were different, how Boston was more at home on a farm in the dirt than in a suit in the city. I found he looked perfect either way, but listening to the quiet yearning in his voice drove home the truth of what Kale had always said.

"I know," I agreed, even though it killed me.

"And you know, for the longest time, I thought home was a place. Thought it was the farm with my parents." He paused, swallowing and shifting a quarter turn, knocking his shoulder into my chest. "But I know better now."

"What do you mean?"

Boston gave me a cockeyed grin, the casual intimacy of it

enough to set off an explosion of feeling behind my ribs. I grabbed him and pulled him closer to me, hip pressed against the quartz kitchen countertop, his gaze turned upward toward my face. Golden rays of sunshine burst through the window, reflecting off his glasses and making the gorgeous hazel of his eyes turn impossibly more vibrant.

I slid my hand around his neck, fingers tangling into the short ends of his hair, a growl rumbling out of me at the perfectly submissive way his lashes fluttered when he leaned back into my grip.

"What do you mean, sweetheart?" I asked again, the taste of hope on the tip of my tongue, better than any whiskey I'd ever had in my life.

"It's you," he said quietly, smiling and closing his eyes. "I love you, Ford Carlisle. My home is with you."

Ford bought me a farm.

Kale still wanted to put us both in the ground and Ford was busy putting his name on an offer for a 124-acre property three hours away from the city that already had a thriving produce business and room to expand. Sitting in a rocking chair on the porch, I texted Shawn to let him know his dreams for the food kitchen were coming true, then I texted my brother.

**Me:** Let me know when you're ready.

His response came quickly.

**Kale:** Fine.

I slid my phone back into my pocket and lifted my feet, letting the chair start to rock. The gentle sway reminded me of being back with my parents, but I could still taste Ford on my tongue, smell him on my clothes, and the things that had meant to the most to me before were so much *more* now.

Behind me at the door, Ford and Lisa said their goodbyes and I vaguely listened as she told him when to expect a response from the seller, but that his offer was fair. She didn't see a reason the property wouldn't sell. I closed my eyes and sucked in a deep breath, the air infinitely cleaner here than in the city. Everything was different at the farm when compared to the city, everything except for one very important thing.

"You look like you could get used to this," Ford said, his voice a low rumble as he sat down in the chair to my right.

"I think I already am."

"We should know by the end of the week," he said.

I nodded, turning my head to the side and opening my eyes to drink him in. The sight of him took my breath away because, between the two of us, Ford was the one who looked like he could get the most used to the comfort and quiet of a farm. I smiled, reaching out for his hand and settling back against the seat once he took it.

"Is this too much?" he asked, letting his chair begin to rock in time with mine. The motion wasn't always perfect and sometimes the opposing forces tugged us in different directions, but his grip on my hand remained steady and firm as we continued side by side.

"Buying me a farm?" I scoffed, containing the noise in the back of my throat. "It's a lot."

"But is it too much?"

It should have been too much. If for no other reason than I had inherited enough of my own money to buy a farm if it was what I truly wanted, but Ford had done it for me. He'd observed and he'd listened and he'd heard what I missed the most in my life, and he'd found a way to give it to me. It should have been overbearing and over the top, but watching the rays of the setting sun disappear past the horizon, it was anything but. Ford trying to buy me a farm to make me smile was the same as the way he washed me in the shower and carefully picked the drying cum out of my happy trail. It was the way he made me coffee in the morning if he got up first and it was the way he would have put himself between Kale and me if it had come down to that. Ford took care of me with his body, his heart, and also with his money. It was a luxury we were both lucky to have.

"Not for you," I said.

"We didn't even talk about logistics." He turned his attention back toward the driveway. "It's quite a commute."

"We don't have to stay here full time," I was quick to say, "I love your home in the city. I even like my apartment. This is...a nice alternative."

"There's a lot of hiring to do." Ford preemptively sounded tired.

"I won't put any of that on you," I promised, giving his hand a squeeze. "You've done plenty. I can talk to my parents and get the backend logistics and anything else."

"So what you're saying is, much like everything else we've done, we'll figure this out as we go."

"It's worked out so far," I agreed, giving him a tug as I stood from the chair. Lisa had already left, and I didn't want to overstay our welcome on property that wasn't yet ours. "But let's get home for now."

Ford pretended to pout, yanking me against his chest and pressing a kiss against my mouth. "I thought home was me."

I smiled against him, returning the kiss. "Home is wherever you are, and bonus points if there's a bed because I do want to finish what we started earlier.

Ford had me in the car before I'd had a chance to stop laughing, and we were off back toward the city. A much longer three hours later, we pulled into the garage around the corner from his house, and then before I knew it, we were in his house, the mess of my clothes and luggage still in the entryway, but finally dry.

As soon as the door closed, Ford had my back against it, his hands furiously pulling at my belt and my zipper while I tried and failed to kick off my shoes without falling. He caught me just as one shoe went flying and righted me with so much force I fell out of the other.

"Now that *that's* sorted," I murmured, the sentiment lost as he slanted his mouth back against mine.

Admittedly, nothing short of the interruption from Kale would have been enough to distract me from how horny I'd been earlier in the day. Ford's mouth against my asshole like that should have been categorized as a wonder of the world, and the exciting stretch as he'd pushed his finger into me...out of this world.

Fast as lightning, Ford maneuvered us both to his bedroom and I was back against the same tangled sheets from the morning, and he was back between my legs like he'd been there all along. I spread my legs wide, no longer nervous about the anticipation of the whole thing.

"Jesus." He rubbed his face across my ass, burying his nose in my crack. "You smell so fucking good."

"It's sweat."

"I love it." He licked my crack from my asshole up to my

balls then back down again. He added a finger sooner than he had in the morning, and I reached down to lift my cock and balls to make more room for him. I couldn't see much of his face, save for his eyes, which were dark and frenzied with lust. He used one hand to work me open, the other shoved between his own legs. I could see the muscles in his arm twisting as he jacked his cock into the sheets, groaning and pushing his tongue into me.

"That feels so good, Ford. So good." I petted my trembling hand through his hair, dropping my head back against the pillows.

"There's lube," he mumbled, pulling himself away enough for me to hear him. "Lube in the nightstand."

I rolled over to grab it, tossing it down to his waiting hand. He was back with his mouth against me and then a searing heat as he pushed two lube-slick fingers into my already wet and ready hole. I arched off the bed, fisting his hair and pulling him closer against me.

"That's a lot," I whined.

"Breathe into it, sweetheart," he whispered, kissing the inside of my thigh. "Let me make you feel good."

He pushed both fingers into me up to the knuckle and I cried out, ready to call the whole thing off. The nerves were back and I knew if I told him to stop, we would stop. Ford changed his position between my legs, stroking his free hand gingerly over the gooseflesh on my stomach while keeping his other hand firmly lodged inside of me.

"I trust you," I rasped, repeating it over and over like a mantra until he started to move his hand. I grimaced, and he added more lube. The sounds coming from my body were beyond indecent, but Ford growled and groaned after every one. A cold sweat broke out across my temples, and then my balls started to *hurt*. Cradling them in my palm, I searched for his face, finding his stare laser-focused on me.

"Do you want this?" Ford asked carefully, easing his fingers out of me. He poured lube over his long cock and teased the tip of it against my hole. "Do you want *me*, sweetheart?"

I didn't just want Ford. I needed him in ways I didn't yet know how to articulate.

Ford had turned my life upside down, and I knew that hadn't been either of our intent, but it had happened just the same. Life had a funny way of giving you the things you asked for, even if those things didn't look the way you expected when you asked for them in the first place.

I'd been yearning for the comfort and safety of home, expecting it to be shaped like California and the faded wallpaper of my childhood bedroom. Instead, I found it looking like a six-foot tall man with careful hands and thoughtful eyes. I found in the way my chest swelled when he smiled at me, the way I felt like a king when he went slack-jawed from release.

"Yes," I whispered, nodding rapidly and digging the back of my head deeper into the pillows.

Ford propped himself with one hand beside my head, the other secured around the base of his cock and then my vision went white. His cock was thicker and longer than his fingers, the stretch of penetration feeling suddenly insurmountable. I screwed my eyes shut, muscles clamping down and stopping him from getting more than an inch inside.

"Boston, sweetheart." He brushed my hair back from my

face, took my glasses off, and bent forward to knock our noses together. "Boston, it's me. It's just me. Relax, sweetheart. Relax."

I heard the words, understood the definitions, but my body was in revolt.

At least, it had been until Ford pressed his mouth against mine. I could taste the familiar flavor of him on my tongue, mixed with my own sweat, and there was something so indecently primal about the combination. I snaked my hand around the back of his neck, holding him down and sealing our mouths together. I breathed into him, through him, and then Ford growled into my mouth as his cock slid deeper into me.

The pain was blinding, and then...

Then...

It was anything but.

"There you go," he said softly against my lips, the simple words nothing more than a praiseful recognition of what I'd given him. "Oh, God, Boston... you feel perfect."

"Do you really mean that?" I murmured, the question barely audible even to my own ears. Ford's hips pressed against the backs of my thighs and he groaned, going still between my legs.

I'd never felt anything like what Ford made me feel, and I was constantly at war with myself when it came to believing it would last. I didn't understand what made *me* so special. Maybe it was because I'd spent my whole life feeling one-upped by Kale, who was always smarter and faster and better at everything, or maybe it was because I was jealous of his relationship with Christian, the easy way they loved each other. It could have been any number of things, none of which I wanted to think about with Ford buried inside of me. He hadn't done anything wrong. He'd been upfront and honest with me from the start, and any issues about either of our pasts had always been mine. It wasn't fair for me to put any of it on him when he'd been so amazing from the gate.

"Never mind," I said quickly, closing my eyes. A strangled groan twisted in my throat and I wanted to focus on him, not the rest of it. "It doesn't matter."

"I mean it more than I've ever meant anything else in my life," Ford answered anyway, dropping his forehead against mine. "I want you to believe that."

"I do. I'm sorry, I really do."

How could I not? The proof was painted across his face, clear as day.

Ford moved his hips back slightly and eased forward, a short and slick pump of his cock in and out of me. Sensation and need flared to life somewhere around the base of my spine and I grabbed him around the waist, fingers digging into his trim muscles. With Ford inside of me, I lost track of everything except the feel of his body moving against mine. When it started to hurt, he slowed down, added more lube, changed position. All the while he kissed and cared for me, finally coming with me on all fours and his chin notched against my shoulder, breath hot against my ear.

The sounds he made as his body went still, hot spurts of cum shooting into the deepest parts of my body, were enough to bring me over the edge. I grabbed my cock and jacked myself once, twice, and then jets of hot cum splattered against my stomach and my fingers. Every muscle in my body convulsed as I spilled onto the sheets, and Ford cursed into my ear, sinking his teeth into the earlobe and rutting deeper into me.

We collapsed in a heap, his cum already trickling down the back of my sac as we fell tangled into the sweat-soaked sheets. Ford rolled me onto my side, his softening cock still lodged as deep in my ass as his body would allow, and he kissed the back of my neck, the top of my head, everywhere he could reach. I wrapped his arms around my chest, my own fingers scrabbling against his wrists to keep him in place behind me.

"You're okay," he whispered, hooking one leg over my calf and pulling us closer together. His dick slipped out of me, pressing hot and wet against my ass. "You're okay. I've got you still."

I nodded, realizing for the first time my entire body was shaking. Without him inside of me, I was free to move, so I turned and buried my face against his chest, relishing the smell of our mixed sweat, the lingering scent of salty cum hovering in the space between us. It awakened something new inside of me, and I licked him from his nipple to his collarbone, grunting with an unspoken appreciation for the way he'd opened my eyes. The way he'd changed my life.

"When your heart rate quiets down, I'll get you into the shower," he promised. "I'll clean you up and take you back to bed and, if you like, we can do that all over again.

I hummed, shifting my weight to push him onto his back so I could sit on top of him in a straddle. Ford's eyes went wide with surprise, then a soft and almost arrogant smile quirked the corners of his mouth.

I dipped my chin against my chest, looking down at the bouncing hardness of my own cock. I'd come all over myself, the evidence of it still drying and dripping down my stomach, but my body showed no signs of slowing down. I grabbed the lube and poured some into my hand, then gave a slow, over-handed stroke of my cock, returning the sly smile.

"How about we skip the shower and get to the doing it again part right now?"

Boston's cock against my prostate managed to force another orgasm out of me, this time the feeling of it rippling over my body from my toes to the top of my hair and back down again. It was consuming in the ways I'd spent my entire life avoiding, but with him, I never wanted another kind of orgasm ever again. I wanted to come like that, with him inside of me and me inside of him, for the rest of my life. Whether it was at my house in the city or on the farm that I knew would be ours, I wanted the rest of my life tied to the man who trembled above me, looking like a submissive prince with his chest puffed out, muscles tense with the force of his own release. His entire body quaked and he fell forward, landing with one hand beside my ear. He reached with the other to pet his way down the outside of my arm, drawing goosebumps in his wake.

"I'm so glad you're home," I said quietly, closing my eyes to enjoy the heat of him against me. "So glad you're mine."

He hummed, giving a little pump of his hips and pushing deeper into me. "So glad I propositioned you for sex."

I chuckled, grabbing him around the waist and tugging

him the rest of way down. "I've never been happier about my reputation than I am every time I get to see you come, sweetheart."

"There should probably be something wrong with that."

Boston moved his hand down to ease his cock out, and I winced as he withdrew. He dropped onto the bed beside me, tucking himself against my side with a content and tired groan. It was beyond late and we were both in desperate need of sleep, but I wanted to enjoy every moment with him.

"Do you remember before?" He kissed my armpit and my cock moved.

"Before you?"

"Not that far back. I was thinking more about the time you tied me to the bed."

My dick gave another valiant twitch, eager to rouse from its previous state of exhaustion.

"I very much remember that," I told him.

In fact, I thought about it often. My relationship with Boston, at least when it came to kink, was different than anything I'd had before. Not to say I had much experience with relationships at all, but I'd always put much more focus on the roles and the formality of it than on the intimacy. Part of that was by design, to keep people at arm's length, but with Boston, he comfortably floated on both sides of my defenses. When he decided he wanted to call me Sir, it was everything, but when he didn't...there was no real loss. Both pieces of him made up the whole, and I was more than happy with the package.

"I want to try more of it," he whispered, scrunching his nose against my ribs. "I know I'm not good at it—"

"Wait, what?" I rolled him onto his back, climbing on top

of him and pinning his arms to the bed. His nostrils flared, and he blinked me into focus from the new position.

"I don't do it right."

"There is no *right* way, Boston."

He looked annoyed, sucking in a breath and rolling his eyes at me. "I don't do it all the time. I don't always call you Sir and I don't always let you be in control."

"Sweetheart." I tutted my tongue against the roof of my mouth, shaking my head. "I'm never not in control here. You don't have to worry about that."

"I don't—"

"Do you remember when you made the choice?" I asked, tightening my fingers around his arms. "The choice to be with me? To let me be in charge?"

He nodded, breathless.

"Just because I'm not always ordering you around doesn't mean that's changed. This kind of thing...it doesn't look the same for everyone, and this is how it looks for us."

"Are you happy with how it looks?" he asked.

"I couldn't be happier," I promised, dipping down and dusting a kiss across his lips. Boston arched off the bed to chase after me, but I pulled away to repeat, "I couldn't be happier, sweetheart."

His lashes fluttered. "I love when you call me that."

"And I love when you call me Sir. And I love that you don't do it all the time so it's special when you do," I said.

"You call me sweetheart a lot." He smiled up at me, eyes still half closed.

"Because it's my job to take care of you, to make sure that you're happy."

"That's why you're buying me a farm?"

I stretched my back, a yawn escaping out of my mouth that was far too late in the evening for me to try to hold back.

"The farm is selfish," I said, swinging my leg around and dropping back down onto the bed beside him. I was happy to have him home and beyond thrilled to talk with him again. It had been so long since we'd had a chance, but if I didn't get him to sleep soon, I was going to pass out.

"How so?"

"If it's here, so are you," I told him.

"I'm wherever you are, Ford."

"Well." Another yawn. "I'm right here, so let's finish this conversation in the morning."

Boston laughed, rolling away from me and reaching back blindly to drag me closer.

"I love you," he whispered, burrowing into the sheets.

"And I love you."

———

The night flew by, and I woke up slowly, reaching for Boston and finding his side of the bed empty and cool. I rolled onto my back, picking sleep from the corners of my eyes and staring groggily at the ceiling as I waited for my eyes to start working. While I stretched my legs, Milo jumped up on the bed, smelling like cat litter and fish pate. He meowed and butted his head against mine, purring like a violent little machine until I untangled my arm from the sheets to pet him. The purring got louder, then he smacked me in the mouth with his tail and jumped off the bed.

I stretched for the nightstand, glad that I'd had the foresight at some point the night before to plug my phone in to charge. It was almost ten in the morning, and I was definitely late for work. A quick scan of my emails revealed I'd only missed one meeting, and I fired off a quick text to my secretary to let her know I'd be in before lunch.

How easily I'd gotten lost in Boston, when before him my life had revolved around random hookups and work and more hookups. I lost track of time with him, happy for the distractions. But now that he was back from California and our relationship was out in the open, it was time to face the real world with friends and responsibilities, and all of that shit we'd both managed to pretend didn't really exist.

I took a quick shower and got dressed in a navy blue suit, grabbing a pair of brown leather shoes and a matching belt, which I carried downstairs. I found Boston sitting in the kitchen, a cup of coffee in his hand and a frown on his face.

"Good morning," I said, voice still thick with sleep. He looked up, eyes going wide when he saw me dressed and ready for the day. "You look miserable."

He raised his phone and gave it a shake before dropping it onto the counter. "My brother just fired me."

I sucked in a breath, and any goodwill I'd ever felt for my friend flew straight out the window and far down the street. I dropped my shoes and belt onto a chair and moved around the counter, taking him into my arms and kissing the top of his head.

"What do you mean your brother fired you?"

"He said he has a rule," Boston grumbled into my chest, arms sliding around my waist and holding me loosely.

"A rule about me," I remembered out loud.

He nodded.

Kale's rule was arbitrary and he knew it. We'd both

enjoyed the game of it. He liked to pretend he had a say in my life and I liked the thrill of the chase. It was a win-win for both of us, even though my jaunt with his assistant before Boston had cost me a pretty penny in the end.

"I'm sorry, Boston."

He wiggled his shoulders until I let him go, then he walked around to the side of the counter where I'd left my belt and shoes. He picked up the belt, running the Italian leather through his fingers a couple of times before returning to where I stood. Without a word, he carefully threaded the belt through the loops of my slacks, bringing it together in the center and doing up the buckle. Boston smoothed his hands over the stitching on the top of the belt, just over my hip, then took a step back and looked down at the job he'd done. It was a simple thing, really. Putting on a belt, but it made my breath catch in my throat just the same.

"I wasn't going to work for him forever," he said, leaning around to get my shoes and then raising a brow at me in question.

I swallowed, managing a nod.

Boston slowly lowered himself to the floor in the middle of my kitchen, then one at a time, slid my socked feet into my shoes and made neat bows of the thin, waxed laces. Instead of getting up when he finished, he rested in that now familiar pose, palms shaking a little against his thighs. I braced myself against the counter, waiting for his next move while also trying to decide if he was waiting for instruction from me.

I studied the top of his head, the thick brown hair still tousled from sleep and sex, then I gently worked my fingers through the messy strands. Boston hummed and leaned into me as I finger-combed his hair.

"It's not a bad thing, is it?" I finally asked, tilting his head back and forcing him to look up at me.

He shook his head.

"This is what you really want to do, isn't it?" I asked.

He nodded, and my dick stirred behind the fly of my slacks.

"You want to serve me when it pleases you," I said, tightening my fingers in his hair. "And you want to go up to your farm and get your hands in the dirt on the weekends. Come home when you've gotten your fill and then give me mine, isn't that right?"

Boston groaned, hips giving a little circle as if to demonstrate just how much he liked the shape of his new life.

"If that's what you want, sweetheart, it's yours."

"I don't think I'm submissive."

"You look it right now," I said.

"Not all the time," he murmured.

"No. Not all the time."

Having him submit the way I used to have my hookups submit would have gotten boring before the month was out. I liked that Boston took what suited him, trusting me all of the time to know what he needed and when. It was a big responsibility and a steep learning curve, but I was sure we would figure it out.

"I made you coffee," he said, sucking in a breath and dragging his hands down the length of his thighs. He squared his shoulders, eyes far more focused than when he'd gone to his knees in the first place.

"I'm late for work, but I have time to have a cup with you before I go." I slid my hand out of his hair and held it out for him. His hand felt so good against mine, and I helped him to his feet, immediately bringing our bodies together so I could get at his mouth. He tasted like sleep and bitter black coffee, and I loved every second of it.

"Thank you for letting me do that," he said, pulling away for a breath. His cheeks were flushed and eyes downcast.

"Do what?"

"Your belt," he whispered. "Your shoes."

"Boston." I took his hand and placed it against my half hard cock. "Thank *you*."

He hummed and smiled, stepping away and turning, then sliding a full mug of coffee across the counter toward me. I crowded in behind him, not ready to be away from him.

"What are your plans for the day?" I asked, raising the mug over his head to take a drink.

"I'm going to clean my mess of clothes out of your entryway," he said, mouth pulled into a tight line. "And then I'm getting lunch with my brother."

THERE WAS ALREADY SOMEONE NEW AT MY DESK WHEN I GOT INTO the office. She couldn't have been older than nineteen, with experience to match, I imagined. She looked overwhelmed and out of her element, eyes going wide when I walked through the door. I didn't have a chance to introduce myself because Kale was already coming out of his office, his mouth tugged down into what I guessed to be a permanent frown.

"I'll be back in an hour, Sarah," he said, tapping the edge of her desk. "You're doing great."

Kale ushered me out of the office, and I waited until we were well beyond her earshot to speak. "She looks like she has no idea what she's doing."

"She doesn't," he said, stabbing the down button on the elevator. "She's everything Ford won't want."

I bristled, stepping into the elevator as it arrived and opened. "I honestly don't know why you're so obsessed with his sex life."

Kale followed me into the elevator and the doors closed.

He folded his arms in front of his chest, tension rolling off of him in waves until we reached the lobby.

"If you want an apology, you're not going to get one from either of us."

The top of Kale's lip twitched, and he stormed out of the elevator, stalking through the lobby. I walked behind him, not in a rush to catch up. He was the one who had reached out and wanted to talk. I knew he had to work through whatever feelings he had about Ford and me being together, but I had sincerely hoped he'd at least done most of it before he decided he wanted to talk to me.

Kale waited for me outside on the sidewalk, and when I came beside him, he started walking. He headed toward Central Park, which was surprising, but with every step, his shoulders relaxed so I didn't say anything about the destination. Even when we came up in front of my favorite gyro cart, I didn't say a word. He ordered two wraps and waters, then we found a bench and sat down.

"I didn't think you liked gyros," I said, unwrapping the foil from mine.

Kale still frowned, taking a bite and chewing slowly.

"I don't like Ford right now either," he said after he swallowed.

"None of this went how you think it did."

"And how do I think it went, Boston?" Kale took another bite, wiping sauce from the corner of his mouth with his knuckle.

"You think Ford set his sights on me after you hired me. You think he seduced me against my will."

Kale scoffed.

"You think I'm incapable of making my own decisions," I went on. "You think I'm a child and not the same age as you."

"You're my little brother."

"Four minutes, Kale. Come on."

"You're not like him." Kale's voice went up an octave. He cleared his throat and stared down at his lunch. "You're not like me. You're better."

"I'm not better. I'm just different."

It pained me to think that my brother felt himself to be less than me. Even though we were the same age, I'd always looked up to Kale. He'd always been surer of the things he wanted. He trusted himself and all of his decisions. He made the right choices, the best moves. I admired my brother beyond words.

"He was the man, wasn't he?" Kale asked. "The one in the office you told me about."

"Yes."

"So, this has been going on awhile?"

"Not terribly long," I answered. "But it's serious, Kale. I love him."

My brother's jaw ticked and I watched his cheek hollow as he sank his teeth into it.

I wanted to tell him Ford loved me too. Wanted to tell him about all the ways Ford had helped me find myself and explore things I'd never even been aware of before him. I wanted to tell him Ford had bought me a farm to keep me close. But even as I watched Kale struggle through the basics of the conversation, I knew he wasn't ready for the full weight of it.

That made me hurt for Ford, who knew from the start his relationship with one of his best friends was going to be on the line for pursuing me. I didn't want to break up their group, and I didn't want to be responsible for ruining their friendship. I hoped one day Kale would understand that Ford hadn't gone into things with me lightly. We'd always understood what was at risk, and if anything, it should show my brother how real Ford's feelings for me were.

"I don't think Ford has ever had a serious relationship, Boston."

It sounded like a warning.

"And I've never been with a man," I interrupted. "We're both learning new ways to be."

Kale licked his lips, then took another bite of his wrap, chewing slowly and swallowing it down. He stared ahead of us at the slew of people who'd come around and gotten in line for lunch, a mixture of locals and tourists, bundled up against the cold breeze.

"How was California?" he asked, changing the subject entirely.

"It was nice," I said, finishing the last bite of my wrap. "Weird to be back home."

"You've always preferred it there."

"I thought so too," I said softly.

Kale groaned, balling up the last bit of his wrap and throwing it into the trash can to his right. "But not now."

"No."

He held out his hand and I dropped my trash into it. Kale tossed it, then leaned back against the bench, stretching out his legs and fiddling with the knot on his scarf. I didn't have my scarf, and I shivered as a particularly sharp burst of air whipped past us. Kale loosened the knot and yanked it off his neck, wrapping it haphazardly around mine, so much like the way our mom used to when we were kids. His fingers shook as he tied a loose knot at the base of my throat, then he immediately twisted the top off his water and took a huge drink.

"I'll get over it eventually, Boston," he said, standing up and rolling his neck to crack it.

"I know."

"Today isn't the day, though."

I worried my lips together between my teeth. "I know."

"Okay," he said.

"You should talk to Ford," I suggested.

Kale scrunched his nose like I'd suggested he go swimming in the sewer. "Another time."

"Okay."

"I need to get back to the office," he said.

"Did you want me to walk with you?"

He sniffed a sharp breath through his nose and rubbed the corner of his eye before shoving his hands into the pockets of his pea coat. "You don't have to."

I recognized a dismissal when I heard one. The simple statement burned, but I tried to put myself in my brother's shoes. He knew Ford well, but he didn't know Ford the way I did. And while I appreciated Kale's concern over my involvement with him, there was no way of convincing him it was unfounded. Only time would tell him that, and maybe a few drinks with Ford would help ease the way. But Kale was so much like our father, stubborn and proud. Just like Dad had left to forge a life with Mom in California, Kale had done the same in New York for us.

The only reason I had Ford—had my life—was because Kale had been brave enough to want more and to not be scared of what that looked like. I would have stayed on the farm forever if not for him, and it was that exact taste for more he'd instilled in me that had given me the strength and the courage to pursue Ford in the first place. I didn't think Kale would want to hear that it was because of him, though, so I kept that to myself. Maybe there would come a day or time down the road for that revelation, but today wasn't the day.

"I didn't mean for you to find out the way you did," I told him. "Neither of us did."

"I don't think you meant for me to find out at all."

"We were going to tell you after the trip. You just got there before we could do it."

Kale cleared his throat, standing tall and proud.

"Does he treat you well?" The question was so softly spoken, the wind almost carried it away.

"Very," I promised him.

Kale gave me a jerky nod. "I'll see you later, Boston."

"I love you, Kale."

"Love you too, brother. But those gyros are still fucking disgusting."

I laughed and settled against the bench, watching my brother walk away from me. I didn't particularly enjoy being left behind, but Kale was a complicated man sometimes and I knew finding out about me and Ford had been enough to send him into a tailspin. The fact he was making an effort instead of locking himself away and getting angry about the whole thing spoke volumes to how well Christian balanced him, and I was grateful for it.

I pulled out my phone and texted Ford to let him know how the meeting had gone, and I also made the suggestion he reach out to clear the air on their side of things. Ford answered with a vomit emoji and then asked if I was going to be at his house when he got home from work. It was an easy yes, though we would need to figure out the future state of our living situations sooner rather than later.

Ford said he had to get back to work, and I found myself left with half a day and nothing to do. After finishing my water, I decided to grab a cab to the soup kitchen to drop in on Shawn. Even though it was barely noon, the cloud cover was thickening and walking didn't feel like an option. I tightened Kale's scarf around my neck and flagged down a taxi outside the park.

After a short drive, I hopped out and jogged up the stairs, the familiar warmth and smells of the place working wonders to soothe the tension that had taken up residence in my bones during lunch with my brother. I found Shawn in the kitchen, chopping up sweet potatoes and throwing them into a huge pot. From the other side of the room, I gave him a wave and Shawn smiled, setting down the knife and wiping his hands off on the half-apron he wore.

"You're out in the daytime," he teased.

"My brother fired me," I said with a laugh, the whole scenario sounding so ridiculous when I thought about it after the fact. "He's mad I'm dating his friend."

"That seems rash."

"He's already coming around, but the job was a bandage anyway. I wasn't going to be there forever."

"No?" he asked.

"Kale gave me the job to keep me in the city, but I've found a better reason to stay."

Shawn rolled his eyes. "That's too sappy, even for me."

I shrugged. "It's true. Do you have time for a break? I want to talk to you about the farm."

At the mention of the property, his eyes glowed warmly, but a glance at the clock had his expression souring.

"I really need to get the rest of these vegetables chopped up."

"Can you talk and cut?" I asked, unwinding the scarf and shrugging out of my jacket. "I'm happy to help and I've got nothing but time."

Shawn took my things and traded them for an apron.

"Talk away, Boston. I want to know everything."

## CHAPTER 40

# FORD

The following weekend, I was getting dinner with Brooks, when Kale showed up. I wasn't sure if it was a setup, but as soon as I saw the steely set of Kale's mouth, I knew it didn't matter. We were sitting at a four-top, and Kale threw himself into the seat across from me, immediately flagging down the waiter and getting himself a drink. Beside me, Brooks tensed, but didn't say a word.

"Didn't expect you out tonight," Brooks finally said.

Kale narrowed his eyes and sighed, leaning back in his chair and shifting his attention from Brooks to me and back again. It was a good thing Boston had decided to stay home, because if this was how Kale acted toward me on my own, I didn't want to see him if we were together. After Boston had lunch with his brother earlier in the week, he'd come home that night smelling like chicken stock and carrots, telling me all about it. To me, it didn't sound like it had gone well, but Boston seemed optimistic about things, so I was happy to wait it out.

"I didn't expect to be out," Kale said. "I'd rather be home with Christian."

"Then why aren't you?" he asked.

Kale cracked his knuckles, and the waiter brought Kale's drink to the table. Brooks and I got refills, and I chewed the inside of my lip while I waited for Kale to answer. I'd known all along that he wasn't going to take me and Boston well, but I hadn't thought the whole thing through to completion when I'd started it. I hadn't truly walked myself through what it would feel like to lose Kale's friendship.

I fucking hated it.

I hated that there was a divide between us now that felt insurmountable, but I wouldn't go back and change what I'd done. Boston had given me so much more than I'd ever expected, ever dreamed of, and I was beyond grateful for him and the life we were going to build together. Kale was my closest friend, but Boston was the love of my life, and I wished the two of them could find peace about it.

"Because Alex called me and said the two of you were out. He said he missed the way things used to be before and he wanted me to fix it."

"Things haven't been right since Beamer moved," Brooks said.

"They were more right than they are now," Kale said. "At least that's what Alex told me on the phone."

"Did he say it was your fault?" I asked.

Kale swirled the ice around his drink. "I told him it was yours."

"Do you really believe that?"

Before Kale could answer, Alex yanked out the chair beside him and sat down. He looked tired, as he normally did, but the corner of his mouth tugged into an amused smile. "Did I miss the fun?" he asked.

"This feels orchestrated," Brooks muttered.

He wasn't wrong.

I hadn't been avoiding Kale, but I'd definitely been giving him time to process. It had been awhile since I'd seen any of my friends, and since Kale wasn't talking to me and Alex was still playing the role of recluse, Brooks was the only option. I'd called him up and he'd said yes to dinner and drinks, but he'd apparently spilled the beans to Alex who felt like causing some trouble by telling Kale. It was the most on-brand reaction any of them could have had to the situation, and I found it impossible to even be mad about. Things were going to come to a head sooner rather than later, better to hash it out in public where cooler heads would have to prevail.

"Kale was just telling us now it was my fault things are weird here," I said, arching a brow. "What do you think, Alex?"

If he thought he was going to start a shitstorm with his meddling and send all of Kale's self-righteous rage down on my head, he had another thing coming.

"I think that Kale is always too worried about who everyone else is fucking," Alex answered with a shrug.

"That's not true."

"You were an asshole to Beamer when he brought Dalton around," Brooks offered.

"You were an asshole to Beamer when you found out I was the one who'd marked him," Alex added. "We're both consenting adults, Kale. Just like your brother and Ford."

"Don't gang up on me, you pricks," Kale grumbled, taking a huge swallow of his drink.

"Don't give us cause to," Alex said.

"Stop being so level-headed."

"Stop being so wrong."

Brooks huffed out a laugh, but quickly smothered it with his drink. I hadn't expected either of them to come to my defense, but I wasn't unhappy with the support.

"If it's any consolation," I interrupted, knowing it was my battle to have and not theirs, "we didn't mean for you to find out the way you did."

"How did he find out?" Alex asked.

"He walked in and found all of his brother's clothes on the floor in front of the door," Brooks answered for me.

"And then found my brother in Ford's clothes," Kale added.

"Better than naked," Alex teased.

I chuckled, shaking my head and turning toward Kale with as much seriousness as he deserved. "I know you don't want to hear this, but I love your brother, Kale."

"You love all of them," he snapped.

"That's not fair and you know it. I've never...it's different with your brother."

"How?" he asked.

"Do you really want me to paint a picture of it for you?" I frowned, lifting one shoulder. "I will, but I don't think you want to know."

Kale grit his teeth, cheeks burning red. "I didn't mean in bed, Ford."

I scrubbed a hand down my face, wishing I had an entire bottle of whiskey instead of just a glass. "I don't know how to explain it, Kale. He makes me want to be better and no one ever has before."

"You've always done anything to seal the deal," he interjected.

I groaned, picking at an itch inside the shell of my ear.

"What do you think then? Do you think this is some long con? I lured your brother into bed for fun to get my rocks off, to ruin my relationship with you? Do you really think I would have risked all of that for a piece of ass?"

"My brother isn't a piece of ass," Kale growled.

"No shit. That's what we've been trying to tell you."

Brooks gave the waiter a wave and ordered a new round for all four of us. I finished what was left in my glass and pushed it toward the edge of the table.

"I love him, Kale. And, frankly, our worries over your reaction to that has spent far too much time between us." Dragging my tongue across the front of my teeth, I gave him a helpless shrug. "And I'm done letting you be there. So, you can get over it or not. I don't want to lose you, but I'm not leaving him to save our friendship."

Alex's eyebrows rose toward his hairline and he threw a wide-eyed glance at Brooks, who leaned toward the edge of the table.

Kale glared at me, swallowing before grinding his teeth together so loud I could hear it from across the table. I knew him well enough to read all the emotions that flashed across his face, from anger to confusion, before finally settling on something that looked a little like tired resignation.

"Good," he muttered, finishing the rest of his drink and pushing his empty toward mine.

Over the years we'd known each other, Kale had managed to be both predictable and surprising at the same time. Flying across the country to kidnap a prince was expected because it was just the kind of person Kale had always been. But his acceptance over my willingness to walk away from our friendship to be with his brother was not a reaction I ever would have expected.

"Pardon?"

The waiter brought us fresh drinks, and Kale drank half of his in one shot, shaking his head like that would clear either the alcohol or his thoughts.

"Good," he repeated, gritting his way through the word like it was covered in razor blades.

"Good?"

"My brother deserves that."

I swallowed. "I know."

Kale set his drink down on the table and drummed his fingers against the edge.

"Good," he said a third time, pairing it with a jerky nod. "If you leave him, I'll cut your dick off."

I snorted, rolling my eyes. "I bought him a farm, Kale. I'm in it for the long haul."

"You bought him a *what?*" Brooks asked, swiveling toward me so quickly he almost fell out of his chair.

"I haven't had a chance to tell him yet. I mean, he knows I put in the offer, but I just got the acceptance this afternoon."

The call from Lisa was a welcome break from the frantic crush of work, and my first instinct had been to call Boston and let him know the good news, but he'd been fresh off lunch with his brother and I did really want to tell him in person. Part of me wanted to get through closing and then tell him by giving him the keys, but I was only making the purchase in name and money. The property was for him, and he needed to be involved in as much of the process as he wanted. I'd planned to tell him after drinks with Brooks, but I wasn't sure how long the night was going to run now that Kale and Alex had shown up.

"Where?" Kale asked.

"Just outside Clintondale."

"How big?"

"Eighty acres," I said.

"That's smaller than where we grew up."

"I know."

"Does he like it?

"Very much," I answered.

"You're not moving away, are you?" Alex asked, his tone a little shaky.

I shook my head. "We're not leaving the city."

Kale let out a long breath and closed his eyes, nodding at my answer. "Thank you, Ford," he said so softly I almost didn't hear it.

That was the first moment I'd ever seen Kale show fear. And I realized how out of his mind he must have been with worry at the thought of Boston packing up and going back to California.

"I just want him to be happy," I said.

Kale cleared his throat with a swish of his drink. He stood up quickly, shoving the chair away from the table with a quick jerk of his arms. "I'll be right back."

All three of us watched Kale navigate his way through the maze of tables toward the bathroom. It seemed like the revelation about the farm was the only thing Kale needed to believe how committed I was to Boston, and if I'd known that, I would have opened with it the weekend before. As it were, I thought my level of dedication to his brother would have been a red flag instead of a green one, but I'd apparently misread the situation. It wouldn't have been the first time I got something wrong about a Sheffield, because up until he'd slid his hand around my thigh in front of his brother's office, I'd been wrong about Boston too. Just went to show how people could always surprise you if you gave them the opportunity.

"So." Alex grinned, clapping his hands together. "That went well."

"It could have gone horribly," I said.

"But it didn't."

"What were you thinking?" Brooks asked, shaking his head.

"I was thinking the three of you are the best friends I've ever had, and something as stupid as Ford falling in love with Kale's brother shouldn't be the thing to ruin that for me."

"So this came from a place of selfishness?" I laughed, raising my glass to toast him.

"Absolutely." He and Brooks brought their glasses up and clinked the rims against mine. "To being a narcissist."

I laughed again, and Kale was back, a little red-faced, but overall looking a thousand times less tense than he had on arrival.

"What are we toasting?" he asked, sliding his glass in a circle around the table, not quite committed to the celebration, but not ready to leave. Relief had flooded my chest when he returned and I flashed him an apologetic smile.

"Being bold enough to fight for what we want," Brooks

answered, reaching across the table to push Kale's glass into his hand.

"To getting what we want," he muttered.

"And what we deserve," I added, clinking my glass against Kale's. He sucked in a breath, then lifted his glass and took a drink.

I'D BEEN AT THE FARM FOR TWO DAYS WITH A CRISIS AT WORK delaying Ford's arrival. He'd called me after lunch on Friday, a little frantic and a lot upset about the holdup, promising that he was going to be on the road before eight at the latest. Normally, I didn't mind his absence at the farm. After we closed on the property, we'd hired out help to run things during the week, but I spent as many weekends there as I could. It was a good balance, giving Ford time to spend with his friends and me time to do my own thing too. Things with Kale were far better than they had been, but neither Ford nor I wanted to test the tentative truce that had settled between the three of us. We'd gone out on double dates with my brother and his boyfriend, but we were careful to not flaunt things. I hoped one day Kale would be fully accepting, but it was okay for now.

"I think that's the last of it," Shawn said, shoving another cardboard box of lettuce into the back of a rented cargo van. He wiped his dusty hands on the front of his jeans and then folded his arms in front of his chest, surveying the amount of food we'd managed to get packed up for him in such a short amount of time. He'd only arrived after breakfast and we'd been hard at work ever since.

"Hopefully you won't hit too much traffic on the way back down," I said.

"There's always traffic."

"I know." I tilted my head back and sucked in a deep breath of the smog-free farm air.

"Are you sure you don't want to make the permanent move here?" he asked, giving me a reasonable amount of side-eye.

A more permanent relocation to the farm was something Ford and I talked about often, but the answer was always a resounding no. He loved the city and I loved him. It was perfect for me to have the best of both parts of my life within arm's reach, and much like how I let things sit with my brother, I didn't want to ruin what already worked for us.

"I'm sure," I promised.

"I'll see you next week then?"

"You know it."

I walked Shawn around to the driver's door of the van and gave him a hug before he climbed in. Gravel kicked up under his tires, but I waited until he was well on the main road before turning around and heading back inside. It was nearly dinner time, which meant I still had hours before Ford was supposed to arrive. Normally, I didn't mind being on the farm alone, but we had plans for the weekend that I'd been very much looking forward to and putting them off felt a lot like my least favorite kind of torment.

I busied myself cleaning up the kitchen and making sure the bed was made, ensuring that everything that needed to be put away was put away and everything that needed to be out was out.

Four months after my brother found out about Ford and me, I moved into Ford's brownstone. I sold my apartment and used a lot of the money from the sale to deal with getting things in order for the farm. Ford had, of course, offered to pay for the whole thing, but there was no way I was going to let him foot that bill. I appreciated that he treated money the same way as my brother, the way I never had. Neither of them ever worried if there was going to be enough, and there always was.

We'd been living together for four months and waking up with him was as magical three days ago as it had been the very first time. Ford gave me the space to explore not just his body, but my own. I'd learned more about my own likes and dislikes in the past four months than I had in the past twenty years. To say I was grateful for him was an understatement.

That was why I had planned the weekend to give him something special.

It was spring and the trees were in full bloom, the garden sprouting up all the new growth for the season. Ford had been salivating at the thought of the weather being good enough to fuck outside, and even though his arrival was delayed, the weather had held.

I was on the back porch checking the sturdiness of our latest purchase when my ears registered the familiar sound of tires on gravel. Immediately, my pulse spiked and my cock jerked against my leg. I knew it was Ford, knew it was the man I loved. I set some supplies down on the small table beside the back door and headed to the front to greet him.

He blew in the front door with his hand around the knot

on his tie, yanking it loose as he kicked both of his shoes off and toed them toward the shoe rack. His hair was perfectly styled as always, but his face was almost frantic, only settling when he saw me in the doorway.

"There you are," he murmured, finishing his tie and loosening the top two buttons of his shirt. He closed the space between us and wrapped me in his arms. "I'm sorry I'm late."

"You're earlier than I expected," I assured him, tilting my head back for a kiss.

Ford crashed his mouth against mine, the strength of his tongue more of a promise than a question. He pushed me against the doorframe and reached between us to undo his belt, knuckles grazing over the quickly growing bulge between my own legs.

"I think I broke the sound barrier getting here," he whispered against my lips, kissing his way up to my ear.

"Good."

He turned his hand and cupped his hot palm around my cock, applying enough pressure that I lifted onto my toes with an embarrassingly high-pitched gasp.

"I'm so ready to have you."

My nostrils flared, and I reached down for the hem of my shirt, rucking it up and pulling it over my head. I'd spent the last hours cleaning, but I would deal with the mess we made later. Ford growled and buried his face into the crook of my neck, kissing and biting his way to my ear, and with his hands around my waist, he walked us both out to the back porch, tearing himself away from me only long enough to observe the handiwork of our latest purchase.

"This is going to be amazing," he murmured, gesturing

with one long finger at the rest of my clothes. "Get those off and then get on all fours."

The purchase in question was a bed swing, which I'd initially laughed at, but Ford was insistent. It was essentially a porch swing, but instead of a bench, it held a full size mattress pad, framed with low slats on three sides. I'd decorated it with some pillows, but there was still plenty of room for spreading out in the middle.

In the last eight months, another thing that happened was I'd gotten a lot better at doing what Ford told me to do. I still pushed and poked him, but I had found an unexpected kind of comfort in submission to him that never ceased to surprise me. So I stripped out of my clothes and climbed onto the swing, sticking my ass in the air and showing him the plug I'd shoved up there earlier as a surprise.

"You're going to give a man a heart attack, sweetheart." Ford smoothed his hand from the small of my back down over the swell of my ass, finger pressing softly against the flared base of the plug.

Toys were another thing we'd brought into the bedroom. I'd worried at first, that the inclusion of toys in any way would be a bruise to the ego, but the only thing they did was ramp up the pleasure for both of us...and sometimes the pain too. I was by no means a masochist, but I had grown to love a good spanking over Ford's lap when the mood struck. That wasn't the norm for us, though. The dynamic between us was soft most of the time, demonstrated more with words and actions than physical displays of pain and pleasure.

Ford still loved to make me come until I cried, though.

I didn't hate that.

"Check the table, Sir," I said, pressing my cheek against

the cushion and facing the table where I'd set out a bottle of lube, a set of leather cuffs, and a spreader bar.

"Oh." Ford's words were breathy and low. "Is this you asking for what you need, sweetheart? You need to be spread out and fucked?"

Just the thought of it was enough to make my cock leak precum.

"I need you," I rasped, dropping a more noticeable arch into my back.

Ford was still dressed, tie loose around his neck and belt undone around his waist. He had the button and zipper of his fly down, the thick bulge of his cock filling the gap. He was quick to get the cuffs around my wrists, latching them onto the clips I'd discreetly hidden beneath the mess of pillows. The size of the swing meant that my arms were spread wide, my chest and face pressed down and putting my ass on better display. There was a moment when Ford stepped back to observe me, but I couldn't see him because of my own position. I swallowed nervously, always wondering what he thought when he looked at me, if he ever felt regret.

Before I could entertain any more of those thoughts, he fastened cuffs around my ankles, then latched the spreader bar between them on the longest setting. The stretch burned the muscles in my legs, and the warm spring air swirled around my erection.

"You're a fucking dream," Ford murmured. Clothes hit the wooden porch, and he yanked the spreader bar toward the edge of the cushion. "You're *my* fucking dream."

"I love you," I whispered. "I love this."

Ford hummed, giving the plug in my ass a tentative pull. "I love both of those things too."

Behind me, I heard the sound of the lube bottle opening, and then Ford groaning as he slicked his cock with an over-hand pull of his fist.

"You look so pretty with this toy in your hole," he said, swirling a lube-slick finger around my rim. "I wish I could fit my cock right next to it, stretch you out even more."

A shiver raced up my spine and the most indecent whimper tumbled out of my mouth. Ford huffed out an amused and almost evil-sounding laugh before he twisted the plug once more and pulled it all the way out of me.

My body didn't even have time to register the absence because, with one smooth glide of his hips, Ford's cock was seated fully inside of me, his balls burning hot against mine. I shouted out his name, the switch from the immoveable plastic of the toy to the hard press of his erection the best thing I'd ever felt in my life.

When it came to sex for the two of us, I preferred to top. There was something that felt *right* about being over Ford, watching my cock disappear into his body and wringing plea-sure out of him, but I didn't hate to bottom. It had become my preference when I was more in the submissive mindset with him, but I topped him sometimes then too. It depended on our moods, and I loved the versatility of the act while main-taining the steadiness of our roles outside the bedroom.

"Fuck, Boston."

I loved when he called me by my name. Ford so heavily favored calling me sweetheart when he was in the mood— and I loved that so much—it was like he forgot himself some-times and the only thing he could remember was my name, the way I made him feel.

"I need you," I whined, something about the arch of my

back and the burn in my legs making me absolutely mad for him. The chains clanked against the wood slats of the swing as I tried to adjust to a position that didn't make a cold sweat break out against the small of my back, but with the cuffs and the spreader bar, there was nowhere for me to go.

"I've got you," he promised, pulling back and easing back in.

With every thrust of his hips, the swing glided in time, the sensation of floating on the clouds a very real thing. I closed my eyes, content to lose myself to the pleasure Ford offered me. In the distance, birds chirped and the sun sank below the horizon, and I'd never been happier in my entire life.

Ford climbed onto the swing behind me, setting it off on a far more noticeable range of motion, driven by every snap of his hips. He reached around my front, leaning down and pressing his chest against my back and taking my cock into his hand. I was hard and hot, his touch almost too much to handle.

"Give me what I want, sweetheart," he whispered the demand into my ear.

His voice was the only thing grounding me, as from the moment he put himself inside of me, I'd absolutely lost all sense of space and time. I didn't know anything except the heat of his body, the touch of his skin, and the promises he made with every pump of his cock.

His hand was heaven on my shaft, and the sensation of being helpless to his touch was like a drug. As he asked, my body delivered, and cum spurted out of my dick, painting hot stripes against the swing and the tight hold of his fingers. I cried out, yanking against the cuffs, against the spreader, against his cock deep inside of me.

"Just like that," he groaned, pace turning frenetic. "You know how I need it, don't you?"

With his fingers still wrapped tight around my throbbing dick, Ford went still behind me, spilling into my ass as he came. My muscles clamped down on him, and I cursed under my breath as he kept up the slow and punishing drag of his fist up and down my cock.

"Ford," I whined, the pleasure of his hand balancing on that line that was ready to slide right into pain.

"I want another one," he groaned in my ear.

His cock was still hard inside of me, his cum sticky and hot as it leaked out of my ass and slid down my thighs and my balls. I didn't think I had another orgasm in me, but that wouldn't have been the first time. Like always, Ford found what he wanted from me and he took it. And tied down beneath him, I was more than happy to give it to him.

Over and over again, for the rest of our lives.

# ALSO BY KATE HAWTHORNE

———

**Trophy Doms Social Club**

Humbled

Edged

Praised

Bound

Shared

**Trophy Doms New York**

All In

Tied Down

Cried Out

Roughed Up

**Giving Consent**

Worth the Risk

Worth the Wait

Worth the Fight

Worth the Chance

**All in Good Time**

Necessary Space

His Kind of Love

The Colors Between Us

Love Comes After

Until You Say Otherwise

## **STANDALONES**

Rebound

One for the Road

Daybreak - Vino & Veritas

Unfettered

Dreams

A Thousand Lifetimes

## **COLLABORATIONS**

**With E.M. Denning**

Irreplaceable

Future Fake Husband

Future Gay Boyfriend

Future Ex Enemy

**With J.R. Gray**

May the Best Man Win

# ABOUT KATE HAWTHORNE

Kate Hawthorne is an author of character-driven LGBT romance, known for crafting emotionally intense stories with high heat and a kinky twist. Creating worlds where passion and angst collide, Kate's books bring you complex protagonists in fearless pursuit of self-exploration and happy —if not sometimes unconventional—endings for everyone.

Visit her website
http://www.katehawthornebooks.com

Sign up for Kate's newsletter
http://www.katehawthornebooks.com/extra

facebook.com/authorkatehawthorne

x.com/katewriteswords

instagram.com/kate.hawthorne

patreon.com/katehawthorne